THE PROTÉGÉE

DAN ZELAZ

First published by Didasko Publishers Corporation 2026

First edition

ISBN: 978-1-962980-22-7

CONTENTS

Chapter One

Hope in the Darkness

In the vast expanse of the universe, among stars and uncharted regions, one bright point shone against the blackness of the cosmos. From a distance, it could have been mistaken for a star, but it was a planet, its dense atmosphere reflecting the splendor of three suns. For that reason, it had long been known as the Kingdom of Light.

For centuries, the Kingdom of Light had endured assault after assault and still remained standing. But its age of victory was nearing its end. Dargos had risen against it, leading the army of the Kronkos: amphibious creatures of towering height, monstrous strength, and merciless speed. They were overrunning the human world with such violence that the threat no longer belonged to one kingdom alone. If the Kingdom of Light fell, the balance of the universe itself would tremble.

The planet had become the stage of a cosmic war, and its defenders were breaking beneath the weight of invasion. Yet amid the ruin, one figure still carried hope. She was not a warrior crowned with victories, nor a conqueror whose name inspired armies. She was a desperate young woman fleeing for her life.

For three days, a squad of Kronkos pursued her across the Suntras Valley. They hunted her with the precision of seasoned predators, following every broken branch, every footprint, every disturbance in the mud until they reached the Enchanted Swamp. Since they could not speak with words, they roared into the night, their fury sharpened by the hunger to seize their fugitive.

The last hope of the Kingdom of Light was about to be cornered. Princess Gemma's determination remained iron, but exhaustion had begun to betray her body. The high-pitched wheezing of the Kronkos pressed against her back; her ears heard nothing but that piercing moan. Her knees trembled so violently that each step felt impossible. The soft ground dragged at her feet, sinking them into puddles of mud and forcing her to stagger whenever she tried to run.

Weariness clouded her senses until reality and imagination blurred. She turned to one side and felt as if an unseen gaze were driving a stake into her back. She turned to the other and imagined something malicious crouched among the shadows, waiting for the right instant to strike. At times, she convinced herself she had only seen a mirage. At others, she knew—without knowing how—that something was watching.

The wind moaned through the treetops. Icy air struck the dry branches scattered across the rocks, and beneath those rocks were caves carved into the earth, dens where strange reptiles hid from the cold. Some crawled out in fear at the presence of a stranger. Others, larger and more patient, remained in their crypts and waited for nature to deliver them food.

The night was blacker than ever. Gemma lifted her eyes to the sky, searching for stars that might guide her, but she found only dense fog and a gray varnish of clouds threatening to release snow over the darkness that covered the swamp.

Only the ancient trees witnessed her flight. Their thick trunks had been battered by centuries, and their roots sank deep into the muddy soil—almost as deep as the despair now pressing against Princess Gemma's soul.

My daughter, listen to me carefully... Don't let the Kronkos capture you. If they get too close, you must strike the mystical sphere against your chest.

The voice of Nótrex, her father, returned to her as if it had crossed the swamp itself.

Don't lose it. Its power is enormous. Only it can protect you from danger.

Another voice rose in her memory, urgent and desperate.

"Nótrex, let Gemma use the mystical sphere!" someone had shouted amid the mob of Kronkos.

"Fight, Kéltrox. I will not risk my daughter's life!" Nótrex had answered.

Gemma was still trapped inside that memory when a Kronko appeared before her.

Before she could turn away, the creature seized one of her legs and hurled her into the mud. She clawed at the ground, driving her elbows and toes into the mire, trying to crawl forward, but the Kronko tightened its grip with every movement.

Cornered, the princess kicked its face again and again until the beast finally released her. She scrambled forward, but her escape lasted only a moment. More Kronkos poured from the darkness, jostling one another as though each wished to be the first to claim her.

They were about to fall upon her when a thunderous command split the swamp.

"Cojeti gaiao turelo!" the Ventu, chief of the Kronkos, roared. "Out of my way, you useless ones!"

The creatures recoiled in fear.

"Nore laia viraleta!" he ordered. "Don't touch her. She has the sphere." Then he approached Princess Gemma.

"Give me the mystical sphere and return with me in peace."

"I don't have it with me," she said, her voice cracking.

"Very well. Tell me where you hid it and come with me, Princess Gemma. I would not want you to be hurt any further." His mouth twisted into something almost gentle. "Dargos does not want you harmed. He has a special plan for you."

The princess pushed herself upright and looked around. The Kronkos shrieked again, closing the circle.

"What are you going to do to me and my family?"

The Ventu opened his arms. "I do not know what will happen to your family. But I know you will be all right."

Before Gemma could answer, a roar like a whirlwind shattered the Kronkos' attention. A massive creature descended from the darkness—winged, clawed, and larger and stronger than any eagle. It landed before the princess with fierce grace. Gemma sprang up, seized its neck, and the creature launched back into the air before the Kronkos could understand what had happened.

"The Bolco took her!" the Ventu shouted.

The Kronkos raised their bows.

"Fly faster, Úniquen!" Princess Gemma cried.

Úniquen zigzagged through the night as arrows rained past them. Some sliced his skin. Others cut Gemma's. But the darkness favored them, swallowing their path and confusing the aim of their enemies.

"Stop, you beasts!" the Ventu shouted in his own language. "Dargos wants her alive."

He seized a bow, took aim, and released a single arrow. It struck Úniquen in the side. The Bolco staggered in the air and screamed, but he kept flying.

"Land!" Gemma cried. "The arrow can kill you!"

"If I land now, it will not be a niti before they catch you," Úniquen stammered, forcing his wings to move faster.

"Land. That is an order!"

"I will not let them catch you."

He turned his head back. Gemma searched the darkness behind them.

"I don't see the Kronkos anymore. Do you?"

"We have lost them for now," he said. "We must find a safe place for you."

His voice weakened. "I'm getting dizzy..." His wings stopped.

"No!" Gemma screamed.

Úniquen fainted, and they plummeted together.

An icy gust pierced the princess to the bone. She clung to his neck with all the strength she had left. "Úniquen, wake up! Wake up!"

He did not wake. They fell so fast that the ground rose beneath them like judgment. Gemma closed her eyes and surrendered her fate to the will of the Overlords.

Only a few meters from the earth, Úniquen opened his eyes and beat his wings with desperate force. The fall slowed, but not enough to spare them from the impact.

When Gemma opened her eyes, she turned toward Úniquen. He lay motionless nearby and seemed not to breathe. The sight struck her harder than the crash itself.

"Úniquen, stay with me... Open your eyes, please."

She tried to crawl toward him. One of her legs barely responded; the other felt as if it had been torn from its place. Still, she dragged herself through the mud until she reached him and wrapped her arms around one of his front paws. She could do nothing more. Without making a sound, she cried.

Silent weeping flooded her face, carving pale lines through the mud on her cheeks. Then, with a sudden ache of memory, she searched for the last gift her father had given her.

At that instant, she felt someone behind her. She turned.

"Malla!"

Gemma rubbed her eyes with mud-covered hands until her eyelids cleared.

But when she could see again, no one was there.

Trembling, she closed her right hand around the mystical sphere and pressed it with desperate force.

Power awakened.

Strength surged back into her body. Her legs, numb moments before, seemed to rise from a deep sleep. The dislocated limb began to set itself back into place. A vibrant tingling spread through her bones and muscles, healing without pain, as if the sphere were reminding her body how it had been made.

Within minutes, Princess Gemma stood again. She hurried to Úniquen and lifted his right wing. The wound was worse than she had feared; the arrow had pierced his side. With trembling care, she pulled it free, tore one sleeve from her dress, and bandaged the wound as gently as she could.

Úniquen was heavy, but the sphere had given her strength beyond her own. She dragged him to the roots of a tree and placed his head on the highest part of them. When she saw that he was still panting, weak but alive, relief nearly broke her. She found a rock and set his head upon it so he could breathe more easily.

Then she tore another strip from her dress, wrapped it around a branch, and made a crude torch. She climbed down the trunk, gathered two stones, dried them with her cloak, and struck them together until fire caught, just as her uncle had taught her.

It seemed impossible that the mystical sphere had healed her. Without it, she never could have dragged Úniquen even a few steps. Now she understood a little more of its nature, though no one had ever taught her how to command it. Her family rarely spoke of it, and in the Royal Council, the sphere had always been a forbidden subject.

Only behind closed doors had her dear friend Rólar once filled her imagination with tales of its mystical abilities. Rumors had spread through the kingdom, but only a select few knew its true potential—or the art of harnessing it.

Chapter Two

FROM THE CLUTCHES OF THE KRONKOS

Before

The royal family slipped through the corridors of Diamondis toward the private chambers. King Nótrex led them, with his brother Kéltrox beside him and the last loyal soldiers guarding Princess Gemma and Queen Krístal.

"Inside," Nótrex said, opening the doors to his daughter's chamber.

"Gemma, you and Krístal will leave through here while we distract the Kronkos."

"Bring that over here!" Kéltrox shouted.

The soldiers dragged a heavy table across the floor and braced it against the doors.

Nótrex turned to his daughter. "Listen to me carefully. Do not let the Kronkos capture you. If they get too close, strike the mystical sphere against your chest. Do not lose it. Its power is enormous, and only it can protect you from danger."

"Then why won't you let me use it now?" Gemma asked. "Maybe I can save all of us."

"No. You must obey me." His voice left no room for argument. "Dargos has a mystical sphere too, and you have no experience. You are no match for him."

Before he could say more, the Kronkos broke through the door and surged into the chamber.

"Here they come!" Kéltrox shouted. "Nótrex, let Gemma use the mystical sphere!"

"Fight, Kéltrox. I will not risk my daughter's life."

The Kronkos flooded the bedroom. Kéltrox and Nótrex placed themselves before the princess and the queen. One of the creatures repeated a harsh word—"Kirko"—as he cut down the few soldiers still standing.

"The half-breed Kronko is dangerous!" Kéltrox cried, rushing toward him.

The Kronko saw him coming and raised his spear. Kéltrox twisted away at the last instant and struck the floor hard, face down.

"Come here!" the king commanded.

He saw his men weakening and knew he had only moments. With his left hand, he pushed Gemma and Krístal forward. With his right, he drove his sword into as many enemies as he could reach, carving a path through the furious mob.

The short distance to the corner seemed endless. Every clash of steel, every groan of the wounded, made the impossible feel nearer.

Each time the king seemed about to fall, Kéltrox's sword came to his defense. Brother beside brother, they fought their way toward the back left corner of the room, where Gemma's bed stood.

They did not need to speak. No cry of "behind you," no warning of "to your right," passed between them. A glance, a movement, the tension in one another's faces—those were enough. At last, they reached the corner. Nótrex shoved Gemma's bed aside and uncovered a trapdoor in the floor. Beneath it, underground stairs descended into a passage lit by torches.

The king seized Gemma first and pushed her toward the opening. She rolled down the stairs and struck her left ankle against the stone. The queen was about to follow when the Kronko chief hurled a spear at her head.

Kéltrox fired an arrow. It struck the spear and changed its path just enough that it only grazed Krístal's back. The queen collapsed a few steps from the escape door.

The sight of his wounded wife broke Nótrex's focus. A Kronko cornered him against the wall and forced the sword from his hand. Kéltrox rushed to help him, but Nótrex shook his head.

The message was clear: take the passage and protect my daughter.

Pain crossed Kéltrox's face. He obeyed, knowing it might mean never seeing his brother alive again. He darted into the passage and saw two Kronkos already racing after his niece, with more preparing to descend behind them.

Gemma ran as soon as she saw them. She did not dare look back. Her ankle burned, her eyes blurred, and the world she had known seemed to be tearing itself away from her with every breath.

She wanted to ignore what had happened in the chamber. She wanted her steps to be fast enough to outrun the truth. But courage rose inside her—not because she felt brave, but because she had no other choice.

She looked back and almost collided with the reality she feared. One of the Kronkos was gaining on her, a dagger clutched in his claws.

At that instant, Kéltrox reached him. He killed the first Kronko before Gemma's eyes, then turned on the second, wounded him, and spun to face the creatures rushing from behind.

"Go, Smally! Go now!" he shouted.

Gemma obeyed. She ran until the tunnel opened before her. Tears blurred the path as she stumbled into the outside world.

Only then did she remember the night her father had awakened her at midnight. Now she understood why he had placed the sphere around her neck. He must have sensed that something terrible was coming. She had seen sorrow in his eyes that night, but surprise had stolen her words.

It was the first time she had seen her father's heart stripped of pride. He had looked filled with despair and resignation, as if he already knew misfortune was near.

That night, Nótrex had taken the mystical sphere, placed it around his daughter's neck, and looked into her eyes.

"Use the mystical sphere wisely."

Úniquen

Úniquen had known the princess since she was a newborn. From that moment, an affection took root in him that surpassed anything he had ever felt for another being. He saw her as his daughter, treated her as his friend, and obeyed her as his queen.

He belonged to the species of the Bolcos, who could live for thousands of years—or tecklis, as solar years were called in the Kingdom of Light. At five hundred tecklis, Úniquen was still young compared to many of his kind.

He had once been companion to Gemma's great-great-grandfather, then to her great-grandfather, and so on until King Nótrex, who followed the family tradition and entrusted the Bolco to his daughter.

Like all Bolcos, Úniquen had a narrow snout that stretched several centimeters forward. His teeth were thin and sharp, like needles fitted closely together. Wide ears hung at the sides of his head, small only in comparison to the size of his body. He stood on four strong legs, carried a long tail, and in his round eyes there was a friendliness that made his fierce shape less terrifying.

Bolcos were rational beings. Their intelligence could equal that of humans, and the passing of centuries often made them wiser than any ordinary creature.

They spoke eloquently and, when something seemed absurd, often revealed their disagreement through sarcasm. Long ago, the Bolcos had formed a covenant with humans. Thousands of them once lived on the planet Bolcania, spending their days flying, playing, and hunting small animals. But in the war remembered as the Six Worlds' War, the Bolcos joined the humans. Only a few survived, among them Úniquen's ancestors.

Princess Gemma

"Listen to me!" Princess Gemma cried. "Do not give up."

She gripped Úniquen's wounded wing, squeezed the sphere in her right hand, and shouted, "Sphere, do it. Work. Now. Heal him!"

She repeated the command again and again. Beyond words, she felt a deep connection with the Bolco through the sphere. Her heart pounded, and with each beat, energy rushed through her body.

"It's working, my friend," she whispered with relief. "The wound is closing."

"It is good that we are away from the furry ones," Úniquen murmured. He opened his eyes, then closed them again.

Gemma smiled through her tears.

"You are still weak. Rest."

"I feel better now," he said without opening his eyes, "but I will stay here a little longer."

He curled his tail, scratched his muzzle with one front paw, and settled his head higher against the rock.

After a silence, Gemma said, "Something extraordinary happened to me when I was running from the Kronkos."

"What?" Úniquen asked.

"In the Valley of Suntras, I heard Malla's voice telling me to run to the Enchanted Swamp. And a few nitis ago, before I used the mystical sphere, I saw her."

Úniquen opened his eyes. "You saw Malla?"

"Yes."

"Malla, Malla?"

"Yes."

"Your imaginary friend?"

Gemma looked away. "You did not believe me either."

"Gemma, I thought you had outgrown that. Many tecklis have passed."

"Forget it," she said. "I remember what everyone told me. But I always said she was real. I thought at least you believed me." For a moment, neither of them spoke.

Then Gemma forced a change in her voice. "You made a spectacular entrance, Úniquen. You left the Kronkos with their claws in the air."

"It was a miracle I escaped at all," he replied, scratching his snout. "I almost died in Diamondis. They held me in custody and chained me. I still do not know why Dargos did not eliminate me."

"How did you escape?"

"Someone helped me. That is the strange part—I do not know who."

"What do you mean?"

"A man released me. He wore a mask, as if he did not want anyone to recognize him. He approached me and removed my chains, though I still do not understand how. I never saw a key. I think he used magic."

"Maybe you did not see clearly," she said, yawning. "He must have had the keys."

"What difference does it make? The important thing is that I arrived on time. You frightened me. I did not know whether you were dead."

"If you had not come, I would surely be..." She stopped. "Do you know what happened to my parents?"

"No. Your father entered the palace after Dargos defeated the remaining soldiers on the battlefield. He ran to find you and your mother, and Kéltrox went with him. Everything happened too fast. The survivors resisted with the last of our strength, but it was difficult for anyone to stand. Then Dargos hurled another fireball at us."

Úniquen lowered his head. "Your father shouted, 'Kéltrox, Dargos is scorching the soldiers!' Your uncle called his best men, and they retreated. That was the last time I saw them."

"Was Rólar among them?" Gemma asked.

"Yes. Marcus too."

"I hope they are alive." Her eyes filled again. "The last time I spoke with Rólar, we argued. I insulted him in so many ways, and now look what has happened."

"What did Rólar do to you?"

Gemma swallowed. "When I think about it now… I believe all he did was tell me the truth."

"Calm yourself, my friend. I know this is hard to understand now, but all will be well. For the moment, I must take care of you. I imagine you must be hungry."

"You do not know how much. I have not eaten for several days, and I am so dirty that my body feels heavy."

"Yes," Úniquen said, "I almost did not recognize you. Even as a little girl, you never managed to get this dirty. But I can help you with that." He stuck out his tongue.

"Disgusting. Take it away, Úniquen!" They both smiled.

Úniquen yawned, scratched his ears against the edge of the rock, and settled his head back into the hollow. Princess Gemma remained beside him. They spoke softly until, without meaning to, both of them fell asleep.

Chapter Three

The Kingdom of Light

Before

Princess Gemma had grown up in Diamondis, the majestic palace of the kingdom. Diamonds, rubies, pearls, and countless precious stones adorned its walls and towers, but none shone more brilliantly than the immense colorless diamond set at its highest point. Each daybreak, it caught the light of the Triplets and scattered their radiance across the palace like a crown of fire.

Around the palace rose smaller towers where the most important nobles lived, and beyond them stood a mansion of many rooms for the servants who chose to remain near the royal family with their own households.

A lake bordered the buildings. Along its shore, domesticated animals grazed beneath fruit trees, ornamental trees, and other varieties brought from across the kingdom.

Among the most exotic creatures were the séritrocs, nórmides, and tíricus—animals whose presence in the palace gardens astonished every visitor to the Kingdom of Light.

Séritrocs, often called the carriage of kings, were tall beasts with seven powerful legs: three on the right, three on the left, and one in the middle. The middle leg was the strongest. They used it to jump and to cushion their landings, folding it beneath them when they walked. Their paws could spring them great distances, though riders had to take care not to slide from their smooth backs. When calm, they were tender and playful. Their red-merlot fur made them visible even in darkness.

They could jump for days without drinking water, and their rugged, armorlike skin allowed them to endure almost any attack without injury. For that reason, people often used them in battle.

Nórmides were more common. They reproduced quickly and gave milk in abundance. Six legs carried their broad bodies, and a massive tail dragged behind them as they walked. Their greenish skin let them disappear among the flora. They were herbivores, fond of water, and were the usual means of transportation for the people of the City of Light. King Nótrex, however, possessed the purest breed.

Those who rode nórmides praised their comfort, for their backs were broad and soft. Their weakness was endurance: they tired easily and could not travel long distances.

Tíricus, by contrast, were rare in the Kingdom of Light. Lighter and faster than nórmides, they had four slender legs and came in several colors, the most common being yellowish. Their small, soft-haired tails resembled tiny spines. They came from Green Plant, the only planet where large herds still remained.

Inside Diamondis, the royal servants decorated the corridors with carpets made from fine furs, paintings, and sculptures of the kings who had ruled before Nótrex.

One of the most majestic statues belonged to King Vargos, the only tyrant ever to sit on the throne of the Kingdom of Light. Centuries earlier, after overthrowing his cousin Normen, Vargos had ordered his own effigy carved. Later, he disappeared after a battle, and no one ever learned what became of him or of the soldiers who followed him. Yet despite the shame of his reign, none of the kings who came after him removed the statue. The work was too magnificent to destroy.

The people loved King Nótrex because he ruled the City of Light with justice and care. They admired his nobility, his intelligence, and the way he protected those who had less. From an early age, his parents had seen in him the gift of leadership, and once he ascended the throne, he proved them right.

Nótrex was calculating, loyal to his wife, devoted to his family, and committed to the prosperity of his kingdom. Yet all the wealth of Diamondis and all the treasures of the palace could not compare to what he cherished most: the love he bore his family.

Princess Gemma had lived a fulfilled life within those walls. Across the planet, both humble citizens and nobles respected her. When she walked through the streets of the City of Light, the people praised her dedication and wisdom. Their admiration was not accidental. At fifteen tecklis, her work among the poor had already surpassed much of what her father had achieved in that area, and she had done it with fewer resources.

After a private assembly, the governors of the regions recommended that King Nótrex include Princess Gemma as an honorary member of the Royal Council. They argued that she possessed the wisdom her mother had shown before suffering what they called her severe mental illness. Gemma was sixteen then.

King Nótrex did not receive the recommendation with joy. Still, after considering the queen's wishes, he allowed Gemma to attend Council meetings without the right to speak, for a period he called probationary.

If Gemma was to become a permanent member of the Royal Council at such a young age, the king decided she would have to pass three tests within a fixed period. To fulfill them, she traveled to the opposite hemisphere of the planet, to an island in the Southern Quadrant of the Luminous Region. There, during his controversial reign, King Vargos had founded the largest library in that hemisphere and renamed the island Artistic.

At first, Gemma wanted to go alone, flying on Úniquen. Both the king and queen opposed the idea, and when Rólar expressed his desire to accompany her, she accepted the family vessel instead. She took Rólar, Úniquen, a few women who served her, and the escort assigned by her father.

She completed the tests in less time than required, to the surprise—and reluctant resignation—of the king. An illustrious sculptor from the island, grateful for her work, carved a statue of Princess Gemma mounted on Úniquen's back. He named it The Protégée of the Overlords.

Laryon, governor of the Luminous Region, agreed to place the statue in front of the library in Artifice, the central city of Artistic Island, if the king had no objection. To Gemma's surprise, Nótrex proudly approved it.

Gemma returned to the City of Light and took her place in the Council. The book The Princess of the Kingdom of Light recounts the three tests King Nótrex entrusted to her and how she solved each one.

By then, King Nótrex had arranged her engagement to Prince Altren, son and heir of King Sortus, AK of the planet Ilucus. Both families had been planning the soul-bonding ceremony for tecklis. The celebration was a declaration of love before family and friends, and it lasted thirty days.

During those thirty days, the lovers remained at each other's side and tied their hands together every night with an emerald ribbon. When the thirty nights ended, the bonded couple danced a joyful song before the guests, and their mothers preserved the accumulated ribbons with those of previous generations. The custom symbolized that their love, like the ribbons, would endure forever.

Gemma still did not fully know Prince Altren. In truth, she had met him only twice, both times when he came to rehearse the bonding dance. Deep inside, she suspected her father wished to strengthen the relationship between Ilucus and the Kingdom of Light through the union. Even so, she did not oppose it. For better or worse, she believed she might one day love Prince Altren, and she longed to find someone who would love her in return.

As a child, Gemma used to walk through the City of Light with her mother in the evenings. They spoke with the people they met and delighted in buying aromatic plants for their rooms.

Then, without understanding why, Gemma lost the magnificent relationship she had always shared with her mother. Krístal's behavior changed, as if her essence had been altered and her inner spark had vanished. Her father explained it as a mental illness, but Gemma never fully accepted that answer.

She knew little of her mother's family. She had heard only fragments about her grandfather Lardo and almost nothing more. After everything that had happened in recent days, Gemma began to suspect that some evil sorcerer might have bewitched her mother. Perhaps that was how Dargos had been able to defeat her father.

Whatever the truth, she knew she had to find a way to save her parents, her friends, and her kingdom from the tyrant who had invaded her planet. The Kingdom of Light had resisted enemy attacks for centuries. Now, dozens of cities and millions of people lay beneath the oppressive shadow of Dargos.

Princess Gemma

In the early morning hours—or nitis, as hours were called in the Kingdom of Light—Princess Gemma awoke to the sight of a Kronko rushing toward her.

Her eyes searched for Úniquen. A group of Kronkos had cornered him between the tree and their weapons.

"Run, Gemma!" Úniquen shouted.

She threw herself from the tree, but before she could escape, the Kronkos surrounded her. The Ventu, chief of the Kronkos, stepped before her.

"Hand over the sphere, and we will not kill you."

"You have orders not to kill me," Gemma said. "If you could, I would be dead already."

The Ventu lunged. He seized her by the neck, lifted her from the mud, then threw her down again. The Kronkos shrieked around them.

Gemma lay with her elbows sunk in the mire, her eyes fixed on him. The Ventu placed his paws on her arms, and his weight pressed her deeper into the mud, nearly breaking her bones. She forced back the scream rising in her throat.

A claw lifted a lock of her hair. His half-open muzzle came close to her face, and slime fell between her nose and mouth. Disgusted, she turned her head and wiped some of the viscous liquid away with her shoulder.

"Where did you hide the mystical sphere, princess?" he asked. "Tell me. Or would you rather I search you myself?" His tone became suggestive. "Dargos does not want us to touch you, but you are giving me no choice."

"You are hurting me," she murmured. "All right. I will tell you. I sank the sphere in the mud near the tree. Let me go, and I will find it and give it to you."

The Ventu grimaced. The Kronkos shrieked again, and Gemma understood the sound as laughter.

"Very well," he said, releasing her with cruel reluctance. "Find the mystical sphere and put it in that chest."

Gemma sat up. "So you cannot touch it?" The Ventu growled.

One of the Kronkos holding Úniquen shrieked.

"What is it?" the Ventu demanded.

The Kronko pointed to Úniquen's side.

"I wounded the Bolco," the Ventu muttered. His eyes narrowed. "So she knew how to use the sphere."

He turned back to Gemma and noticed the thick chain around her neck.

With a leap, he sprang toward her. He snatched the mystical sphere from her hand, jumped back, shook his claws, shrieked in pain, and released it.

The sphere fell into the mud.

Gemma threw herself after it.

"Use it, Gemma!" Úniquen cried.

The Kronkos struck his muzzle.

"How?" she asked, terrified.

Then her father's words returned to her.

She looked at the Ventu. He looked back.

Gemma gripped the mystical sphere and struck it hard against her chest.

"No!" the Ventu cried.

The sphere touched her chest, and a fountain of energy burst from her body. The Kronkos stared in terror. The sphere fastened itself to her as if it had become part of her flesh. Gemma rose from the ground. Light filled her eyes and arms. Her red hair darkened, a radiant cloud gathered above her head, and a current of air wrapped around her body.

"What is this place?" she asked, looking around.

"You are at the edge of the Forest of Weeping," a woman's voice replied.

"Everything is different. I recognize nothing."

"That is because you perceive it differently. You are looking at it from a higher plane. Do you see those shadows over there?"

"Yes."

"They are the Kronkos, your enemies. The one by the tree is your friend, Úniquen."

"Who are you? Where are you?" Gemma asked.

A silhouette flew toward her: a young woman who looked exactly like Gemma, though surrounded by a halo of light that made her almost incorporeal.

"I am you," the woman said, "and I am here."

"I do not understand. How can you be me?"

"When you struck the mystical sphere against your chest, it amplified your being and your inner energy to their highest capacity."

"But how can I be the one answering my own questions?"

"Because your understanding has multiplied. You can now communicate with your inner self. You are in battle against the Kronkos. Do not rush. Your perception of time has changed, so everything appears slower. Now you must defend yourself."

"How?"

"Like this."

Gemma lifted her index finger toward the largest group of enemies. Bursts of light shot from her glowing hands and burned several Kronkos.

The Ventu and the others fired arrows and spears at her.

"Do you see those points coming toward you?" her inner self asked.

"Yes."

"Those are their arrows and spears. Stop them."

"How?"

"You know how."

Gemma raised both hands. A halo of energy surrounded her, and the weapons froze before they could pierce the light.

"The girl already knows the power of the sphere!" the Kronko chief shouted.

Gemma watched the Kronkos retreat.

"They are gone," Úniquen said. "Do not worry."

She closed her eyes and slowly descended.

After a while, Gemma awoke and saw Úniquen standing before her.

"I feel dizzy," she said.

"That is normal until you learn to use the sphere." His eyes brightened.

"Gemma, that was amazing."

"It was not me. It was the sphere."

"I am serious. Do you know how long it took your father to throw fire?"

"How long?"

"Tecklis, Gemma. Many tecklis. When he was learning, even levitating was difficult before he fainted."

"I was in a strange place," she said.

"What do you mean?"

"It was this same place, but it looked different. My sight could penetrate deeper. Have you ever heard of anything like that?"

"The king used to say the sphere gave him access to a higher dimension," Úniquen replied, scratching his muzzle.

"I also spoke with myself. Did the same thing happen to my father?"

"No. What do you mean, with yourself?"

"I saw myself and spoke to myself, though she looked a little different—older, wiser, more peaceful." Úniquen fell silent.

"What are you thinking?" Gemma asked. "Do you know something about this?"

"Your father never mentioned anything like that. Neither did your grandfather or great-grandfather."

"Then why are you looking at me that way?"

"There is an ancient book with a story about someone who saw something similar. According to the book, it happened millions of tecklis ago."

"I have read nothing like that in Diamondis, and I think I have read the entire library."

"The book was part of the royal collection for centuries, until King Vargos..."

"The one with the statue?"

"Yes. He fled Diamondis and took the book among his belongings."

"I heard he ran away from his cousin," Gemma said. "If he was fleeing, why would he choose to take a book?"

"It was not just any book. The Book of Origins is coveted, and very few copies exist. Your father tried to discover which worlds possessed the others. Your great-grandfather used to tell your grandfather a story from that book by memory."

"What story?"

Úniquen hesitated. "I do not think your father would appreciate me telling you that."

Gemma frowned. "Do you see my father here?"

"Well..." Úniquen shifted his paws. "It was a story passed from father to son for generations. In that story, something similar happened to someone else."

"Then my family must have considered it important. I wonder why Father never told me."

"Trust me, King Nótrex has his reasons." Úniquen stroked her shoulder with his tail. "I know you are curious, but right now you must take care of yourself. We need food and rest."

Gemma looked down at her hands, her feet, and the torn dress clinging to her body. "I am exhausted and starving. But we must seek help and reclaim our kingdom. My parents. Rólar. By the disgrace of the Overlords, Dargos holds their lives in his hands. They could be dead already. What am I going to do?"

She wanted to cry, but her eyes were too dry.

"Think, Gemma," Úniquen said. "What matters most now? Dargos just sent a squad of Kronkos after you. His army—or Dargos himself—could come at any moment with his mystical sphere."

She breathed in slowly. "You are right. I must be prepared. I need to understand what I can do with the sphere."

"Then I think we should go to the Weeping Forest."

"Yes. It is a good place to practice, and there are wild fruits." She climbed onto Úniquen's back. "We cannot escape to any of the Seven Regions. I heard Father say the Kronkos had taken our boats."

"That is true. We cannot remain on this planet."

"After we eat and I practice, we will go to the Pirutus and travel to Ilucus."

"To the Weeping Forest, then. Hold on, Your Highness." Úniquen took flight.

The Bolco brushed his tail over the treetops, climbed until the branches looked like ants beneath them, then swept downward to touch the leaves again. Gemma closed her eyes, raised both hands to the sky, and let the wind strike her face.

She smiled.

"It has been so long since we have done this," she said. "You know how much I love flying, do you not?"

"I know. Since you were a child." He rotated through the air.

"That is so wonderful."

"I only want to make you feel better."

They left the Enchanted Swamp behind and saw the green meadows of the Weeping Forest spread before them. Animals frolicked among the trees. Some bathed joyfully in crystal streams along the hillsides; others raced over the grass beside rivers that formed small islets crowded with roses and fruit trees.

By day, birds filled the forest with songs of love, and the movement of their feathers seemed to carry peace through the fresh wind, filling the souls of travelers who entered that paradise.

"I like that river," Gemma said. "There are fruit trees all around it."

"I will land so you can eat."

Once they reached the ground, Gemma climbed a tree and plucked a ripe fruit.

"Try this one."

"You know I cannot eat that. It makes me nauseous." Úniquen watched her move toward a branch. "What are you doing, Gemma?" She swung from the branch and jumped into the river.

"I needed water to wash off the mud. You know I like to be clean."

She braced herself, swam to the shore, and shivered. "Ah, how wonderful it would be to have my aromatic leaves and a warm dress."

Then she looked down at her ruined clothing. "I am going to wash this. Better wet than filthy. Turn around." Úniquen obeyed.

"I once saw a peasant girl do this," Gemma said. She dipped the dress in the river, struck it against a rock, and repeated the motion several times. "It works. At least it is not so muddy."

She put the dress back on, trembling.

"Yes," Úniquen said, "you are cleaner."

Gemma held the mystical sphere. "Can you imagine if it could dry the dress?"

"Hilarious. You know that is not the purpose of the sphere."

He paused. "What are you doing?"

Gemma did not answer. She stared at the sphere. Her eyes glowed faintly, and the sphere lit in response.

"It is reacting to you," Úniquen said.

"I need to know more about you," Gemma whispered to the sphere. "Can you defend me from Dargos?"

"Who are you talking to?" Úniquen asked, flapping his wings until he stood before her.

Gemma remained unblinking.

"I know you hear me. I can feel you." Her voice rose. "Answer me." She struck the mystical sphere against her chest.

As before, Gemma levitated. Light filled her eyes. Úniquen became, to her vision, a small dark shape below. She turned toward the river and heard the current as if she were inside it. She saw a spout of water, then the drops joining to form it. She sensed she could look deeper still, down to particles smaller than she wished to see.

"Where did you go?" she asked. "I know you are listening. I feel you. But why are you silent? I need to know how to defend myself against Dargos. If he finds me before I leave this planet and I cannot protect myself, it is over. My parents will die. My friends will die. Rólar. The Kingdom of Light and its legacy will perish."

Without meaning to, she detached the mystical sphere from her chest.

She fell into the river unconscious.

"Gemma! Can you hear me?"

Úniquen's voice reached her from far away. She opened her eyes and found him standing over her. She lay on a river rock, her dress wet at the bottom though almost dry near her chest.

"What happened?" she asked.

"You fell into the river, and I had to pull you out."

"Truly?"

"Yes. You fainted, and the sphere sank. The current almost took it away, but I caught the chain before the water carried it off."

He pointed with his snout to the mystical sphere beside her.

"My head hurts. How long was I unconscious?"

"Almost two nitis. What happened?"

"I do not know. I was trying to speak with myself."

"Like the first time?"

"Yes, but I do not know why she—why I—would not answer. I could feel her presence, just as before, but she did not speak to me." Gemma rubbed her forehead. "That sounds insane."

"I am glad you know."

She sighed and stood. "It is getting late. I must hurry."

She reached for the sphere and prepared to strike it against her chest again, but Úniquen pushed her hand aside with his muzzle.

"What are you doing?" he asked, upset.

"I have to practice. Time is short. Dargos—"

"No. No, Gemma. That is enough practice for today." His voice was sharper than she had ever heard it.

"Calm down," she said. "It is all right. I have never seen you like this." She hung the sphere around her neck again.

"The mystical sphere is not a game," Úniquen said, more calmly now.

"Many have died because they underestimated its power."

"I beg your pardon, Your Highness," Gemma said.

They both smiled.

"I am sorry, princess. You know I care for you."

She nodded.

"Come," he said. "We must find a safe place to sleep before the Triplets hide. You know what they say about this forest."

By daylight, the Weeping Forest was beautiful. But when night fell, its horror lived up to its name. The wind whipped the branches until they sounded like cries, like whimpers, as if the trees themselves were alive and grieving.

Many said mysterious spirits lived among those trees and possessed the hearts of animals that lurked in the shadows. Others claimed the specters formed dwarf whirlwinds that destroyed small bushes and vanished without explanation, as if darkness itself wished to disturb anyone foolish enough to walk through that frosty solitude.

It was also said that, on nights when the spectral portals opened wide, creatures from other dimensions could cross into the forest and walk its hidden paths.

Chapter Four

The Seven Regions

Unlike other Sibling Worlds, whose progress was measured by machines and greater technological wonders, the Kingdom of Light still crossed its own regions mostly by sea. Its vessels were not entirely unlike those of other planets, yet one feature made them unmistakable: their complex system of sails.

Like spiderwebs stretched across the body of the ship, hundreds of thin ropes—light, strong, and almost innumerable—interconnected the sails overhead. Five sailors controlled them from a wooden panel under the orders of the second captain, whom most people called the captain of sails. Through a series of levers, the panel tightened or loosened the ropes as needed, changing the shape and tension of the sails with remarkable precision.

The system looked archaic beside the inventions of more advanced worlds, but its efficiency was undeniable. When the sails shifted into the proper positions, they formed a kind of channel through which the wind was gathered, redirected, and used again, giving the ships a speed that astonished travelers who judged them too quickly by appearance.

Ships were not the kingdom's only means of transportation. Balloons also existed, though they had never earned much affection among the people. Some kings and nobles had used them, but King Nótrex despised them. Kéltrox often claimed that his brother feared balloons because many kings had died in them during ocean crossings. Nótrex always denied it.

The kings of the Kingdom of Light were expected to visit the Seven Regions once every teckli. Nótrex, however, often delegated the journey to his brother. Kéltrox accepted the duty with barely hidden joy, moved by his tireless love of the oceans, the scent of salt, and the freedom of open waters. If any man knew the six oceans, the twelve seas, and the Seven Regions of the kingdom, it was Kéltrox.

On her fifteenth teckli, Princess Gemma undertook the customary journey by ship to visit the Seven Regions. Whether prince or princess, the heir was expected to travel with only one chosen companion, arrive at the central city of each region, attend the feast organized by its ruler, and then continue the voyage.

King Nótrex nearly broke the Law of Light trying to cancel the trip. When the law left him no way to do so, he attempted instead to impose Kéltrox as Gemma's companion, arguing that his brother could protect her. But the same law that prevented parents from joining the journey also forbade them from choosing the heir's companion. When Princess Gemma reminded him of this, she chose Rólar.

Rólar, surprised, asked why she did not prefer her uncle or Úniquen. Gemma laughed and told him the decision had been simple: she did not want relatives on her journey, nor anyone who could fly away if the voyage became boring. Her refusal to accept the companion her father desired later brought consequences—not royal ones, but paternal ones.

Princess Gemma left the City of Light riding a séritroc with Rólar at her side and a group of soldiers escorting them only as far as the ship. That afternoon, she sailed from the port of Brilliant Sea. Two days later, she had crossed the borders of the Region of Light. On the third day, she arrived at the Main Port of Artistic Island, which belonged to the Luminous Region.

A formal retinue awaited her there. Among them stood the region's ruler, Laryon, accompanied by his daughter, Larnesa, who was in charge of the Pirutus and, at thirty-two tecklis, was the mother of ten-year-old twins.

Before Gemma descended from the ship, she noticed that Larnesa was staring at Rólar with unmistakable intensity—and with contempt.

"Rólar, that woman is looking at you strangely," Princess Gemma said.

"She is," Rólar replied. "Almost as if she is angry. But why?"

"Do you know her?"

"No. She must be Laryon's daughter."

"She's leaving," Gemma said.

"How strange. I wonder why."

"It is rather rude to leave without welcoming me properly."

"Bah. Put your royal ego away and let's go down," Rólar said.

The two descended and came face to face with Laryon.

"The Luminous Region welcomes the princess of the Kingdom of Light and her companion," Laryon said with a bow. The retinue, made up of some of the most distinguished men of Artistic Island, followed his example.

"Thank you, Ruler Laryon, and all of you, for the welcome," Princess Gemma replied. "I could not help noticing that someone had to leave." She gestured toward Larnesa, who was hurrying along the wooden harbor with her children by the hand.

"Let go of that rock," Larnesa told the boy holding her right hand, and the child obeyed.

"My daughter is dizzy," Laryon explained. "She has also been busy with her children. They are sickly."

"That is understandable," Princess Gemma said diplomatically.

"Good. The banquet in your honor will be held tomorrow night. In the meantime, your rooms are prepared in my house in Artifice."

Princess Gemma and Rólar left Artistic Island two days later. They arrived at the port of Invosconia, also in the Luminous Region and the largest depository in that territory, rested there, and on the fourth day set sail toward the Thundering Ray Region.

The chronicles of Princess Gemma's journey record a series of events that no careful reader could call ordinary. A massive fire broke out in the City of Rumble and spread to the room where she slept in the ruler's house of the Triplet Thunderbolt Region. An assassination shook the Streetlight Region. A seemingly simple voyage turned into a battle in the Lightning Region. In the Matron Region, the princess endured a terrifying encounter with rebels.

In the Flash Region, she witnessed a ghostly apparition.

These and many other episodes are told in The Princess of the Kingdom of Light, which insists that none of those events were accidental.

The Matron of the Triplets

The oldest historical record of the Kingdom of Light claims that the planet's first inhabitants were not human. They were an extinct race of arachnid-like beings who carved into stone the story of their escape from a homeworld destroyed beneath the flares of its own star.

Apart from the paintings and statues they left behind, little is known about their exact appearance. The surviving record shows with certainty only that they had many legs, extraordinary intelligence, a deep curiosity for astrological truth, and remarkable artistic skill.

Interpreting their accounts began in the era of the First Kings, when the new human inhabitants of the Kingdom of Light grew fascinated by them. Among those humans was a group of the Perfect Ones, who gave the vanished race the name "Chroniclers" because of their contributions to history, exploration, and the analysis of events both on their planet of origin and in the Kingdom of Light. Unlike many other races, they did not possess a traditional written language.

Among their most important surviving works were two sculptural essays, each told through tiny figures carved in sequence. One recorded a true event; the other preserved a fiction that became legend.

The first story tells how a group of Chroniclers escaped the cataclysm of their world. The carvings show the explosion of their star, the burning of the sky, violent earthquakes, and showers of fire. Shortly before the planet turned to ash, one caste of Chroniclers, fleeing between seismic tremors and stellar storms, fell through a crack in the earth. There, deep underground, the fire awakened a rugged portal hidden beneath the surface.

The Chroniclers emerged in a lake. Those who could swim reached the shore. Not all survived. Charred bodies floated on the water, and others drowned before they could escape. Because the illustrated account never explains this detail, some human scholars—including masters from the Kingdom of Light, scholars of Green Plant, and scientists from several other worlds—have argued that the Chroniclers did not know how to swim. Their theory seems reasonable, since none of the surviving accounts mention lakes, rivers, or seas.

Others believe the drowned had already been wounded, while the most widely accepted theory is simpler: some could swim, and others could not. Not knowing where they were or how they had arrived, the survivors explored the place and discovered they stood on an island in a different world. Much later, humans would name that island Artistic Island and call the waters the Lake of the Chroniclers.

Though fictional, the second story became the more famous of the two. Its ingenuity lay in the way it transformed an event the Chroniclers could not explain—an event that occurs every teckli in the Kingdom of Light—into myth.

The tale says that one night, a young girl stood on a beach of Artistic Island and asked her parents what kind of star shone in the darkness. Her parents did not know it was the kingdom's natural satellite; their home planet had possessed no such moon. So they invented an answer, and the answer became a folktale, later carved into a cave near the Lake of the Chroniclers.

They said the night's luminary was called Matrona and that she had given birth to three children: the Triplets, whose light turned night into day for days at a time.

That phrase—night becomes day for days—describes a phenomenon that occurs every teckli in the Kingdom of Light and, according to many scholars, gave rise to the kingdom's name. The planet and the Matron align in such a way that the Triplets reflect their light upon the Matron with great intensity, illuminating the nights for seven days. After the seventh day, darkness returns. Then, on the ninth day, the planet moves away from its stars, and winter—brief but merciless—lashes the entire world for ten days.

In the City of Light, this short winter is harsh but bearable. In other regions, survival requires preparation. Beneath each house, the people built underground shelters connected to a common steam-heating system, fed by provincial chimney equipment and linked through a network of pipes.

Chapter Five

OMINOUS SECRET

"Look over there," Princess Gemma said.

"A hut?" Úniquen asked. "What would a hut be doing in this place?"

"It will be dark soon. We should ask for shelter."

"There is something strange about this place, Gemma."

"What do you mean?"

"How many times have we come to the Weeping Forest?"

"Many," she replied. "I do not know. Too many to count."

"Exactly. We have been here more times than either of us can remember, and I do not recall ever seeing a hut."

"You are right," she said. "Let us see what is happening."

She climbed onto Úniquen's back, and he rose into the air. The cool breeze stirred her wet dress. Drops of water ran down her body and fell from her back onto Úniquen's tail.

"You are getting me soaked," he complained.

"Where is the hut?" she asked.

"There it is. No... how strange. I saw it a moment ago."

"I cannot see it either. Go back to the river."

Úniquen turned and descended. The princess jumped from his back as soon as he landed.

"Look," she said. "There it is again."

"I do not like this."

"Maybe that is why we have never seen it before. It could be some kind of optical effect."

"Optical what?"

"Forget it. I read about something like that long ago in one of my mother's old books."

They walked toward the hut for a while, until Úniquen slowed.

"What is that?" he asked.

"It looks like a wooden fence."

Before them stood a barrier made of cut logs, nearly as tall as the princess and stretching far across the land. Beyond it rose an old tree with a thick trunk.

"Whoever built this intended to keep visitors away," Úniquen said. "It is a barrier meant to separate whatever lies inside."

"Look," Gemma said. "The fence goes up the mountain. I cannot see where it ends." She stepped closer to the tree. "There is a metal plate embedded in the trunk."

"It is rusty. What does it say?"

"Sequetari novitico semite," she read. "Do you know what that means?"

"No. But whatever it means, I suggest we leave."

"And sleep in the Weeping Forest?"

"Do you not think it is strange that we saw the hut from the river, but not this fence?"

"Yes. It is strange. And stranger still that we did not see the fence or the hut from above. But I want to know what this is."

She began to climb. Úniquen flapped his wings, caught her gently by the arms, and carried her over the barrier. On the other side, he set her down near a small stream.

"Let us speak to that boy bathing there," Gemma said. "Maybe he lives in the hut."

They approached the shore. A boy sat on a rock beneath a narrow fall of water, motionless, staring downward.

"Child," Princess Gemma called, "would you come here, please?"

The boy did not answer. He remained seated under the stream, his head bowed.

"Hey, little one," Úniquen said. "Where are your parents?" Still, the boy gave no sign that he had heard them.

"Something is wrong with him," Gemma said.

She rolled up the hem of her dress and stepped into the stream. As she approached, the boy remained silent, and Gemma's feet sank into the mud beneath the water.

"You are going to get soaked again," Úniquen warned. Then his ears lifted.

"What is that sound?"

"It is the boy," Gemma said after a pause.

"How can he make a sound like that? Is he laughing?"

"No," she whispered. "It is more serious than that. It sounds as if he is crying."

"Boy," Úniquen called, "are you looking for something in the water?" The child did not move.

"No, Úniquen," Gemma said. "He is looking at his reflection."

"Get out of there, Gemma."

"That is exactly what I was thinking."

She turned to leave, but before she could take a step, the boy sprang from the rock and landed on her back. His small legs tangled around hers, and his arms locked around her neck. Gemma jerked violently, but he clung to her with impossible strength and forced her head beneath the water.

She kicked and twisted, but she could not free herself.

Úniquen shot toward them, seized the child in his claws, and lifted him away. The boy struck at Úniquen's talons until he broke loose, then dived into the stream and vanished beneath the water.

Princess Gemma staggered onto the shore and collapsed, coughing.

"That boy is mad," she gasped.

"I do not know how he escaped my claws," Úniquen said. "I held him tightly."

"He was strong, Úniquen. Too strong."

She sat up, gathered herself, and they continued toward the hut.

Along the path, several animals watched Princess Gemma and Úniquen with unsettling attention. Their gestures seemed almost expressive, almost deliberate, as if they were warning the strangers to turn back.

Children moved through the countryside. Some rode unfamiliar beasts. Others carried pieces of wood, cleared dry leaves, worked small fenced fields, or filled baskets with fruit from the trees surrounding the hidden village. The abundance of vegetation astonished Gemma.

"Gemma," Úniquen said, "do you see the two kinds of animals those children are riding?"

"I have never seen either kind before."

"The one ridden by the thinner boy is unknown to me," Úniquen said. "But the other one, near the fence, was supposed to be extinct. I remember seeing an animal like that nearly three hundred tecklis ago. Was I with your great-great-grandfather then, or with his father? I am not sure."

"Look, Úniquen. There are more huts up there."

"They look old," he said. "Very old. But I see only children. What kind of place is this?"

"The city of orphans," she said.

They both smiled, though neither felt at ease.

When they reached the hut, Princess Gemma knocked several times.

"There does not seem to be anyone inside," Úniquen said.

Gemma looked through a window and saw an old man within.

"The door is open!" the old man shouted.

Princess Gemma and Úniquen exchanged a glance. "I do not fit," Úniquen said.

"No, you do not. Stay close."

She entered the hut, and Úniquen pushed his head through the window.

The interior was neat and clean. To the right, two armchairs faced what looked like a fireplace. On the left wall hung several pointed objects resembling weapons, and beneath them lay a sword whose handle alone was visible beneath a black cloth. In the center of the room, logs had been assembled into a table, with smaller logs arranged as chairs around it. Along one wooden wall stood a shelf filled with books of many sizes, all placed with perfect symmetry.

Princess Gemma was studying the books when she met the old man's eyes.

"We are passing through," she said, "and wished to ask whether you could offer us shelter for the night."

The old man did not answer at once. He observed the princess, then turned toward the window and met Úniquen's gaze. Slowly, dragging his cane along the floor, he walked forward until his knees struck one of the log chairs. With the same peculiar slowness, he turned and sat down.

"You are of the nobility, are you not?" he asked in a weak voice.

Úniquen and Princess Gemma looked at each other.

"Why do you say that, sir?" she asked.

"Sir, you say? Very convenient." His mouth bent into a faint smile. "You may call me Vilo."

"Could we sleep here tonight, Mr. Vilo?"

"You could. But, as you know, everything in life has its price."

"We do not travel with silverets or goldets," Úniquen said, "but if you allow her to sleep here—"

"I did not say I wanted currency. How crude."

"Then what do you want?" Princess Gemma asked.

"Information. Answer a few questions, and you may stay."

"Let us go, Úniquen."

Úniquen motioned for her to remain.

"Ask," he said.

"She has already answered my first question," Vilo said.

"I do not understand," Gemma replied.

"I asked whether you were of the nobility. Now I am certain you are. And you are not merely noble, are you?"

"Are you using magic?" Úniquen asked.

"Magic?" Vilo laughed softly. "I have no need of it. Besides, all the magic you could imagine is found in knowledge." He pointed toward the books.

"How do you know anything about me?" Princess Gemma asked. "My dress is dirty, and—"

"Listen and learn, princess," Vilo interrupted. "The delicate dress and the Bolco at your side are one matter. Education is another. You entered my house with more confidence than any ordinary person would dare, almost as if everything you saw already belonged to you. Therefore, there were only two possibilities. You were either the daughter of a noble of great importance to the king, or you belonged to the royal core itself. And since you are a woman, the possibilities narrowed further: the queen, or the princess of the Kingdom of Light. I discarded the first the moment you decided to leave."

"How does he do that?" Úniquen murmured.

"Very simply," Vilo said. "It is part of knowing how to use knowledge, which is itself knowledge. Had you been the daughter of some principal of the king, you would not have taken long to identify yourself. But the queen would not do that, and neither would the princess of the Kingdom of Light. She would not need to say who she is in order to be known. If someone failed to recognize her, that person would bear the shame of his ignorance. She would not feed the knowledge of an ignorant man. She would not need to prove who she is, because she knows it."

Princess Gemma and Úniquen were speechless.

"Of course you may stay tonight, princess of the Kingdom of Light," the old man added. "After all, everything is yours."

He stood, made an exaggerated bow, and disappeared into another room.

"How does he know I am the princess and not the queen?" Gemma whispered to Úniquen.

"Easy," the old man shouted from the other room. "Because you have not bonded!"

His laughter burst through the hut. Gemma and Úniquen turned to each other again.

Before dawn, Princess Gemma and Úniquen awoke in alarm at the sound of moaning inside the hut. Úniquen pushed against the window sill with his snout until his head appeared inside. Still disoriented, Gemma looked down the narrow hallway, where a rudimentary torch threw dim light across the bedroom door.

"The old man is screaming," Úniquen said.

Gemma hesitated only a moment between the terrible groans and Úniquen's worried gaze. Then she ran to the door.

"It will not open!" she shouted.

She struck the primitive lock several times, then pressed her eye to a narrow crack in the wood.

She could not see Vilo himself, but she saw the shadow of a deformed hand beating against the floor. The fingers bent strangely, then seemed to shrink with each blow. The old man's groans grew louder, almost unbearable, until an unexpected silence fell, followed by a strange sigh.

Gemma froze with her eye against the crack. The shadow of the hand appeared again, now smaller, and moved slowly beyond the narrow edge of her sight.

"Mr. Vilo?" she asked.

"Gemma, tell me what is happening!" Úniquen shouted from the front window.

She saw the shadow of a small hand rise from the floor. Daylight slipped through the cracked wood of the hut. Then the bedroom door opened wide, and a boy stepped out.

The princess jumped back and retreated into the room. The boy walked toward her. They faced one another in silence while Úniquen watched a small figure, dressed in clothes far too large for him and wearing a grumpy expression, emerge into the living room.

"Who is that?" Úniquen asked.

Gemma did not answer. She continued backing away until her shoulders struck the front door.

The boy glanced at Úniquen's snout pressed awkwardly against the lattice. He seemed as if he wanted to laugh, but instead he frowned, sat on one of the log chairs, lifted his feet onto another, leaned back against a cushion fastened to the partition between the living room and the bedroom, reached with small hands toward one of the half-open books in the loft, and sighed.

"Are you going to stay at the door, princess?" the boy asked in the deep voice of a grown man.

Gemma startled and struck the door again.

"Let us go, Úniquen." She tried to open the door several times, but it would not move.

"It is me, Princess Gemma," the boy said. "Vilo."

"Why can Gemma not get out?" Úniquen shouted.

"You are turning the handle the wrong way, princess," Vilo said.

"Is it truly you?" Gemma asked.

"Get out of there, Gemma," Úniquen interrupted.

"Well..." She straightened herself as much as she could. "Thank you for your hospitality, Mr. Vilo, but we must leave."

She opened the door and stepped outside. Vilo rose and walked after her.

"You do not want to leave, Princess Gemma," he said. "I can help you with what you need."

"Get on, and let us go," Úniquen said, spreading his wings. "This place is unsettling."

"The princess will need all the knowledge she can gather about the mystical sphere if she is to defeat the one who overthrew her father." Princess Gemma returned to the doorway.

"How do you know someone overthrew my father?"

"It is clear you were running from someone when you came here. And what enemy could force the princess of the Kingdom of Light to flee her own palace? It points to an irrefutable fact: if the princess is running, she is running from the one who has overthrown the king."

"And how do you know I need to learn more about the mystical sphere?"

"Gemma, let us leave," Úniquen repeated.

"Last night," Vilo said, "I saw the sphere hanging from your neck between your wet dress and the firelight. Come inside. Let us finish our conversation."

"What do you know about the mystical sphere?" Gemma asked.

"Many things. For one, there is one in each of the thirteen Sibling Worlds."

"Thirteen?"

Vilo waved his tiny hands, inviting her back into the hut. She followed him inside and sat across from him. Úniquen pushed his head through the window once more.

"It is astonishing, is it not?" Vilo asked, brushing his slender fingertips along the line of books arranged in the loft.

"What? The books?"

"The knowledge that emanates from them," he said. "The immense source of wisdom preserved in objects so simple, so small, so harmless in the eyes of the ignorant, and yet, in the hands of the wise, among the most lethal weapons ever created. A book can give life and take it. It can do good and provoke evil. It can become the origin of happiness or misfortune. It is discreet enough to hide between sheets or in a dark corner, yet it carries a power capable of inspiring wars and conquering worlds. The most splendid creation of perishable beings was made to endure." He sighed, and Gemma nodded.

"For a long time," Vilo continued, "I have wished to leave this village and have not been able to. Yet I have traveled through the Sibling Worlds. I have met civilizations, learned magic, and discovered wonders I could never have imagined, all from here, sitting beneath that loft, reading night and day." Gemma nodded again, then exchanged a look with Úniquen.

"Vilo," she said, "could you tell me what you know about the powers of the sphere and the Sibling Worlds?" Úniquen turned his gaze to Vilo.

"You like to read, princess, do you not?" Vilo asked.

"Yes, Vilo. But I would be grateful if you told me what you know now. My enemy's army may already be looking for me."

"And I will. But first, tell me: who attacked our world?"

"Dargos, from the planet Gálax."

"No. I do not know him." Vilo leaned back in thought. "I have been out of touch with civilization for some time. Has Diamondis changed? Has the palace been torn down, or does it remain intact? The precious stones, the paintings, the statues?"

"Mr. Vilo," Úniquen interrupted, "I do not know whether you understand the gravity of the situation. Our world is in danger. Could you please answer the princess?"

"Oh, I understand," Vilo said with a smile.

"Did you say there are thirteen mystical spheres?" Gemma asked.

"That is right. Each mystical sphere belongs to one of the Sibling Worlds."

"Sibling Worlds?"

"Yes. Thirteen planets, scattered across different galaxies, are called the Sibling Worlds. It is said the name was given to worlds of human ancestry." Princess Gemma and Úniquen looked at each other.

"Are the human beings of those planets the same as the humans of the Kingdom of Light?" she asked.

"The same race, expanded across different worlds of the universe," Vilo replied. "The essence of humanity has not changed. What has changed are the abilities humanity has developed in each Sibling World."

"Abilities?"

"Yes."

"What kind of abilities?"

"For example, some humans have lived for centuries on worlds whose natural conditions allow them to live longer. On other worlds, though not all, humans have developed the potential of the mind far beyond what is common here."

"I have heard that humans on Green Plant can read minds," Úniquen said.

Vilo nodded.

"Why does that name sound familiar?" Gemma asked.

"King Nótrex and Kéltrox went there once," Úniquen replied.

"What do these Sibling Worlds have to do with the power of the mystical sphere?" she asked.

Vilo bowed his small body toward her.

"Your Highness, I mean no disrespect, but you should have known all this. It is essential knowledge for someone of your position. And seeing your hunger for learning, I know ignorance did not come from weakness of character. Your education was careless." Gemma's expression tightened.

"But do not worry," Vilo added. "I will explain. The reason the mystical spheres exist is to protect the Sibling Worlds. Each planet must have a sphere and a wizard protector."

"A wizard protector?" Princess Gemma asked, startled.

Úniquen lowered his head.

"Did you know this?" she asked him.

"Some of it," Úniquen replied.

"Why did no one tell me?"

"Your father wanted to keep you away from all this. He believed you would be safer."

"Away? Safe?" Her voice sharpened. "Do I look away from it? Do I look safe to you? I am trapped in it up to my neck, and because of his arrogance and pretension, I am not ready." Úniquen did not answer.

Gemma turned back to Vilo. "What are the Sibling Worlds called?"

"Green Plant, Senters, the Shared Kingdom of Dóriton, Gálax, Ilucus, Humus, Germovas, Kekarta, Salfinio, Corazo, Carcania, Tántum, and, of course, the Kingdom of Light."

"I will ask Prince Altren whether Ilucus has alliances with any of those worlds," Gemma said, turning briefly to Úniquen. Then she faced Vilo again.

"Before we go, tell us where I can find one of these wizards."

"Princess Gemma, you must forgive me, but I have important matters I cannot postpone, not even for your sake. I must be absent during the day. We will continue the lesson when I return."

"But this is imperative, Vilo. If Dargos and his army of Kronkos find me here, they could wipe out this entire village." Vilo burst out laughing.

"Dargos and his army of Kronkos? No, princess. They will not be able to follow you here."

Gemma and Úniquen looked at each other.

"Then we should still be on our way. I cannot take that risk." She rose from her seat.

"Have you heard of the Book of Origins?" Vilo asked.

Úniquen frowned. Gemma nodded.

"Good. Tecklis ago, while plowing the land, I found a hidden chest. The insignia of Diamondis was impressed into the metal. Inside were scrolls and ancient writings. Beneath them lay a book. My surprise was indescribable when I discovered that the Book of Origins was inside that chest." Gemma did not move.

"I will return the book to its rightful owner," Vilo said. "To you, Princess Gemma. And at sunset, when I return, I will answer all your questions." Úniquen examined the loft.

"No, my Bolco friend," Vilo said as he left the hut. "I would never place such a treasure among those other books. The Book of Origins is well hidden—and well guarded."

Chapter Six

SEARCHING FOR ANSWERS

Vilo dashed away with a speed that looked less like running than a small, frantic gallop. Every few moments, he glanced over his shoulder, stealing a wary look at Princess Gemma before facing the path again.

From the riverbank, Gemma and Úniquen saw a group of children gathered on the opposite side, near the slope of the mountain. A few animals emerged from among the trees and joined them. Vilo crossed the river and began climbing the hill, and the children and animals followed him in a line.

"This keeps getting stranger," Úniquen said.

"It does," Gemma replied, watching the animals carefully. "Look at them, Úniquen. I know it sounds absurd, but they move as if they are thinking beings."

"They are all going in the same direction."

"Where do you think they are going?"

"I do not know, Gemma. And that is exactly why I think we should leave this place as soon as possible."

"If Vilo truly has the Book of Origins," she said, "we may find something that can help us defeat Dargos."

"And do you not think it is too great a coincidence that he has it?" Úniquen asked. "Do you know how long your father searched for that book?" Gemma kept her eyes on the hill.

"Then let us find out."

"Find out what?"

"What Vilo is doing with those children and animals. Besides," she said, climbing onto Úniquen's back, "I want to understand this village."

They followed from the air, flying low and keeping their distance. Úniquen moved behind trees, rocks, strips of cultivated earth, and curtains of wild grass. Ahead of them, the line of children and animals climbed with the tense obedience of creatures summoned by danger. From time to time, one of them looked back, as if sensing unseen eyes behind them.

"Gemma," Úniquen murmured, "I have been thinking about what Vilo said. What do you think he meant when he said the Kronkos cannot enter the village?"

"I do not know," she whispered. "Sometimes it feels as if we are not even in the Kingdom of Light anymore."

"This region was supposed to be uninhabited."

They reached the top of the hill and advanced a little farther. At last, the crowd stopped before a tree growing in a plain enclosed by three mountains and a great ring of stone. Princess Gemma and Úniquen lowered themselves behind a dry trunk on a nearby rise, lying close to the ground where they could see without being seen.

Vilo climbed onto the rock, cupped his hands around his mouth, and gave a sharp hoot. The children and animals fell silent.

"Chief Mantus will lead this emergency assembly, as always," Vilo announced, then stepped aside.

A child climbed onto the rock.

"Condemned inhabitants of the Cursed Village," Mantus said.

The voice did not belong to a child. It was a man's voice, firm and authoritative, coming from a small body with a posture too old for its face.

"Did he say cursed?" Gemma whispered.

Úniquen nodded.

"Everyone knows the reason for this convocation," Mantus continued.

"For the first time in several centuries, visitors have entered our village. Our isolation has ended. Strangers breached the enchantment barrier. We do not yet know how. However, if anyone wishes to leave, he may do so."

A murmur spread through the crowd.

Princess Gemma and Úniquen stared in disbelief as children spoke in the voices of grown men, and animals answered them with the same grave understanding.

"Those animals are talking," Gemma whispered.

"I cannot believe it," Úniquen replied under his breath.

Mantus raised both hands.

"Silence. Silence, please." The murmurs faded. "Apparently, the spell has weakened. But we have not fully returned to our original forms."

The crowd stirred again. Gemma and Úniquen exchanged a troubled glance. "Listen!" Mantus called. "You are making too much noise."

"Go on, Mantus," Vilo said.

"We must discover who the strangers are and how they entered."

"I think they are wizards," one animal said.

"Did you see her clothing?" another asked.

"I do not think they are from this world," said one of the boys, again in the voice of a man.

Mantus turned toward him.

"And how can you state that they are from another planet? None of us knows the outside world anymore, you dullard." Vilo stepped before the crowd.

"Do you hear what you are saying? You are mistaken. They are only two travelers passing through. They asked for shelter in my house, and I gave it to them. They are not wizards. They are not from another world. And they did not come here to harm us." Mantus studied him.

"Vilo, your wisdom, your magical ability, and your former place as the king's advisor give you more experience than most of us possess. Can we trust the strangers?"

"Yes," Vilo answered. "They are harmless. We have nothing to fear from them."

"What about the séritroc we found?" asked one of the animals.

Vilo's face sharpened. "What séritroc?"

"They say someone—or something—was riding it," Mantus said. "And that it was hiding among the trees."

"I heard nothing of this," Vilo replied.

"A séritroc?" Úniquen whispered.

Gemma's breath tightened. "Do you think the Kronkos found us?"

"I understand your claim that the visitors are harmless," Mantus said to Vilo. "But the spell failed when they entered our village."

"As you said," Vilo replied, "I am the oldest among you, and I know magic. I assure you they have nothing to do with this." He paused, then lifted a finger. "Give me one day to prove it. Tomorrow, I will bring you an answer regarding these events. Otherwise, you may proceed as you see fit."

"Be it as you say," Mantus replied.

The assembly agreed. The meeting ended, and the children and animals began to disperse.

"We should return to the hut before someone discovers us," Gemma whispered.

"Climb on," Úniquen said.

They rose into the air.

"This does not feel right," he added.

When they reached the hut, Princess Gemma went inside, rubbed two dry branches together until the fire caught in the fireplace, chose a book from the loft, and sat on one of the cut logs nearest the warmth. Úniquen remained by the window, watching over her while she read.

After a long while, Vilo returned and collapsed onto a log.

"I was right about you, princess," he said. "I see you are passionate about reading."

Gemma lowered the book and smiled faintly.

"Nothing would comfort me more than reading the Book of Origins, as you promised this morning."

"And who would not want to read the Book of Origins?" Vilo sighed. "The book of books. A formidable thing of incalculable value." He looked toward the fire. "Did you know it was written by a perishable?"

"A perishable?" Úniquen asked.

"Yes. Though in my opinion, he is no longer one."

"What is a perishable?" Gemma asked.

Vilo smiled as if the question pleased him.

"I could answer you now, if you wish. But why waste the pleasure of seeing the essential mysteries of the universe with your own eyes? Why deprive yourself of such delight?"

Gemma's patience thinned.

"Where is the book, Vilo?"

"That is the question," he said, rising. "The great question." He approached a cracked board near the loft and knocked on it.

"Since ancient times, men and women, kings and slaves, have asked the same thing. Some, obsessed with possessing it at any cost, sacrificed their own lives and the lives of others. They destroyed civilizations. They crossed human worlds and worlds belonging to other races."

The cracked board gave way. Vilo reached into a hidden space and pulled out a golden chest engraved with ancient markings on a strip of silver fixed to its lid.

"And despite all their futile efforts," he said, turning to her, "here it is, princess, in your fugitive hands."

"Is the book inside the chest?" Gemma asked, standing. "Not the entire collection. Only the first volume." He placed the chest in her arms.

"So there are other volumes?"

She knelt, set the chest on the floor, released three latches, and opened it.

"Seven," Vilo said.

Then he went still.

His head froze. His eyes stared at nothing.

Gemma let the chest fall and stepped toward him.

"Vilo? Vilo?"

He did not answer.

"Try to shake him!" Úniquen shouted.

She placed both hands on Vilo's small shoulders and pulled back at once.

"He is burning."

"Pour water on him."

Gemma started to rise, but Vilo lurched forward and collapsed at her knees. His hands clenched the rug. A man's voice tore from his throat. His eyes filled with tears, and between his screams, Gemma heard a dreadful sound, as if his bones themselves were changing. Veins rose across his face. His hands swelled and twisted. His fingers bent backward. He spun on the carpet, and the childlike shape began to disappear. His body lengthened. His soft face wrinkled. The boy was becoming an old man.

Later, Vilo opened his eyes.

His head rested on a bundle of rags. Through heavy eyelids, he saw Princess Gemma sitting on the carpet near him, the Book of Origins open in her hands.

"He is awake," Úniquen said from the window.

Gemma lowered the book.

"Why did you turn into an old man?"

"Because of a curse I would rather not speak of." He sighed. Gemma returned to the page.

"Is it what you expected?" Vilo asked.

"I have barely begun," she said. "I waited until your fever passed."

"Did you find a small twig inside the book?"

"No. What twig?"

She turned a few pages, then stopped.

"Oh. Here it is."

"It is for you," Vilo said.

Gemma touched the tiny shoot with her fingertips. She studied its texture, and for reasons she did not understand, tears rose in her eyes. She looked at Úniquen, then at Vilo.

"What is this?" she asked, her voice trembling.

"A gift given to me long ago by the prime minister of Green Plant." Vilo's voice softened. "Now tell me, princess. How do you feel?" Gemma swallowed.

"Sad."

Úniquen shifted at the window.

"Gemma, what is wrong? Why are you crying?"

"Do not interrupt her, Bolco," Vilo said. "Let her drain the sorrow. Go on, princess."

Gemma's shoulders trembled.

"I am afraid to use the sphere. Almost every day, I dream that the Kronkos torture me. I only want to be somewhere safe." A low groan escaped her.

"What did you do to her?" Úniquen demanded, forcing his snout harder against the window frame.

Vilo opened his trembling arms.

"Come here, princess. I will tell you how to ease your pain." Gemma rose and stepped toward him.

"Gemma, wake up!" Úniquen shouted, digging his claws into the wood.

"I am tired of fighting, Úniquen," she said, her voice distant.

"Come closer," Vilo whispered.

When Gemma reached him, she knelt. Vilo caught the chain that held the mystical sphere. Outside the window, Úniquen roared as the wood began to crack.

Gemma looked down at Vilo's hand and took hold of the chain herself.

"Let it go, princess," Vilo said. "Let it go, and your pain will disappear. I promise."

She released the sphere.

Vilo held it as if he had recovered a piece of his own soul. He caressed it. His eyes shone. Úniquen shouted louder, but Vilo ignored him. With the sphere in his hand, he rose from the floor with sudden strength.

"I have been considering what to do with you, Princess Gemma," he said.

"I sincerely wish there were another path to regaining my kingdom."

"Your kingdom?" Gemma stammered from the floor.

"You see, Princess Gemma, I have not been honest with you. But it is naive to believe that everything a stranger says must be true. I do not blame you for that. You have the same thirst for knowledge I had at your age. I blame your deficient education and those responsible for it. A king who neglects his daughter's preparation does not deserve to be king."

He looked down at her, the sphere gleaming in his hand.

"Vilo was the name of my advisor. My true name is Vargos. Long ago, I ruled the Kingdom of Light. And now, thanks to you, I will reclaim what is rightfully mine."

Gemma's face went pale.

"As for you," Vargos continued, "I meant what I said. I wish there were another way. But those who hold power must sometimes make decisions others will never understand. I thank you, Princess Gemma. After so many tecklis, I will leave this rotten cursed village. And I will take revenge on Faltron."

He struck the mystical sphere against his chest.

Energy burst around his body. Vargos rose into the air as the power covered him. At the window, Úniquen pounded the wood with his claws, tearing deeper into the frame.

The former king lifted his hands toward Princess Gemma. A small flame kindled around his wrists, then grew.

Before he could strike, a man burst into the hut and seized him from behind. In one swift motion, the stranger tore the mystical sphere from Vargos's chest and drove a dagger into his heart.

The light vanished. Vargos stopped floating, and both men crashed to the floor.

Gemma blinked, as if waking from a dream.

"What happened?" she asked, releasing the small shoot from her right hand.

"You gave the sphere to Vargos," Úniquen said from the ruined window, "and then someone came in and killed him."

"Who is the man who saved me?"

She crawled toward Vargos's body. Blood soaked him. Beneath him, partly hidden by a travel-worn cloak, lay the man who had burst into the hut.

Princess Gemma rolled Vargos aside with shaking hands. The stranger's face was covered by the cloak, but his body bore the marks of a brutal journey.

She pulled the fabric away.

Her astonishment matched Úniquen's.

"Uncle Kéltrox?" she whispered. "Is it you?"

Kéltrox sat up.

For a moment, neither of them spoke. Then Gemma threw her arms around him, and he held her tightly.

Chapter Seven

Little Kéltrox

Unlike other children, who played with sticks and dolls, Kéltrox spent his childhood in the palace gardens swinging a wooden sword at trees and stones. Even then, his desire to join the army of Diamondis burned in him with unusual force, and he trained tirelessly with the only weapon his parents allowed him to carry.

As happened every teckli, the winter gale, brief but merciless, lashed the walls of Diamondis. During that season, King Lardo and his wife, Katty, rulers from the planet Gálax, visited King Dervinán and Queen Ardnas of the Kingdom of Light.

The rulers of Gálax left the Pirutus and reached the City of Light at dusk on the fifth day. Some citizens rode nórmides through the torch-lit streets, clearing a path for the five tíricus-drawn chariots that surrounded the royal carriage.

That afternoon, as usual, Kéltrox had disguised himself in rags so no one would recognize him. Without permission, he slipped past palace security and met the children of the city, who were waiting anxiously for him before the gates of Diamondis.

"Morico the warrior is here!" one child shouted.

Kéltrox raised his wooden sword, and the children rushed toward him.

They divided into two armies: one calling themselves the Destroyers of Men, the other the Humans of Morico. With sticks for weapons and frozen earth for a battlefield, they fought until the gardens rang with victory cries and the whispered last words of the fallen. Each child surrendered fully to the role. Kéltrox, whom they called Morico, moved among them with fierce agility, swinging his wooden sword as if it were a blade worthy of command.

Then King Lardo's carriage stopped before the gates of Diamondis.

Lost in the force of his imaginary war, Kéltrox did not hear the chariot arrive. He leapt forward, then back, striking at the invisible enemy he called the Chameleon. Still caught between fantasy and the world around him, he spun with his sword raised and collided with King Lardo just as the visiting king stepped down from the carriage with Katty beside him.

The children froze. As if waking from a dream, they saw their swords become sticks again. The dead rose from the frozen ground, slowly and solemnly, as though the wounds of their game had truly pierced them.

King Lardo's general saw the ragged, mud-streaked boy stagger toward his sovereign and mistook him for an orphan. He drew his sword and swung a dagger toward Kéltrox's head. To the astonishment of everyone present, Kéltrox ducked by instinct, avoided the deadly blow, and struck the general three times with his wooden sword: first across the head, then on the right arm, and finally, with all his strength, at the man's feet.

The general fell flat on his back.

Those who had accompanied King Lardo burst into laughter, and the children, their dreams restored, raised their sticks and shouted again in triumph.

Humiliated, the general rose and thrust the point of his sword toward Kéltrox's chest. Before it could touch him, King Lardo blocked the blade with his own.

"Leave the child alone," King Lardo said, "and do not behave like a savage."

When Queen Ardnas learned what had happened, she scolded Kéltrox for leaving the palace gates. Yet she could not stop King Dervinán from retelling his son's achievement with pride night after night.

Princess Gemma

"Is that a wound?" Princess Gemma asked, kneeling before Kéltrox.

"Insignificant," he said, dropping onto one of the logs.

"It does not look insignificant. It is covered in something that is not blood. Let me see." She untied the rough, tattered cloth wrapped around his side and threw it aside. "What kind of bandage is this?"

"I think it was part of a tunic," Kéltrox said. "Or a cloak. I tore it from a body."

"If we do not find some kind of ferment among Vilo's belongings, we will have to burn the wound." Kéltrox sighed.

"Check my case. I threw it over there. I have dry sticks, some clothes, and a bottle of oil."

"Why did you bring oil?" Gemma asked.

"Remember that you can use the mystical sphere," Úniquen said from the window.

"No," Kéltrox said sharply. "Your father does not want her using it unless it is the last resort."

"It was the last resort," Úniquen replied. "She healed herself, healed me, and defeated a squad of Kronkos." Kéltrox stared at him.

"How did you defeat a squad of Kronkos?"

"With fireballs," Úniquen said.

"Fireballs?"

Without answering, Gemma crossed to Vargos's lifeless body, retrieved the mystical sphere from the pool of blood, and poured water over it from a pitcher. Then she returned to Kéltrox and knelt before him.

"I want you to heal," she said, taking his hand.

"Wait, wait. What are you doing?"

"I am telling the mystical sphere to heal you. That is how it worked with Úniquen."

Kéltrox laughed despite the pain.

"It is strange that it worked that way. You do not need words."

"How was I supposed to know that if no one taught me?" Gemma asked.

"Then teach me."

Kéltrox grew serious.

"Hold it tightly in your right hand. Touch the wound with your left. Close your eyes, clear your mind, and desire the healing." She obeyed. Almost at once, the wound closed.

Kéltrox looked at his side, then at her.

"Do you know how long it took your father to heal someone? Or to throw fire?"

"Úniquen told me."

"I always knew you could do it." Gemma lowered her eyes.

"I know. Unlike my father, you have faith in me." Her voice cracked. She drew a breath and continued. "I overheard part of the conversation you and Father had several nights before he gave me the sphere." Kéltrox watched her in silence.

"What conversation?"

"You know which one."

Before — King Nótrex

King Nótrex arrived at the Fountain Table with Rólar beside him. Kéltrox and a small group of high-ranking soldiers stood over the map, moving silver statuettes shaped like men across its surface.

"Rólar just told me," the king said. "Are we certain it is him?"

"Yes, brother," Kéltrox replied. "Dargos has come to the planet." Nótrex dropped into a chair.

"With the Tolorons of Sinella?"

"No. With the Venturians. The dome of Ventus has joined him with a massive army of Kronkos."

"Which route did they choose?"

"Úniquen saw them after they left the Pirutus," Kéltrox said. He slid his index finger across the map. "They divided the army into three groups. The one commanded by Dargos took the desert of Nale."

"He intends to come here," the king said.

"He is flying on his Bolco, and the Kronkos are fast," Rólar added, frowning as he moved one of the figures. "They will reach the City of Light in three or four days."

"The Ventus commands the other two groups," Kéltrox said. "They are headed for the Shining Sea and the Waters of Salavera."

"Dargos sent them to seize the regions by taking the ships," Nótrex said, then sighed. "How many?"

Kéltrox's expression hardened.

"Too many. Millions, brother. The regional armies will not resist them for long, and we cannot protect them."

"Why not?" Rólar asked. "According to my father, no human being can use the mystical sphere as skillfully as you, my king." Nótrex and Kéltrox exchanged a glance.

"Your father told you that?" the king asked.

"Yes. I was only a child. He told me you defeated an army of chameleons by yourself." Rólar looked from one brother to the other. "What is wrong?" Nótrex did not answer him. Instead, he looked at Kéltrox.

"Why would Dargos take this risk now, knowing my mastery of the sphere?"

"Leave us," Kéltrox ordered.

The soldiers withdrew.

"You too, Rólar. Go to your father and help him prepare the defenses." Rólar obeyed.

When they were alone, Kéltrox spoke in a lower voice.

"Brother, Dargos has discovered that you cannot use the mystical sphere."

"Did the informant report that to you?"

"The news came too late. He told me Dargos had been staying in the shared kingdom of Dóriton. The informant overheard a conversation between Dargos and Tolan."

Nótrex tapped the table with one finger.

"Then someone close to us, one of the few who knows about Krístal, has betrayed us. Otherwise, Dargos would never have dared attack with only the Venturians. We must discover who the traitor is."

"For now, we must plan our defense."

At that moment, Princess Gemma, awakened by the commotion, passed before the door. She had been about to open it when a murmur stopped her. "You must tell Gemma to use the sphere," she heard Kéltrox say.

"No," Nótrex objected. "She is still too young."

"She is the same age Krístal was when she bonded with you. Brother, think carefully. The future of our planet depends on it."

"I am thinking of the kingdom," Nótrex said, "but I will not send my daughter to certain death."

Kéltrox heard a gasp and rushed to the door, but Gemma had vanished.

Mantus

Before daybreak, Princess Gemma woke to the squeak of the turnstile. Her eyes still heavy with sleep, she saw Kéltrox standing in the doorway of the hut, one hand on the frame and the other on the half-open door, staring intently outside.

"Get ready to run," he whispered, then closed the door.

Gemma rose quickly but quietly. She crossed to the window and peered through the lattice.

"They have been there for some time," Úniquen said.

Gemma searched for him and did not see him at first. She leaned through the window opening, looked down, and found him crouched between the thick sticks that served as beams for the hut.

"The children and those strange animals have surrounded us," Kéltrox said.

"What do they want?" Gemma asked.

"Nothing good, from the look of it," Úniquen said.

"Some of them are armed," Gemma whispered.

"Then they are suggesting we will not leave without a fight," Kéltrox replied.

The boys with men's voices drew closer to the house. One of them, the one they called Mantus, shouted, "Come out of the hut calmly and unarmed."

"Gemma, stay here," Kéltrox said. "I will speak with them. If they attack, you and Úniquen leave. Do you understand?"

"I can defend us with the mystical sphere."

"Your father does not want you using it unless-"

"We told you she already used it against the Kronkos," Úniquen interrupted.

Kéltrox looked from the Bolco to Gemma.

"All right. We go together. But do nothing unless it is strictly necessary."

He stepped out of the hut with firm, controlled steps, his fingers brushing the hilt of his sword without drawing it. Gemma and Úniquen followed. The Bolco kept his wings half-raised.

They stopped before the children and animals.

"We have not come to harm you," Kéltrox said, meeting Mantus's gaze.

"Then where is Vilo?" Mantus asked. "Mericul saw you stab him last night."

He pointed toward another child.

"If Mericul saw clearly," Kéltrox said, "then he also saw that your friend Vilo tried to kill her and declared himself King Vargos while doing it."

He gestured toward Gemma. The man-voiced children and the animals murmured among themselves.

"We saw a bright light come from the hut last night," one of the animals said. It was grotesque, broad and powerful as a bear, yet with a head too small for its body.

"Then you should have asked your friend about it, whatever his true name was," Kéltrox replied. "He was the one who made that light appear." Mantus studied him.

"Who are you?"

"I am Kéltrox, brother of King Nótrex and general of the Army of the Kingdom of Light." His voice turned commanding. "Why do you not know me?"

Some of the children laughed. Gemma and Úniquen exchanged a glance.

"Do you even know where you are?" Mantus asked. "We can only explain your presence here if you used magic to break the spell barrier. Are any of you wizards?"

"What spell?" Gemma asked.

Mantus looked at the others. Several children and animals nodded, then fixed their attention on him again.

"We have lost count of the tecklis," Mantus said.

"Go on," Kéltrox ordered.

"King Vargos had usurped the kingdom from his cousin Normen, and the men loyal to him fled Diamondis with him. For days, they tried to recover the throne. They ambushed us several times, but they never defeated us. We warred against them for months, cutting them down one by one until we had eliminated them all. King Normen was the only survivor. He was an agile warrior, and he fled to this village to hide."

Mantus paused. He looked toward Vilo's hut, then toward the mountains, the trees, and the scattered dwellings.

"This place was beautiful when we arrived. The people plowed the land and lived in peace. Animals and children played and bathed in the streams. But we cared only about killing Normen."

"Did the villagers hide him?" Gemma asked.

"To their misfortune," Mantus said, "and ours." He drew a breath before continuing.

"When we found Normen, we executed him before the community. Then King Vargos ordered us to kill every living being in the village as punishment. One of our soldiers begged him not to commit such an atrocity. He pleaded for mercy again and again. Vargos pierced that soldier's chest with his sword and shouted, 'Does anyone else wish to contradict my orders?' Seeing what had happened to him, we kept silent. Then we drew our swords and murdered every living creature here. Men. Women. Children. Elders. Animals. All of them. Afterward, we gathered the bodies in one place." Gemma went still.

Mantus lowered his gaze.

"When it was time to move the body of the soldier Vargos had killed, we saw an old man climb over the fence. He was tall and carried a cane. Though he walked without difficulty, he stopped before the tree and raised his hands toward its branches. We did not hear what he said. Soon after, a metal plate with an inscription appeared on the trunk."

"Seketari novitico semite," Gemma said.

Mantus glanced at her, then continued.

"We dropped the soldier's body, raised our weapons, and took position to attack. The old man walked toward us until he stood before King Vargos." Mantus's voice changed slightly, as if repeating words carved into memory.

"You should have listened," the old man said, pointing at the dead soldier.

"What do you seek, old man?" Vargos asked.

"I could not stop your atrocity," the old man replied, "but I spoke through the soldier you killed, the one who opposed this massacre."

"We laughed," Mantus said. "Then the old man struck the ground with his staff, and the mystical sphere hanging from King Vargos's neck flew into a bag he carried. He said he would return it to the Kingdom of Light, where it belonged. He also said his name was Faltron, or something like that. We did not understand him well. We were too shocked to understand anything."

"Faltron the wizard?" Kéltrox asked.

"Yes. The one who wanders the Sibling Worlds judging evil acts. He pronounced our sentence." Mantus closed his eyes.

"I hereby declare you guilty of causing harm to this land. In the name of justice and for the betterment of humanity, I condemn you to assume the shape of the innocent children and animals whose lives you have callously destroyed. As long as this planet exists, the memories will keep you captive. Every murder you committed will haunt you in nightmares so vivid that you will feel them as if they are happening again. The torment will become so great that you will beg for death and long for perpetual sleep. No one will see you again. None of you may escape, for any who cross the fence will become ash. I have marked the fence and hidden the village. This will be your invisible cell. Every thousand tecklis, one of you will die until none remain." He opened his eyes.

"It happened exactly as he said. He had barely finished speaking when we transformed. Some became animals. Others, like me, took the shape of the children we had murdered. The rest of the curse also came true. Since then, five thousand tecklis must have passed, because five of us have died in our nightmares. Three others crossed the fence and became ash. Fifty-two of us remain."

"Has anyone come here before us?" Kéltrox asked.

"You are the first visitors since then."

"Why did Vilo call himself King Vargos?" Gemma asked.

"Vilo was King Vargos's right hand," Mantus said. "Now we understand that Vargos must have taken Vilo's identity to preserve his own life. When the wizard cursed us, we were confused. All of us had changed form, and no one knew what body the others had taken. We were enraged because our obedience to Vargos had condemned us, and many wanted to kill him. But Vargos escaped in the chaos." Mantus looked toward the hut again.

"We questioned one another until nightfall, trying to discover who was who. Then, taking advantage of the darkness, Vargos raised his voice and cried, 'I hate you, King Vargos! I hate you! I followed you wherever you sent me, but I will not follow you to death.' Then he took a sword and cut off his advisor's head."

Gemma's eyes narrowed.

"He killed the real Vilo so no one could expose him."

"Exactly," Mantus said. "And it worked. We all believed King Vargos had been beheaded. Now we have told you everything. Tell us, then: how did you break the barrier of the enchantment?"

"We are leaving," Kéltrox said. "If the enchantment is broken, then you may leave as well."

He started forward, and several children raised their weapons.

Kéltrox drew his sword.

"We are leaving," he repeated.

Gemma clutched the mystical sphere in her right hand. Before she could press it against her chest, Mantus spoke again.

"You said you were the general of the Army of the Kingdom of Light. If that is true, why is a man in your position guarding a young girl and her Bolco?" He circled Gemma, studying her dress and face with unsettling precision.

"Who are you, young lady? You must be the daughter of a nobleman, must you not?"

"Yes," Gemma replied carefully. "I am the daughter of a nobleman." The man-voiced child continued to circle her.

Gemma leaned toward Kéltrox and whispered, "This cursed little man in a child's body is terrifying me. I am going to use the sphere."

"Not yet," Kéltrox whispered back. "Wait for my signal." Úniquen lifted his wings discreetly.

Mantus stopped.

"Not every noblewoman has a Bolco as a mount, nor a bodyguard who commands the army."

"What do you mean?" Gemma asked.

"Are you related to the king? His niece, perhaps?" Mantus stared harder. "No. I see it now. You are the king's daughter. Yes. You are the king's daughter."

The children and animals exchanged glances. Some tightened their grip on their weapons. Others lowered them at once. "Stop!" Mantus shouted. "Put away your weapons." Then he looked at Gemma with sudden awe.

"You possess the mystical sphere. That is how you entered this place. That is what made the light in the hut last night." His face changed. "So that is why the barrier broke. Vargos fooled us all during the assembly. That villain wanted to keep the sphere for himself."

"Do not take another step," Kéltrox warned, his sword raised.

Mantus glanced at the others and repeated more sharply, "I said put away your weapons."

He turned back to Kéltrox.

"Go freely. No one will interfere. We have already received our sentence for what we did to this village. We do not wish to learn what would happen if we harmed the princess of the Kingdom of Light."

Kéltrox lowered his sword to waist height and watched as Mantus, the children, and the animals stepped aside.

"I will gather supplies," Gemma said.

She ran back to the hut, collected what little they had, took the Book of Origins from the carpet, wrapped it in the blankets Vargos had kept there, and tied the bundle to Úniquen's back.

They had not yet crossed the fence when they heard movement behind them. Mantus was hurrying toward them with both hands raised. A bundle of intertwined rags hung from his back, swinging with each step.

"What does he want now?" Gemma asked.

"He is in a hurry," Úniquen observed, wrinkling his muzzle.

"At least he is not armed," Kéltrox said.

Mantus reached them breathless, half-bent, his small hands planted on his knees.

"There is something else I want to tell you," he gasped.

"Speak," Kéltrox said.

"Allow me to join your journey. I served King Vargos faithfully. I helped him plot against his cousin Normen and take the throne. It is time for me to repair what I helped destroy and serve a just cause."

"No," Kéltrox said at once. "Go back."

"You may come," Gemma said. "I believe you could be useful." Kéltrox turned to her.

"Useful for what?"

"It is not a good idea," Úniquen added.

"Why not?" Gemma asked.

"Many reasons," Úniquen said. "Traveling with a five-thousand-teckli-old boy cursed by a wizard, trapped in a haunted village, complicit in a war between kings, and guilty in the murder of children and animals is not exactly my preferred kind of company."

"I know this land," Mantus said. "I can guide you."

Kéltrox looked at Gemma, leaving the decision to her. She nodded. "If you do anything strange," Kéltrox told Mantus, "I will kill you."

"You will not regret this," Mantus replied.

Úniquen brought his snout close to Gemma's ear.

"You did that to contradict him," he whispered.

"Yes," she whispered back, loud enough for Kéltrox to hear. "I am not a little girl anymore, and he still wants to decide everything without asking me. We are no longer in the palace, and he is not my father." Kéltrox said nothing.

He climbed the fence and dropped to the other side. Úniquen beat his wings, lifted Gemma, and crossed with her. Mantus remained frozen where he stood.

"Why do you not finish crossing?" Gemma asked, watching him through a gap in the fence.

"I am coming," Mantus whispered.

He climbed the fence with surprising agility and sat astride the top.

"Are you crossing or staying?" Kéltrox demanded.

Mantus looked down at Úniquen's paw.

"Do you see that black spot beneath your right paw?" Úniquen nodded and stepped back slightly.

"That is the ash of my best friend. He crossed the barrier right there. He fell where you are standing now, Bolco."

Úniquen moved farther away.

"What happened to him?" Gemma asked.

"At first, nothing," Mantus said. "Then he began to scream. Not only his voice. I heard something cracking inside his skin, and I knew it was his bones. They grew, stretched, widened. His face and skin swelled. He looked at me, and I saw terror in his eyes as they throbbed and grew larger. Then it ended. He had the shape he possessed before the curse. He laughed. He looked at his hands. He touched his face. I was sitting on this fence, exactly as I am now, and I was about to jump when his skin began to darken. His cheeks sagged. His whole body seemed to collapse. He tried to scream again, but there was no time. Before my eyes, he became ash." Mantus stared at the black mark.

"So forgive me, princess, if I am not fully convinced I will survive the crossing. You were able to pass through, yes. But that does not mean I can."

"Then do not come," Úniquen said.

Mantus inhaled slowly.

"Move farther, Bolco. I want to land where my friend landed."

Úniquen stepped back.

Mantus threw himself from the fence and landed on the black spot.

Princess Gemma, Úniquen, and Kéltrox watched him in silence.

Chapter Eight

Honor of Cowards

"Are you going to stand there forever?" Úniquen asked.

Mantus stood motionless on the blackened earth, eyes closed, as though he were listening for a sentence only he could hear. At last, he opened his eyes. He touched his face, examined his hands and feet, and turned slowly in place.

"Do you see anything different in me?" he asked.

"Different, as in you turned to ash?" Úniquen said.

"Do you feel different?" Gemma asked.

Mantus looked at his fingers again, then at his toes.

"I do not think so. I am the same."

"Why did you remain a child?" Gemma asked.

"I have no answer."

"Then let us move," Kéltrox said. "If Dargos does not come after Gemma himself, he will send more Kronkos."

"I told Úniquen we would go to Ilucus for help," Gemma said.

"A sound decision," Kéltrox replied. "King Sortus AK will not refuse you, especially with the bond promised between you and Prince Altren."

"If you intend to leave the planet," Mantus said, "you must reach the Pirutus."

Kéltrox nodded.

Úniquen lifted his ears and turned his head toward the fence.

"What is that sound?"

One man in the shape of an animal and several others in the bodies of children were climbing over the fence.

Mantus stiffened.

"What are you doing?"

"We are coming with you," one of them said, jumping down to the other side.

The child-shaped man landed in the pasture and stood still. Everyone watched him, waiting for the curse to strike.

Nothing happened.

"Come," he called back. "I told you. If nothing happened to Mantus, nothing will happen to us."

Four men trapped in the shapes of boys and one animal with a man's mind leapt from the fence and landed in scattered places along the grass. For a few breaths they remained upright. Then they dropped to their knees and screamed.

Their skin swelled. Their limbs stretched. Faces lengthened. Bones cracked and shifted beneath their flesh until the bodies of children and beasts became the bodies of men.

"It is me again!" one cried, touching his own face and laughing.

Another froze.

"Wait. Why did Mantus not change like—"

He never finished. All of them collapsed at once. Their skin loosened, their cheeks caved in, and their bodies crumbled into ash. A gust of wind scattered what remained.

For a moment, Gemma, Kéltrox, Úniquen, and Mantus could only stare.

"How did that not happen to you?" Úniquen asked.

Mantus looked shaken, but he forced himself to speak.

"Perhaps Faltron, or whatever the wizard's name was, granted me one chance because I am helping you."

"Or perhaps the mystical sphere protected you," Kéltrox said, more skeptical than convinced.

Mantus stepped before Princess Gemma and bowed.

"I will not turn away from you." Then his gaze shifted.

"What is that over there?" he asked, pointing toward a tree.

"Cortus," Kéltrox said. "My séritroc. I hid him there."

"So that is the animal everyone spoke of," Mantus said.

"Which route do we take to the Pirutus?" Úniquen asked.

"The shortest path crosses the Nale Desert," Mantus answered.

"And the most dangerous one for travelers on foot," Úniquen said.

"Both are true," Kéltrox said, fastening the supplies to Cortus. "The Nale Desert is the shortest route and the most dangerous. Unfortunately, we cannot spare the time. We will need water, shelter at night, and distance from the Weeds. A sandstorm could bury us in our sleep."

They walked until they reached the river where Gemma had washed herself earlier.

"How will we carry enough water?" she asked.

Mantus dropped the ragged bundle from his back and drew out three medium-sized pitchers. He filled them at the river.

"That is not enough to cross a desert," Úniquen said.

"He is right," Kéltrox said. "Drink as much as you can now."

Then he unloaded three more pitchers from Cortus and filled them as well.

"We will ration the rest."

They secured the pitchers to the séritroc and set out north.

Gemma walked for a while in silence before turning to her uncle. "Before you left Diamondis, did you learn anything about my parents?" Kéltrox's face softened.

"No, smally. I am sorry. I only know your father wanted me to find you. Several soldiers helped me escape Diamondis. They gave their lives for it. Only three of us survived."

"How did you escape?" Gemma asked.

Kéltrox looked toward the northern horizon, as if the answer still lived in the smoke of the ruined palace.

"After I left the tunnel, I ran after you. I had advanced only a few meters when ten Kronkos surrounded me. While fighting them, I saw you enter the Enchanted Swamp. That, at least, gave me relief. I had already killed five of Dargos's soldiers when one of them shot an arrow at me. I saw it too late to dodge. Then someone pushed me aside and saved my life."

"One of our soldiers?" Gemma asked.

"He was short and wore a hood, so I could not see his face. He said nothing. When I rose, several Kronkos lay dead around me, killed before I even noticed him moving."

Úniquen narrowed his eyes.

"He may be the same one who freed me from my chains."

"Perhaps," Kéltrox said. "Before I went after you, I saw Dargos and his Bolco leave Diamondis from your chamber window. I assume he had captured your parents by then.

When he did not find you with them, he realized you had fled with the sphere. I heard him shout orders for the Venturians to pursue you." He paused.

"Two dozen Venturians left the palace. I followed the path you had taken, trying to reach you before they did. But they were fast, and soon they were behind me. Their breathing filled the trees. I had nowhere to hide." Kéltrox's voice lowered.

"I saw a great boulder and thought I might climb it before they caught me. Then hands grabbed my belt and pulled me down. I drew my sword by instinct as I fell, but I did not strike. Something in me knew it was not a Kronko."

He glanced at Gemma.

"I landed on dry leaves and branches. Those trembling hands dragged me into a narrow opening I had not seen because shrubs covered it. It was a tiny cave. Inside were two young men pressed against the rock, shivering so violently they shook me with them."

Ahead of them, Kéltrox had heard the Kronkos thunder past, crushing fallen branches with their heavy feet. Only a curtain of foliage separated the soldiers from death.

"You can let me go now," Kéltrox had whispered to the two men.

"Do not make a sound, sir," one had whispered back. "Take it easy."

"Who are you?" Kéltrox had asked.

"We are yours, sir," the other said. "You should wait until the Kronkos pass. You can follow them later."

"I do not remember your faces. Names?"

"Mayon, sir."

"And I am Nornos, sir. We are twin brothers."

"I would never have imagined," Kéltrox said dryly.

Then he gave them his orders: they would pursue the Kronkos, find transportation, and protect Princess Gemma if the enemy reached her first.

Nornos lowered his head.

"Sir, we must confess something."

"What is it?"

"We are alive because we did not fight in the battle." Kéltrox's anger rose.

"Are you soldiers of the Kingdom of Light or not?"

"Yes, sir. We wanted to be. Well... our father wanted us to be."

"Stop saying sir. You are making me sick."

"Excuse me, sir," Nornos said, and Kéltrox nearly lost patience entirely.

He called them useless. He accused them of shame and cowardice. They accepted every word.

"It is better to be ashamed than dead, is it not, sir?" Mayon said. "We are alive. That matters."

"Then you will not help me?" Kéltrox asked.

"You see, sir—"

"Enough. If either of you says sir again, I will kill you both. Is that clear?"

"Yes, sss—" Nornos stopped himself, terrified. "We know you are not a murderer."

They tried to persuade him to hide with them. They said the war was already lost. They knew how to hide very well.

"Lost?" Kéltrox demanded. "What do you mean, lost? Have you no honor?"

"No honor, sir. None," Mayon said.

Nornos lowered his eyes.

"Our father always said there is no honor in cowards. He said that is what we were: Mayon and Nornos, a pair of cowards. He never understood how he could have sons like us. He said we would achieve nothing and never have honor."

They looked ashamed, yet Kéltrox could see that their fear was still greater than their shame.

"Cowards," he said. "Then the name fits. I will go alone."

Kéltrox returned to the palace courtyard by crawling among the bodies. Kronkos filled Diamondis, celebrating their victory by clashing swords against jewels and walls. He moved slowly toward Cortus, who was still tethered near the palace animals.

Before he could mount the séritroc, a Kronko seized him from behind.

Dargos stood on the stairs of the main entrance. When he saw Kéltrox captured, he laughed.

"Caught by one Kronko?" Dargos said. "Who would believe it? Bring him to me."

"Kill me now," Kéltrox said. "What are you waiting for?"

"Why the rush? We would spoil the fun. Tie him to the gates." Dargos turned to the Kronkos.

"Listen well. Many stories have been told about the man called Kéltrox. Look at him now—bound and helpless at my feet."

The Kronkos made their harsh, shrieking sound. Kéltrox thought it must have been laughter.

They chained him before the entrance to Diamondis. For several nitis, they celebrated, gathered spoils, and roamed among the dead. Then, before the Triplets rose, Kéltrox saw what looked like a corpse crawling toward him through the bodies.

Mantus interrupted.

"What do you mean, a corpse?"

"A spear was lodged in the soldier's chest," Kéltrox said. "Blood covered so much of him I could not see the color of his skin. I was certain he was dead. Yet he crawled toward me with his eyes closed. When he came close enough, someone slipped out from beneath the body and gave me the keys to my chains."

The whisper came from Mayon.

"Sir, it is me. My brother is looking for your séritroc. When you are free, I will signal him."

The Kronkos saw them and rushed forward. Kéltrox fought with the shackles as they approached, but before they reached him, Nornos appeared riding Cortus. The séritroc leapt before them.

"We jumped onto Cortus and escaped into the Valley of Suntras," Kéltrox said. "A Kronko shot the arrow that gave me the wound Gemma healed. After several nitis of flight, we stopped so Cortus could rest. He had carried three people over too great a distance."

When they dismounted, Kéltrox realized Mayon was wounded. An arrow had pierced the middle of his back.

"Do not worry," Kéltrox had told him. "We will remove it." They laid him face down and bandaged him to slow the bleeding.

Mayon clenched his teeth.

"It is not so hard to be brave after all."

"Rest," Nornos said, trying and failing to hide his panic. "You will be better soon."

"You know, sir?" Mayon whispered. "I can call you sir now, can I not? I think I earned it."

"Yes," Kéltrox said. "Though I would rather you not spend your strength talking."

Mayon's breath trembled.

"I never wanted to be a coward. My brother never did either. Father tried to teach us the sword. We learned, but we never became what he wanted. We only wanted to please him, and we never could."

"Your father is a soldier?" Kéltrox asked.

"One of the best," Nornos said.

"His name?"

"Marcus," the brothers said together.

Kéltrox fell silent.

"Marcus has children?" Gemma interrupted, tears already rising. "But Marcus came from Gálax with Rólar. He had no children in the Kingdom of Light."

"He did, smally," Kéltrox said.

Back in the memory, he had stared at the twins.

"Then Rólar..."

"He is our older brother," Nornos said. "Our half-brother, as Father always reminds us. Rólar does not know we exist."

Kéltrox could hardly believe it. "Why did Marcus never recognize you?"

Mayon answered with a bitter smile. "We were too cowardly to be his sons. We lived with our mother. He only loved one woman—Rólar's mother."

Nornos explained that they had been enlisted for a long time, but they chose every safe duty they could find: washing clothes, carrying dishes, cleaning what others did not wish to clean. Anything to avoid fighting.

Mayon blinked against the pain.

"It hurts, but not as much as I thought. Do not worry, brother. Even if I am a coward, I will not die without honor." Kéltrox took his hand.

"You are one of the bravest men I have ever known, Mayon." Mayon's voice broke.

"How can you say that?"

"My father used to say that the greater a man's fear, the greater his courage when he acts."

Nornos pressed Mayon's hand, trying to smile through his sobs.

"Courage is the honor of the coward," he whispered.

Kéltrox nodded.

"Courage is not the absence of fear. It is action despite fear. Today both of you conquered the enemy that ruled you most: your own terror. Mayon, you are facing your end with honor. It has been a privilege to know you." Mayon's eyes filled with gratitude.

"I wish Father had heard that. He respected you. Did you hear, brother? We have honor. Thank you, sir. Thank you."

Then Mayon closed his eyes and did not open them again.

Gemma wiped her face as Kéltrox finished.

"What happened to Nornos?" she asked.

"We were ambushed when we had almost reached you. I ordered him to run while I fought the Kronkos. He must have hidden well, because I never saw him again. I hope he survived."

"And Rólar?"

"The last time I saw him, he was fighting beside me in the vanguard. When our losses grew too heavy, Nótrex called Rólar and Marcus to help us reach you and Krístal. Marcus was wounded on the way. I pray they are both alive, by the mercy of the Overlords."

"So do I," Gemma said, rubbing the moisture from her eyes.

Before — Rólar

Earlier that same day, the ordinary meeting of the Royal Council was nearing its end. King Nótrex, after concluding several matters, took the floor again.

"Since every ruler has presented the progress of the regions," he said, "I would like to introduce the individual who, as of today, has been formally confirmed as a nominal member of the Royal Council. In the history of our planet, he is the youngest active member after my daughter."

With a sullen glance toward Gemma, he added, "Does any nominal member or ruler wish to speak about Rólar?"

Princess Gemma and several members bowed their heads forward.

"Nerminio," the king said. "Speak."

"Rólar is a brave young man," Nerminio said. "He has imitated the irreproachable conduct of his father."

He looked at Marcus, smiled, and then turned again to Rólar.

"As everyone knows, I do not know how to wield a sword, but I know how to recognize skill. The kingdom gains much by adding this young soldier to the Council, just as it gained much from Marcus."

"Not to mention that Marcus is a severe father," Kéltrox said. "I would not want one like him."

Several members laughed. Marcus laughed too, but Rólar lowered his head.

Marcus rose.

"I disciplined him harshly at times. I did not know whether my son would endure such training." Rólar snorted softly.

"Son," Marcus continued, "today, though it is an unusual gesture for me, I wish to acknowledge your bravery before everyone. Your mother, whose energy the Overlords have scattered through the universe like starlight, would be proud of you."

The council applauded.

After the members were dismissed, King Nótrex, Queen Krístal, Princess Gemma, and Rólar remained at the Fountain Table.

"You embarrassed your father before the Royal Council," the queen said.

Nótrex sat at the end of the table with his arms folded, staring at Gemma.

His brow was furrowed, his breathing uneven.

Gemma sighed.

"So that is why he looked at me that way through the whole meeting. Father, I only said that if we want other planets to trade more with us, we should build land routes from the City of Light to the Pirutus through the Nale Desert. Those who reach our world through the portal would be able to travel both ways more easily."

"Your father does not wish to speak," Krístal said coldly. "And I know what you said. I was here."

"Am I not allowed to give my opinion? I am a member of the Royal Council." Nótrex finally spoke, controlling himself with visible effort.

"How could you speak of the Weeds?"

"Father, the subject of the Weeds matters not only to the security we provide other planets, but also to our own people. And I gave no details. I only suggested that you should judge the Weeds. That is my opinion."

"The opinion of a child who does not understand!" Nótrex shouted, losing the battle with his temper. "I do not know why I allowed you into the Royal Council."

Gemma lifted her chin.

"You allowed me into the Council because the regional governors pressed for it. Unlike my parents, they all gave me their support."

"Just because the Overlords blessed you with wisdom," the queen interrupted, "does not give you the right to contradict your father, much less suggest that he or anyone else should follow your advice. The king is the head of the kingdom. The Overlords placed him there. No one should contradict him, especially us. That is how subjects learn reverence and respect. That is how a kingdom prospers."

Gemma stared at her mother, wounded more by the words than the rebuke.

"Contradicting the king when necessary makes him humble, and therefore wiser. A wise monarch places the needs of the kingdom above his own desires. That is how a kingdom prospers, Gemma." The queen's expression hardened.

"Who told you such nonsense?"

"You did, Mother. On the day I turned five tecklis."

"It was not me. It must have been your imaginary friend." Gemma recoiled.

"Now you mock me?"

"Enough, Gemma!" Nótrex shouted. "There are too many things you do not know, too many things you are not fit to know, and we will not discuss them with you. Do not contradict me before the Council again."

"If you do not want me to contradict you, remove my seat. Oh, I forgot— according to the Law of Light, you cannot do that without a reason of weight, and merely having an opinion is not such a reason."

"Go to your room until I send for you," Nótrex said. "And do not dare come out."

Then he pointed at Rólar.

"And you. Go find a lepedo."

"My king, Princess Gemma and I were going to—"

"Go."

Rólar left the chamber and crossed into the front yard of Diamondis.

In her room, Gemma paced from one side to the other, clutching a pillow in one hand and striking it with the other. Then she heard a sound in the garden. She hurried to the lattice. At first, the leaves hid whoever stood beneath her window, but she knew who it was before she saw him.

She ran to the balcony.

"Rólar?"

"I knew you would be crying," he said.

"Your mistake. I never cry." A single tear slipped down her face.

"Yes, of course," he said gently. "I know. I just do not like seeing you like this."

"Bah. I am fine. Did you find the lepedo?"

"Hilarious. I do not remember ever seeing your father so angry."

"And I do not remember ever seeing a living lepedo in the Kingdom of Light."

She smiled despite herself.

"What are you doing here?"

"I came to see if you were ready."

"Ready for what?" He smiled.

"I am grounded," she said, blinking several times and baring her teeth in exaggerated obedience. "Very obedient."

"Hilarious."

"How do I get down?"

Rólar pulled a rope from the bundle hanging from his shoulder.

"Or you could ask Úniquen to help you."

"Knock on his door."

Rólar crossed to the small house before the balcony, a structure that resembled a mausoleum. Before he could knock, Úniquen's voice came from within.

"I heard both of you from here," the Bolco said, poking his snout through a porthole. "Tell Princess Gemma I will not participate in her shenanigans."

"Are you disregarding the orders of the princess of the Kingdom of Light?" Rólar asked.

"I am sorry. I cannot hear you because I am asleep. If I were awake, I would have to inform King Nótrex of the princess' ongoing adventures into the city."

He withdrew his snout.

"Boring," Rólar said.

Gemma covered her head with a blanket and descended the rope carefully. Together, they left Diamondis on Rólar's séritroc. After crossing the palace gates, they mounted an old nórmide tied to a tree, changed into humble clothes from Rólar's bundle, and entered the city unnoticed.

"I am impressed," Gemma said. "You are becoming an expert."

"Yes. The day your father discovers I have been taking you into the city unescorted, he will appoint me ambassador to the Weeds."

"At least you would go down in history as the ambassador with the shortest term."

They rode slowly through the rocky streets among nórmides and people on foot. Shops lined the way. Musicians played near the art houses, whose walls displayed notices for theatrical works. Then a harsh shout broke through the music.

"Your decrepit nórmide knocked down my fruit!" a merchant yelled.

His moving cart wobbled, and several fruits rolled across the ground.

"Mivitor, you struck his nórmide," said a woman beside him.

Mivitor raised a dagger toward her.

"You are loathsome," he hissed.

Gemma started to speak, but Rólar stopped her.

"They may recognize you," he whispered near her ear. "Wait." He dismounted and faced the merchant.

"There is no reason for rudeness. Tell me how much the fruit costs."

Mivitor looked at Rólar's rags, the old nórmide, and the hooded girl beside him. Then he lowered the dagger.

"You do not look as though you have enough currency. Two silverets and one goldet, or I take your nórmide."

"Expensive for a few fruits, do you not think?"

Rólar reached into his rags, removed two silverets and one goldet, and handed them over.

Then he pointed to the woman.

"Does she work for you?"

"By the misfortune of the Overlords, she does," Mivitor said.

Five men behind him, each with a fruit cart, laughed.

Rólar turned to the woman.

"How much does he pay you?"

"Two silverets every twenty-nine dawns," she said. "It is not much, but I have a sick daughter. I cannot leave the work." Mivitor laughed again, and the others joined him.

Rólar handed the woman four goldets.

"Here is enough for a thousand dawns. Start your own trade." She stood frozen. Then tears filled her eyes, and she bowed.

Rólar mounted the nórmide again.

"Wait!" Mivitor shouted. "I made a mistake. The fruit was worth five goldets."

The woman stared at him.

"Five goldets, Mivitor? That is one thousand two hundred and fifty dawns."

"I will not give you anything else," Rólar said.

Gemma leaned forward, but he asked her with a glance to remain silent. "Oh, no?" Mivitor raised his dagger again. "Then I will take your nórmide."

"Do not hurt them!" the woman cried.

"Give me the old beast, or we will take it."

Mivitor shoved the woman aside and advanced. The five merchants abandoned their carts, drew swords, and surrounded Rólar's mount.

Rólar jumped down, drew his sword, and waited.

Mivitor struck at his head. Rólar dodged and hit him with the hilt of his sword. Mivitor fell on his back. Another attacked his right arm; Rólar shifted aside, seized the man's sword, and kicked him in the chest.

The remaining men rushed him.

Then Princess Gemma removed her hood.

"It is Princess Gemma," the people murmured.

The armed men froze and bowed at once.

"If I hear that you have not left the City of Light within three days," Gemma said, "I will deliver you to my father's judgment."

Still on their knees, the merchants backed away without lifting their eyes, then fled.

Gemma turned to the woman.

"What is your name?"

"Maltra, Your Highness," she said, bowing.

"You were brave to stand against injustice, Maltra. If you wish to move to Diamondis, come to the gates before dawn with your daughter. Someone will be waiting for you. We need women like you—women willing to be fair, even with strangers."

"My daughter is small and not in good health."

"We have the best healers," Rólar said. "Do you not know that?" Maltra bowed again, tears on her face.

"I will never forget your benevolence, Your Highness." Gemma and Rólar turned back toward Diamondis.

After a while, Rólar glanced at her.

"Were you frightened? You have been quiet."

"I was not frightened."

"If I were you, I would be. Your father will certainly discover that you escaped."

He studied her more carefully.

"Wait. There is something else. What is wrong?"

"Why do you ask?"

"Because of that look."

"If I tell you, you will think I am crazy."

"Crazier, you mean." They both laughed.

Gemma looked back toward the street where Maltra had stood.

"That woman, Maltra... I think I have seen her before. I do not know how. I only have a powerful feeling, as if she, or something about her, is connected to me."

"It is true," Rólar said. "You are a little crazy."

She narrowed her eyes at him, then changed the subject.

"You liked Maltra, did you not?"

"What? No. Why do you say that?"

"I saw your face."

"No. I mean, she is beautiful, but I am interested in someone else." Princess Gemma did not ask him to say more.

Chapter Nine

The Alliance of the Five Kingdoms

Before — War of Dargos against the Kingdom of Light

The light of the Triplets had begun to sink beyond the horizon when the army of Venturians advanced on Diamondis. They moved swiftly through the deepening dusk and took position a short distance from the palace gates, where the rocky road forked toward Diamondis on one side and the City of Light on the other.

The soldiers of the Kingdom of Light blocked that road with drawn weapons and silent faces. Behind them, the city waited in dread, praying for a miracle strong enough to keep the conquerors from its doors.

The Venturians grew restless. Some shrieked. Others scraped their claws over the stones of the avenue, filling the night with a sound like blades being sharpened. At last, the Ventu, chief of the Kronkos, stepped forward. He moved like an emissary of horror, slow and deliberate, with the invading horde crouched behind him.

It was not mercy that delayed the assault. It was the thin, useless diplomacy that sometimes stands for a moment between two armies before slaughter begins.

The soldiers of the Kingdom of Light held their ground. They knew Dargos had not come to spare them. They knew the hand of their enemy would bring death without pity.

Still, they stood firm before the gates, determined to remain there until death itself moved them aside.

Dargos descended from the sky on his Bolco and landed before the entrance of Diamondis, where the Ventu was already waiting. He dismounted, took two long strides, and fixed his gaze on Nótrex. He seemed almost amused by the presence of Kéltrox and the other high-ranking soldiers beside the king, among them Marcus and Rólar.

"Age has not favored you, my enemy," Dargos said mockingly. "I confess I am torn. I have waited so long for this moment that, seeing you standing there, I do not know whether I should kill you or embrace you."

Nótrex held his stare and answered with a cold, sarcastic smile.

"You have not changed at all," Kéltrox said. "Still as arrogant as ever."

Nótrex snorted. Dargos laughed aloud.

"I heard about Krístal," Dargos said. "Believe it or not, the news struck me. After all, without her, I would never have become who I am today."

"I see Tolan allowed you to come alone," Kéltrox said.

"He is conquering one of the planets of his decaying alliance," Dargos replied.

Nótrex and Kéltrox exchanged a glance.

"You are surprised I would tell you," Dargos continued, spreading his arms slightly. "But what use is there in hiding my glory from the dying?"

"You are very sure of your victory," Nótrex said.

"You are wise," Dargos replied. "You are also sure of it. Come now, Nótrex. You cannot use the mystical sphere. Why let me slaughter this army? Surrender. I will even honor you. What do you call it on this planet? Ah, yes. Soul-bonding. I could link myself with your daughter. They say she is the living image of her mother." His smile darkened.

"Of course, how could I link my soul to anyone when I no longer have one?" Nótrex did not answer. His eyes held all the ruin of the past they shared.

Before — Princess Krístal

On Gálax, the icy ocean battered the slopes of the Frozen Mountain Range with violent waves, as it often did during the planet's long winters. At the summit, before the gates of the Acropolis, more than a hundred men and women selected by the Royal Court had gathered to witness judgment.

From the windows of their igloos, the people of the City of Concor watched in solemn silence.

Inside the Acropolis, a subdued crowd wrapped in white furs moved through the main corridor toward the Ice Columns. King Lardo walked at the front with Queen Katty. Behind them came the young twin princesses, Krístal and Nilda, followed by the royal advisor Dalan and his son Dargos.

Two men carried a stool adorned with precious stones.

"You are shivering," Dargos said.

He removed the lepedo-fur cloak from over his white robe and stepped toward Krístal. Her small hands were numb, and the skin along her bare neck had bristled in the wind. But before he could place the cloak around her shoulders, she looked him in the eye and shook her head.

"I like the cold," she murmured.

Then she released Nilda's hand and moved forward until she reached her father's side.

"A word, Father," Krístal whispered near his ear.

King Lardo slowed his pace.

"Speak quickly, daughter. We must not delay the ceremony."

"The information from the trial does not match." Queen Katty, walking beside the king, heard her and nodded.

"What do you mean?" Lardo asked.

"Nulerto," Krístal said. "I have thought it over. He seems to have been framed. He has no reason to betray you."

The king paused. He looked at Krístal, then at Queen Katty, and continued walking.

"Krístal, he is... he was my friend. Nothing would give me more relief than his innocence, but the evidence is irrefutable."

"What about the coins?"

"What about them?"

"I am sure he does not know."

"Daughter, I have just received news. It appears Nulerto wishes to confess."

"All the more reason to doubt it," Krístal said. "Do you truly believe a counselor as wise as Nulerto would carry out a perfect conspiracy and then leave obvious evidence in his own room? And who sent the anonymous letter? Could it be the same person trying to incriminate him?"

"They concluded the anonymous letter was sent by the soldier who took his own life," the king said.

"And do you believe that?"

"Enough," Lardo said, though pain trembled beneath his authority. "You are making this harder. Proof is proof, and assumptions are assumptions."

They reached the front stalls of the Acropolis. Above them, rock and ice formed a natural roof. In reverent silence, the crowd sat on wooden benches set on an islet surrounded by hot springs rising from the ground. Before them stood a man locked inside a wooden cage.

In the center of the hot springs, barely above the water, lay a white marble stone flattened into a platform and pierced with six holes. Two men fixed the legs of the jeweled stool into them. King Lardo stepped into the warm water, crossed to the stone, and sat before the crowd.

"Members of the Justiciar Tribune," he said, "we are gathered at the Pillars of Ice to judge an act of treason."

The members of the Tribune rose from their benches, joined hands, and pointed their linked fingers toward the king's crown. Then they released one another, closed their eyes, opened them again, and sat.

"Present the evidence to the Justiciar Tribune," said the king.

"A word, my king," said the man inside the cage.

"Speak, Nulerto," Lardo answered.

Nulerto sighed. His arms protruded through the bars, his elbows resting on the wooden supports. He looked into the king's eyes, then toward the Justiciar Tribune.

"I wish to accept blame for my transgression without defending it." A murmur rose behind the king.

Krístal searched the crowd until she found her sister beside the queen. She hurried to Nilda and leaned close to her ear.

"Nilda, I need you to do something."

Nilda's pupils widened. Without a word, she slipped out of the crowd and left at a quick pace.

"Nulerto," one member of the Justiciar Tribune asked, "do you remember what it means to accept your crime?"

"I remember, and I accept the punishment," Nulerto said.

"Why are you rushing?" another asked. "If we examine the evidence, we may discover this was all a mistake and acquit you. The king himself would hope for that."

King Lardo nodded. His hand rose absently to his right eye, and a couple of tears condensed beneath his lashes.

"I know," Nulerto said, glancing toward Counselor Dalan and Dargos, "but I would rather have it done."

"As is customary," the king said, "the accused is granted one request in exchange for confession."

"I have one, King Lardo." The king nodded.

"I ask that my daughter be allowed to leave the planet."

"Where do you wish her to go?"

"To any other planet within the Alliance of the Five Kingdoms."

"Which do you prefer? The Kingdom of Light, Humus, Ilucus, or Green Plant?"

"I have always had an affinity for the AKs," Nulerto said.

"Are you certain you do not wish to send her outside the Alliance? To Corazo, for example?"

The king looked at Krístal. She nodded faintly. Dalan and Dargos exchanged a hidden glance.

"No. Ilucus is sufficient," Nulerto said. "Why would I send my daughter to Corazo?"

"It is a simple request," the king said. "She would only need an escort to the portal. But I have a doubt: why send your daughter to one of the Five Kingdoms? Do you believe she is in danger here?"

"I am going to confess the crime I committed, King Lardo. For the sake of the friendship that once united us, spare me the shame. Grant this gesture for my daughter without further inquiry."

The king and Krístal looked at each other again. Krístal glanced toward the entrance of the Acropolis.

"Let us proceed, then," the king said.

One member of the Justiciar Tribune rose.

"Nulerto, successor to the eminent legacy of your father Numaleto, do you confess that you betrayed your king and your planet, Gálax? Do you confess that the failed plot to poison the king, the conspiracy to kill Queen Katty and the princesses of Gálax while they slept, and the attempt to steal the mystical sphere were born from your ambition?"

"I confess," Nulerto said through tears. "I confess that I sullied the legacy of my predecessors. I planned the conspiracy. My accomplices lie dead among the fallen soldiers of the night of the attack." Dalan and Dargos looked at each other.

The king lifted his left hand. A man dressed in black emerged from the Justiciar Tribune, crossed to the king's stone, and placed three small wooden boxes on it.

"As tradition commands," Lardo said, his voice almost breathless, "we allow the confessor to choose his end."

"Daggers are for brave men and warriors," Nulerto said. "To drown in another man's hands would be to surrender my final power. I choose the poison of cowards, the same poison that almost blinded the eyes of the great King Lardo forever."

The man in black opened the middle box, removed a vial, and walked toward the cage. Just before he could place it in Nulerto's reach, a voice cut through the hall.

"A dissenting word from me," said Krístal.

The man drew the vial back. Nulerto stretched his arms through the bars, straining toward the poison. Dargos frowned. Dalan snorted.

"Speak, daughter," said the king.

"The night of the attack, one of the soldiers who tried to kill me was struck down by Dargos, who, by the grace of the Overlords, happened to be passing in front of my chamber at the time."

She glanced briefly at Dargos, then continued.

"The soldier was near death, with Dargos's sword still driven through him. He lifted his hands toward me, and I understood that he was ashamed. I asked who had sent him to kill me. He could not speak because blood had filled his throat, but he pointed toward his satchel. When I searched it, I found coins hidden inside one of its compartments."

"Forgive the intrusion, Princess Krístal," Dalan called from the crowd.

"This matter has consumed us for days, and while the last thing I desire is to see a counselor like Nulerto die, I see no reason to postpone the inevitable." The king looked at Dalan, then back at Krístal.

"Finish."

Krístal looked toward the entrance of the Acropolis again. Then she turned to the cage.

"Nulerto, could you tell King Lardo and the Justiciar Tribune how much you paid the soldier?"

"The details of the attack were reviewed during the Previous Tribune," Nulerto replied.

King Lardo and Krístal exchanged another look.

"I did not mention the amount when I gave my account before the Previous Tribune," Krístal said.

"How could I remember such insignificant details as the payment to an expendable soldier? Your question is absurd."

"Answer me, Nulerto," the king said, "and I will grant your request concerning your daughter. Otherwise, I do not believe the Justiciar Tribune should proceed with execution before every piece of evidence is presented." Dalan snorted and looked toward Dargos.

"I paid him a few hundred niquiteros," Nulerto said.

"That is incorrect," Krístal replied.

The members of the Tribunal murmured among themselves.

"I told you I do not remember exactly. I had many things to prepare."

"It would have been logical for the soldiers to be paid in niquiteros, our currency," Krístal said. "But contrary to what one might expect, they were paid in carnelian, the currency of Corazo." King Lardo stood.

"Members of the Justiciar Tribune, if you agree with me, there are matters in this trial that must be clarified."

The members whispered among themselves. Then one of them rose into the silence.

"We agree, King Lardo. Someone is forcing Nulerto to incriminate himself."

"No, no, please!" Nulerto cried, throwing himself against the bars. "Give me the poison, King Lardo. I beg you."

"Where is your daughter?" Krístal asked.

"I do not know where they are holding her now! I do not know!" Nulerto sobbed. "Just give me the poison, or she will die."

At that moment, a scream came from the entrance of the Acropolis.

"Stop the execution!"

Nilda ran toward them with five soldiers and a young woman. King Lardo and the Justiciar Tribune rose as they approached. Nulerto lifted his head, saw his daughter's face, and wept with a smile on his lips.

"You were right, sister," Nilda said, her voice breaking. "We found Gilly blindfolded and bound inside her igloo. Two soldiers guarded her. Neither survived."

"Who did this?" the king demanded.

Through tears, Nulerto shouted, "The true traitor is—" An arrow pierced his heart before he could finish.

Everyone ducked. Above them, a figure fled across the natural roof of the Ice Pillars. Soldiers rushed after him, but he vanished into the frozen heights.

Before — Dargos

Torchlight reflected on the dense ice that covered the avenues of Concor. Beneath the distant glow of the Seven Red Star, Dalan and Dargos stood before the wall that separated the city from the inhospitable zones, not far from the magnificent sculpture of Kerisetale of Gálax.

"Now I do not know what I will tell Peritis," Dalan said. "I can hardly believe you are my son."

"Why do you blame me? I am not responsible for the king postponing the cup."

"They found Gilly," Dalan said between his teeth. "And if you had not saved Krístal, none of this would have happened. She would never have insisted on testing the king's poisoned cup on that stupid lepedo. She would never have discovered that we framed Nulerto."

"You promised me you would not kill her. You know I love her."

"You are so innocent, Dargos."

"What do we do now?"

"What can we do? Nothing for the moment, except hope we are not caught."

"So that is it? We are not going to steal the mystical sphere?"

"Of course we will steal it. But we must wait until the princesses' banquet."

"There will be too many people there, Father. They say the other four kingdoms will come."

"Precisely. Tell Tolan to come with you tomorrow. Your servant has proven more useful than you."

Dargos lowered his head.

"If not for Tolan, Nulerto would have exposed us."

"Yes, his escape was impressive," Dargos said, "but he is still my servant, Father, not yours." Dalan's eyes hardened.

"Calm yourself. Listen carefully. You are my son, but I will not allow you to become the ruin of my legacy. Forget that woman. She chose another man." Dargos stared at him.

"What did you say? How do you know she chose?"

"Do not be naive. Everyone knows. In a few days, at the celebration of the twenty-third winter of the princesses of Gálax, King Lardo will announce the Merger of Spirits between Krístal and Nótrex of the Kingdom of Light." Dalan left him there.

Dargos's eyes filled with tears.

Before — Nilda

The following day, a caravan of children strolled through the streets of Concor, Princess Nilda walking at their head. Half a dozen soldiers, several adults, and a few nobles accompanied them.

"And this enormous sculpture to your right," Nilda said, "does anyone dare tell me whom it honors?"

Dozens of children raised their hands.

"Velita, you have not said anything today. Are you sure you do not wish to answer?"

"I do," the girl said.

She pulled some kind of candy from her mouth and pointed at the sculpture.

"It was built in honor of our mage protector, Kerisetale."

"That is right," Nilda said. "Many centuries ago, a girl mysteriously arrived in our world. Today, we suppose a portal opened temporarily and she crossed by accident. The Concor family adopted her and gave her the name of their deceased daughter: Kerisetale. That is why our city bears their name." She smiled at the girl.

"Velita, do you wish to add anything else?"

"Yes. Is it true our mage is dead?"

"We do not know. We only know that after the Contaminated Wizards appeared, she vanished."

Nilda turned toward the adults arranging the children into rows. "We have finished the excursion. Your parents will arrive any moment."

"Nilda! Nilda!" someone called from the crowd.

She turned.

"What are you doing here?"

"Can you come here for a moment?" Dargos asked.

She stepped closer and studied his face.

"You look terrible. You look as though you have not slept in days."

"Is it true your sister will merge her spirit with that jerk Nótrex?"

"Now he is a jerk?" Nilda asked. "You always give him a different nickname. Do you dislike him so much?" Dargos snorted.

"Listen, Dargos. Why do you not find a woman who returns your feelings?"

"You know I do not want another woman. I want her."

"Friend, you are obsessed with my sister. Why do you not talk to her?"

"I have tried, but she always avoids me."

"Well, there is your answer."

"What does Krístal say about me?"

"What I discuss with you, I discuss with you. What I discuss with my sister, I discuss with her."

Then she embraced him. Dargos rested his chin on her shoulder.

"If you knew something terrible was going to happen, but denouncing it would harm your family, what would you do?"

Nilda drew back so she could look into his eyes. She placed both hands on his shoulders.

"I think nothing is more important than family," she said. "But of course, that depends on how serious the matter is. Why are you asking?" Dargos hesitated, then sighed.

"It is nothing serious."

"Are you going lepedo hunting this afternoon?" she asked.

"You know I do not like hunting."

"True. Last time, you could not kill the wounded lepedo."

"Stop teasing."

"Go," Nilda said. "Try to speak with my sister. I would like things to be right between you."

Before — Nótrex

The clash of swords rang between the columns of Diamondis. King Dervinan and Queen Ardnas descended the stairs, crossed the Fountain Table, and stepped onto the front lawn, where a crowd of soldiers and nobles had gathered around two combatants.

"Do not lower your guard, Prince Nótrex!" a noblewoman called from the stands.

Nótrex resisted the assault with strength and agility, and the crowd cheered. Then one blow knocked him to the ground, sending his sword skidding from his hand. He saw the edge of his opponent's blade descend toward his neck and stretched desperately toward his own weapon. His fingers barely grazed the hilt before cold steel touched his skin.

With the blade still at his throat, Nótrex gasped. Then he gave a disappointed smile, moved the weapon away with his hand, and accepted the hand his brother Kéltrox offered him.

"I beat you again," Kéltrox said.

"The worst part is not that," Nótrex replied. "The worst part is that I am becoming accustomed to it."

"Everyone back to your duties!" shouted King Dervinan.

He approached his sons with Queen Ardnas.

"You must stop fighting during labor nitis," the queen said.

"Have you heard the news?" Dervinan asked.

Nótrex and Kéltrox looked at one another and shook their heads.

"King Lardo has invited us to a special banquet to celebrate his daughters' winter."

"And," Queen Ardnas added, "we have agreed to announce the soulbonding between Nótrex and Krístal that night."

"They call it spirit fusion," Kéltrox said.

Queen Ardnas touched his head, though he clearly did not enjoy it.

"And is there still no one to stir your heart?"

"We leave for the Pirutus in four dawns," the king said, sparing Kéltrox an answer.

When their parents walked away, Kéltrox smirked. "It seems your little love letters worked." Nótrex returned the look.

"And did you have any luck with Nilda? I can tell you like her."

"Well... she is a little cold with me, you know."

"Perhaps it is the weather on Gálax." Nótrex patted his brother's back.

"Very funny," Kéltrox said. "Last time we visited Gálax, I noticed she was very close to Dargos, Dalan's son."

"Krístal says they are only friends."

"I also heard King Lardo made a covenant with a Bolco on Dargos's behalf for his last birthday." Nótrex sighed.

"That only means Dargos has the king's esteem. It is not all about combat, brother. Work on your charms, or you will end up bonded to your sword." Kéltrox snorted.

Before — The Banquet

Guests from the other four kingdoms entered Gálax through the Iceberg Portal. First came the kings of Ilucus: Tuloris AK, his wife Sonari AK, and their son Sortus AK, riding in a steel chariot drawn by nórmides. Behind them came Crelison, acting prime minister of Green Plant, with his wife Liliani and their sons, Lyson, the budding prime minister, and Creslo, his younger brother, all mounted on tíricus.

The Chosen Sentinel of Humus, Vinerila Carbunclo, arrived next with her daughters, Deliria and Ilira Carbunclo, on the backs of séritrocs. Last came the rulers of the Kingdom of Light: King Dervinan and Queen Ardnas, accompanied by their sons, Princes Kéltrox and Nótrex, also riding séritrocs.

The long caravan of nobles departed the Iceberg Portal under escort from the soldiers of Gálax. After two days of travel, they reached the Acropolis. Once the customary greetings were complete, the guests took their places at King Lardo's table, set high in the main hall like a balcony overlooking the entertainment prepared for them.

Enchanters made objects disappear and levitate. Actors performed dramatized tales, and singers filled the hall with songs. On a side stage, an orchestra of dozens of musicians played beneath chandeliers suspended by silver chains from the picturesque ceiling. The great door bore a frame carved with animal figures and coated in burnished bronze.

"Vinerila Carbunclo," King Dervinan said, "you have been walking since you arrived, and so have your daughters."

Kéltrox and Ilira Carbunclo exchanged glances and smiled.

"We do not wish to draw as much attention as last time," Vinerila replied.

The kings, queens, princes, and nobles of the Five Kingdoms talked, laughed, and ate for a long time.

Halfway through one performance, King Lardo rose and signaled for the music to stop.

"Attention, dear guests. It is a pleasure to welcome you to the celebration of the twenty-third winter of the princesses of Gálax. As you all know, this is the age at which our heirs begin their training to rule this planet. The Overlords have blessed my daughters with intelligence, insight, wisdom, and love for others."

He looked toward Krístal and Nilda with pride.

"In that spirit, we also wish to share magnificent news. The rulers of the Kingdom of Light, Dervinan and Ardnas, and my wife, Queen Katty, and I are pleased to announce the merging of spirits, or soul-bonding, as it is called there, between our children: Prince Nótrex and Princess Krístal."

Applause filled the hall. The guests rose with cheers and congratulations.

Across the chamber, Dalan and Dargos watched Nótrex and Krístal from a separate table.

"At least we are seated far from the kings," Dargos said, gritting his teeth.

His gaze collided with Krístal's.

"I arranged it because of the visitors from Green Plant," Dalan said. "They possess powers that are not in our favor. They could expose us. Dargos, could you at least pretend? Unclench your fists and relax."

"I am trying."

His fists had been so tight that when he opened them, his nails had left marks on his palms.

"That is better. Now breathe and smile. Better. Tell me, do you still wish to save her?"

"Of course not."

"At least something good came of this. Prepare the rest."

"Everything is ready."

"Tolan?"

"Where we agreed."

"Your Bolco?"

"Where it belongs."

"That is how I like you: focused. Now go, and let us begin the game."

Dalan headed toward King Lardo's table. Dargos was leaving the hall just as Kéltrox approached Nilda.

"Princess Nilda, I am pleased to see you again," Kéltrox said.

Nilda blushed, turned her head, and saw Dargos slipping out of the hall.

"Excuse me," she said.

She followed him. Once outside, she saw Dargos heading down the corridor that led to the royal chambers. She ran after him and caught up.

"Wait, Dargos!" He turned in surprise.

"Nilda, what do you want?"

"I came to see how you are."

"I am fine. Go back."

"Come here."

She stepped toward him with open arms. Dargos saw her approach and broke into tears again. At that same moment, he noticed his father leaving the hall in the distance with King Lardo.

"I wish I had loved you," Dargos whispered. "I have to go." He left her there.

King Lardo and Dalan saw Dargos and Nilda standing in the hallway that led to the chambers.

"What is happening with your son?" the king asked. "Why is he leaving?"

"He has not been feeling well," Dalan said.

"He was affected by the announcement of my daughter's spirit fusion, was he not?"

"You are very observant, my king. Such are the pains of love." The king studied him.

"Tell me, Dalan. What did you wish to say, and why did it require leaving the hall?"

"Something extraordinary has happened, my king. You were right all this time. We have finally received a visit from our mage."

"What? Kerisetale is here? But she was missing. Why now?"

"I do not know. She contacted me moments ago. She is waiting for us in her room. She said something terrible is about to happen and that she must speak with us immediately."

"Now? Are you certain?"

"Absolutely, my king."

"Then summon my escort."

"As you wish. Though, if I may, were I in your place, I would go alone. She clearly said she wished to speak with the two of us. I do not know whether another presence would offend her." The king hesitated only a moment.

"Very well. Let us go. I must return to the guests as soon as possible." They advanced down the corridor and found Nilda standing ahead of them. "Nilda, why are you not with the guests?" King Lardo asked.

"I stepped out only for a moment, Father. I will return." She frowned.

"And you? Where are you going without your escort?"

"I will return soon," the king said without answering.

Nilda went back to the hall and stopped before the king's table. She searched for Kéltrox, only to find him speaking attentively with Ilira Carbunclo. Krístal noticed her, released Nótrex's hand, and moved through the guests until she reached her sister.

"It seems Kéltrox wants to speak with you," Krístal said.

Nilda looked at him again.

"He appears very entertained with Ilira Carbunclo."

"Your mind is elsewhere." Krístal handed her a drink. "What is wrong?"

"Have you seen Father?"

"I saw him outside the hall with Dalan a moment ago. It is dangerous for him to walk without an escort while the culprit behind the attack remains unknown."

"Without an escort?" Krístal said. "How strange. And why would he leave the guests like that?"

She scanned the hall.

"I do not see your friend either."

"Dargos? Yes. He left a moment ago. He seemed strange during the announcement."

"What did you expect? That he would leap for joy? You know this news was difficult for him. Why did you never speak clearly to him?"

"What is clearer than the obvious? I never encouraged him, and you know it."

Krístal's expression shifted.

"Still, now that I think of it, something else may be happening. I remember Dalan and Dargos whispering a great deal tonight. Have you noticed anything strange about him?"

"Have I noticed anything strange about Dargos?" Nilda asked dryly.

"I keep thinking he knows something about the attack. It troubles me that he was near our chambers that night. And Dalan was the only one who protested when the time to investigate Nulerto's alleged treason was extended."

"You are imagining things. What would he know about—" Nilda stopped.

"There it is," Krístal said. "What came to mind?"

"Dargos asked me an unusual question the other day, as though something terrible were about to happen."

"And now neither Dalan nor Dargos is here, nor our father." Krístal signaled for Nótrex to come closer.

"Keep smiling, sister. We do not want to alarm the guests over a suspicion." Nótrex embraced Krístal lightly when he reached her.

"You look worried, yet you smile."

"We think my father may be in danger," Krístal said. "Call Kéltrox and meet us in the hallway. Be discreet. It is only a hunch."

"Your hunches are usually right."

Krístal, Nilda, Nótrex, and Kéltrox slipped out quietly and reached the royal chamber. The door was open. A trail of blood ran into the hallway.

"Finish it quickly," Dalan's voice hissed from inside. "Kill him. We already have the mystical sphere."

Kéltrox entered first. Nótrex followed, then Krístal and Nilda.

They found Dargos holding King Lardo with a dagger buried in the king's abdomen. At Dalan's feet lay the king's silver knife, slick with blood, while Dalan himself bled from the arm. Behind the door, the soldier who had guarded the chamber lay in his own blood.

"Help!" Nilda shouted toward the guards. Her voice carried into the distance.

"Kill him and let us go!" Dalan ordered.

Dargos pulled the king before him, pressing the dagger's edge against Lardo's neck as he and Dalan retreated toward the window.

"Do not do this, Dargos!" Nilda cried.

"Be quiet, Nilda. He is my father. You said it yourself. Nothing is more important than family."

"You have no escape," Krístal said. "It does not have to end this way."

"Now you speak to me?" Dargos said. "If I had known this was all it would take to gain your attention, I would have killed your father long ago."

"Let us go, son," Dalan said.

Nótrex saw the mystical sphere hanging from Dargos's neck. "You already have the sphere," he said. "Is that not what you wanted?" Kéltrox's hand remained on his sword, though he had not drawn it.

"Leave," Nilda said. "Leave my father alive, and we will not follow you." Wings beat outside. Tolan flew past the window on Bartigo, Dargos's Bolco.

"Back!" Dargos shouted.

"I told you to kill him!" Dalan snapped. "That is what we were ordered to do."

Then Dalan drove the same dagger into the king's chest.

King Lardo fell face down. Blood splashed across Dargos. Nilda bowed her head as if the sight had struck her physically.

Dalan gripped the dagger and prepared to leap through the window.

"No!" Krístal shouted.

She looked at her dead father on the floor, then at the blood-soaked dagger in Dalan's hand. She raised both arms toward him.

Dalan turned unwillingly. His eyes met hers. For a few seconds, the room seemed to stretch into silence. Everyone watched as his eyes began to bleed. His body trembled, but he could not look away from Krístal. Her eyes glowed.

Dalan lifted the dagger in his shaking hand. He screamed, raised it higher, and plunged it into his own chest.

"What have you done?" Dargos shouted.

"How did you do that without the sphere?" Nótrex and Kéltrox demanded at the same time.

Krístal collapsed unconscious.

"Get on, Dargos!" Tolan shouted from Bartigo's back.

The soldiers flooded into the chamber.

"After them!" Nilda cried.

Nótrex, Kéltrox, and the soldiers rushed toward Dargos.

"They killed my father!" Dargos screamed.

He climbed onto the windowsill and slammed the mystical sphere against his chest. At once, he was lifted into the air outside the room. Bartigo recoiled.

Then dark energy poured through him.

Dargos began to bleed. His head swelled. His eyes bulged as though they would burst from their sockets. His hands bloated, and his skin turned blue, as if unseen fingers had closed around his throat. He screamed in agony.

Tolan threw his arms around Dargos's neck, tore the sphere from him, and flew away on Bartigo over the gates of the Acropolis, carrying Dargos unconscious.

The soldiers loosed arrows after them, but none brought them down.

Chapter Ten

THE CONVERGENT SPECTRUM

Princess Gemma kept rearranging the blankets tied across Úniquen's back whenever they loosened. With her head covered against the glare, she watched the Bolco's legs flatten the clay soil beneath him. Behind them, Kéltrox guided the séritroc while the water jugs bounced against the animal's armored hide, rubbing together with every step. The squeaking did not test the others' patience, but Úniquen's sweaty ears twitched each time.

"I am going to roast," Úniquen muttered.

"We have not even entered the desert yet," Princess Gemma replied.

"There it is... That's the Nale Desert," Mantus said. They spotted a mass of reddish sand; the light of the Triplets reflected on the dusty surface, and they could not make out the end of the path.

According to legend, a warrior named Nale had once explored the desert and returned alive, the only man known to have done so. Each time he came back to Trasto, his hometown on the northern edge of the wasteland, he told of unknown places that appeared before him as he traveled south—cities, towers, rivers, and lands that vanished whenever he tried to approach them. Some in Trasto dismissed those visions as mirages. Others, including Nale himself, believed the desert touched other worlds because of its nearness to the Pirutus and to the dark matter that gathered there.

"It looks like burning lava, not sand," said Úniquen.

"For some reason, the light of the Triplets burns brighter in this natural graveyard," said Mantus.

"I heard that dangerous beasts prowl the desert," said Úniquen. Mantus nodded his head.

"Yes, but there is something more worrying than animals," said Princess Gemma.

"You're right. The Weeds," said Kéltrox.

"I met one of their clans a long time ago. I was returning from the Pirutus with several soldiers, escorting your grandfather Lardo before you were born. The Weeds attacked us, and only by luck were we able to escape."

"I have heard they are savage cannibals who obey no law other than their customs," said Úniquen and wrinkled his snout.

"Let's take advantage of the daylight," said Kéltrox and climbed onto Cortus's back. Mantus tried to climb onto the animal, but his small hands slipped. Kéltrox grabbed him by the lapel of his rough leather garment and pulled him up. Princess Gemma mounted Úniquen, and they took flight. The hot wind mixed with sand made it difficult for Úniquen and Princess Gemma to see; Cortus made high jumps, sometimes his head almost brushed Úniquen's claws or tail, and he would fall again, his thick paws buried in the sand, and he would jump again.

They advanced for a while until the desert opened before them into a great chasm.

"What is that over there?" asked Princess Gemma.

"It is the Endless Abyss," said Úniquen.

"Let's go down; Cortus won't be able to jump that," she said. When they landed, Cortus came down only a short distance from the cliff's edge.

"Cross with Úniquen, I will jump the endless abyss," said Kéltrox.

"Your séritrocs won't be able to; the abyss is too vast," said Princess Gemma.

"Did you hear that, Cortus? Your princess underestimates you," Kéltrox said, stroking the animal's pointed ears. "Smally, I have crossed chasms with Cortus more times than I can count. I will see you on the other side."

"Cortus is carrying Mantus, not just you; besides, he's carrying the water pitchers... We'd better go around the abyss," she said again.

"That's at least two days late," said Mantus.

"A séritroc like this can jump that chasm," said Úniquen.

"Wait for us on the other side," Kéltrox said again. Princess Gemma and Úniquen flew over the Endless Abyss, and from the edge, they saw Cortus running in the opposite direction.

"What are they doing?" asked Princess Gemma.

"They seem to be gaining momentum," replied Úniquen. The séritroc charged toward the abyss, its paws kicking up sand and raising a curtain of red dust behind it. Kéltrox clung tightly to the animal's armored skin, kept his eyes straight ahead, and patted Cortus's back vigorously.

"Slow down," said Úniquen, shook himself, threw Princess Gemma away from the edge, flapped at a vertical angle, overtook Cortus's elevation, and waited for him to arrive. Cortus's front legs struck the far edge and half sank into it. Half his body remained on the cliff; the other half dangled over the void. Kéltrox clung to Cortus's ears, Mantus held tightly to him, the pitchers with water broke, and their fragments fell into the void.

Úniquen hooked his claws around Cortus's neck and flapped hard backward, the weight pulling him into the abyss. Kéltrox felt Mantus's fingers slide slowly across his shoulders, tried to grab him, swung to reach the other end, and his hands began to slip away as well. Cortus managed to embed part of his middle leg in one of the sockets of the cliff wall; Úniquen continued to pull the séritroc, and, little by little, they began to ascend. When Cortus felt the firmness of the edge with his central paw, he jumped and fell into the sand. Kéltrox let go of the animal's ears, and Mantus fell into the sand beside him.

"I don't know what happened to Cortus," Kéltrox said, nearly breathless.

"He was too heavily burdened, as I warned you," Princess Gemma replied.

"We can't cross the desert without water," said Úniquen.

"Trasto is to the north, a few nitis from here," said Mantus panting.

"How is it that you always have an answer for everything?" asked Úniquen almost breathlessly. Mantus frowned. "I mean... You've been a prisoner for centuries; how do you know where the village is?" Princess Gemma and Kéltrox looked at Mantus.

"It was the first place we looked for King Normen," he said. Úniquen stared at Mantus carefully.

"What are you looking at, you impertinent Bolco?" Mantus asked. Úniquen snorted.

"Let's go; I have some silverets and goldets in my bag; we could buy water and spend the night in Trasto," said Kéltrox, and they headed north.

They advanced on foot for a while toward where Mantus was leading them.

"You don't look tired, princess," Mantus commented.

"Well, that's because every time I feel a little exhausted, I touch the mystical sphere," she replied.

"Trasto should not be far away now," said Mantus.

"Look over there," said Kéltrox.

"It's not the village. It's more like... a castle?" asked Princess Gemma.

"What's a castle doing in this place?" asked Kéltrox.

"Are you all seeing what I'm seeing?" asked Úniquen simultaneously.

"Yes... The castle seems to have no foundation," answered Kéltrox.

"It's floating," Princess Gemma whispered.

"Get back!" Kéltrox shouted.

"I can't move," Úniquen said—and collapsed.

Princess Gemma fell beside him. Kéltrox released Cortus and tried to rush toward them, but before he could take another step, his body failed him as well. He fell facedown in the sand. The last thing he saw was Mantus standing over the three of them.

Dala

"Are you awake, Princess?"

A high, melodious voice reached Princess Gemma through the numb haze of waking. She rubbed her eyes and saw a woman dressed in white standing beside her, smiling gently.

"Gather the others," the woman said, turning toward a round, glowing door whose frame was carved with symbols Gemma did not recognize. "They must know what is happening."

A slender, human-shaped figure stood before the door for a moment, then passed through its light without opening it.

Only then did Gemma realize where she was. She lay on a wide bed between silk sheets, surrounded by soft cushions and tables laden with food. Still, her thoughts would not settle. Everything felt dreamlike. Her body seemed weightless. She felt neither hunger nor thirst, neither heat nor cold.

"Your uncle and the others who came with you are safe," the woman said.

"Am I dreaming?" Gemma asked.

"No. Humans often touch this reality through dreams, but this world obeys laws beyond ordinary human reason. When you are brought here, your material body is drawn beyond its usual state."

"Are you a celestial being?" Gemma asked, sitting on the edge of the bed.

"Some human cultures would call me that," the woman answered. "But what does celestial mean? A perfect divinity? A supreme being? If that is what you mean, then no. I am not." She extended her hand.

"Come. The others woke before you."

Gemma slid from the bed, took the woman's hand, and walked beside her through the illuminated door.

"Who are you?" Gemma asked.

"I am Dala, guardian of the Convergent Spectrum."

"So that is the name of this castle," Gemma said. "But this place is in the desert. How did you—?"

"The Convergent Spectrum is not in the desert, Princess. In truth, it is not in any physical location."

"But we saw it."

"You saw a portal from the Nale Desert. Nothing more."

"How did I get here?"

"You entered our domain because we allowed you to."

"Whom did you want?"

Dala's smile softened, though something ancient and sorrowful passed through her eyes.

"You will know everything when the time comes. For now, I was given only a little time to speak with you."

"My mother told me a story once," Gemma said.

Dala stopped. Her pupils widened.

"Are you all right?" Gemma asked.

"Yes. You merely reminded me of something. Please, continue."

"My mother told me about someone who came to a place like this. She called it the Realm Beyond Imagination."

Dala repeated the words with a faint smile.

"The Realm Beyond Imagination. It is a good name."

As they walked through the corridors, Gemma took in the beauty of the place. It was broader than she had first understood and more beautiful than any palace she had known. Parts of the walls and floor opened onto landscapes she first mistook for paintings, until she realized they were transparent spaces showing other places. They were portals.

At first, she recognized some of them: parts of the Nale Desert, the Weeping Forest, and other lands she knew by sight or by map. Then the visions changed. She saw lush jungles teeming with animals, gigantic pyramids, endless waters, distant constellations rushing close and vanishing again, civilizations on planets she had never seen, and living forms so strange that no story in Diamondis had ever prepared her for them.

"What is all this?" Gemma asked, pointing toward the floor.

"The Convergent Spectrum belongs to no territory, yet it touches all territories," Dala said. "There are no planetary borders here, no boundaries of place as you understand them. The only true boundary is found in living beings themselves. What you see beneath your feet is the physical world, seen through the portals scattered across the universe." Gemma stared through the floor.

"I feel as if I have been asleep all my life, and only now have awakened to reality. Dala... how do I know I am not imagining this?"

"This place is real, Princess, even if most beings cannot perceive it."

"When people die, do they come here?" Dala laughed softly.

"You are not dead, Princess. Nor is this place a paradise for the virtuous, if that is what you mean. Those who reach this place do so in two ways. Most come by means of immense energy, like the force contained in the sphere you wear around your neck. Others, rare souls of extraordinary sensitivity, cross the boundary through their perception of what cannot be touched. They come to understand that there is a world they cannot taste, but can feel. A world beyond the common senses." She paused.

"Some of them are here even now."

"Can you help me recover my planet?" Gemma asked.

Dala placed a gentle hand on her shoulder.

"Gemma, you do not know how long I have waited for you. But for now, I cannot answer that question, nor can I tell you everything I know."

"Do I know you?" Gemma asked, searching her face.

"It is curious that you should ask me that," Dala said.

She opened another door, and a beautiful garden appeared beyond it.

Kéltrox, Úniquen, and Mantus stood there waiting.

"You woke up," Kéltrox said.

"You slept too much," Úniquen added.

Mantus only smiled.

"How long have we been here?" Gemma asked.

"Time here does not behave as it does in your physical world," Dala replied.

"But outside, two sunrises have passed."

"How is that possible?" Úniquen asked. "We have been here only a few nitis."

"Where is Cortus?" Gemma asked.

"Animals cannot enter this place," Dala said. "You will find the séritroc where you saw the castle. Do not worry. He is being cared for, though you will not see the hands caring for him when you return."

"Can we go now?" Mantus asked.

"Why are you so eager to return to the desert?" Úniquen asked.

"You may leave whenever you wish," Dala said. "First, I want a brief word with the princess."

Gemma and Dala walked through the garden in low conversation. After a short time, they returned. Dala pointed to another door, and they passed through it.

Before — Dala from Senters

So many years have passed since those days that the human mind would fail if it tried to count them. There was an era when the laws governing the universe were still mysterious, and what later generations would call impossible had not yet been given a name.

In a remote corner of a planet called Senters, one of the first human cities in the universe witnessed an event that would leave its mark across the ages, though few understood it when it happened.

The village of Narvos was a natural sculpture carved by time. Thousands of flat rocks stretched across the tops of three mountains, and from the heights one could see the violent swell of two seas breaking against the foothills below.

Only about fifty inhabitants lived there. They survived as a family, protecting one another from a deadly enemy that threatened to erase them. Among them grew a restless little girl named Dala, a child marked by an event that crossed the borders of time—not by apparent merit, and not by any gift she knew she possessed.

"Dala, do not run near those rocks," Pina called to her six-year-old daughter. "You might get hurt. Where are you going now? No, come down from there. You might fall."

"It is so much fun, Mommy," Dala answered, leaping from rock to rock.

"Come with me. Please, I want to play."

"Where do you get so much energy?" Pina asked.

The child often passed too near the cliffs, and though it frightened her mother, it was not unusual in Narvos. The city had been built among huge rocks and steep mountains. Its people made homes in carved stone hollows and in caves prepared for living.

"Gather your things," Pina said. "The Community meets tonight, and I must take you. They are going to tell a story all the children must hear."

"Can I stay a little longer? Please, Mommy. Please say yes."

"For a little while. Then we leave. We must be presentable before the Community."

"Yes, Mommy. Just a little while."

Then Dala spotted a small bird near the edge.

"Look at that pretty bird, Mommy. Come, little bird, come..."

She jumped toward the rocks bordering the cliff. The bird flew away as she approached.

"No!" Pina screamed. "No, no, no!"

The rock beneath Dala's feet slid slowly into the void. For a heartbeat the little girl swung with it, trying to keep her balance while the wind pushed against her. Pina ran toward her, but before she could reach her daughter, Dala, rock and all, fell.

Pina stared down into the abyss, terrified. Then she shuddered—not only from fear, but from the impossible relief of seeing her child alive at the bottom, standing safely on a rock without a scratch, as if the fall had never happened.

"Dala! Are you all right? How did you get there?"

"They put me here, Mommy."

"They put you there? Who?"

"I do not know who they are, but they are friends. I am going upstairs now."

"No! Stay where you are. I will come down for you."

Pina descended as carefully as she could and took her daughter in her arms.

"I have you now. Let us get away from here."

"Thank you for helping me," Dala said, looking upward.

"Are you talking to me?"

"No, Mommy. To my friends."

"What friends, love?" Pina asked, tears still running down her cheeks.

"One is big and shiny. The others I cannot see."

Dala paused, turned toward one corner of the cliff, and smiled as if listening. "All right," she whispered. "I will not tell."

"What was shining?" Pina asked.

"Yes, Mommy. It shone a lot. But they do not want me to say anything."

"When I saw you on top of the rocks, you were alone. No one was beside you."

"They left after playing with me for a while."

"How could they play with you if you were here?" Pina asked. "I do not understand. Explain it slowly, Dala."

"We walked in a beautiful place. I played there for a long time. Then they fed me, and I rested for a while before they brought me back here."

Nótrex

Daylight reflected from the columns of Diamondis, yet it failed to reach the dungeon where Nótrex had lain since his capture. The place seemed darker than he remembered. His eyes had begun to adjust to the lack of light, but he could no longer tell whether the world outside was trapped in dawn or buried in night. Time itself seemed to have stopped at the bars of his cell.

The smell of death had once been unbearable. Now even that had grown distant.

Through the bars he could see part of Diamondis, ruined and occupied. His only company was the group of Kronkos sleeping near the cell. From time to time, one stirred, opened its eyes, examined him, and returned to sleep.

Then footsteps sounded on the stairs.

Three Kronkos descended, dragging a woman between them. Nótrex had to look twice before he was sure it was his wife.

They opened the cell, shoved Krístal inside, and closed the bars again.

"Where have you been?" Nótrex asked, moving toward her. Then he stopped. "They healed your shoulder."

Fresh white bandages showed beneath the torn edge of her silk dress. Somehow she still looked like herself: clean, composed, and faintly perfumed, as though the ruin of the kingdom had not been able to touch the habits of a queen.

"I have something to tell you," she whispered.

Nótrex sat on the floor and placed his hands over his head.

"What have you done?"

"What kind of question is that?" Krístal said. "I have done nothing. Dargos made me a proposal to save your life."

"A proposal? What proposal?"

"He says he might spare your life and Gemma's if I bond with him."

"I do not care about my life anymore!" Nótrex shouted, striking the bars.

The Kronkos rushed toward the cell. One entered and stood in front of Krístal, as if guarding her from her own husband.

"So now the Kronkos protect you?" Nótrex said.

Krístal looked at him with weary disapproval and sighed.

"Perhaps you do not care about your life," she said, "but what about Gemma's? Do you no longer care about your daughter?"

"You know I would do anything to save her."

"Then listen. Dargos says he could spare you and Gemma if he and I bond our souls."

Nótrex closed his eyes.

"As if our lives were his to forgive," he murmured. "As if we had done something wrong."

He opened his eyes again.

"Before the war, Dargos told me he had heard about you. He said the news had shocked him. He knows our secret, Krístal. I am sure of it. That is why he attacked us."

Krístal's face tightened.

"Is it impossible for someone to want me for myself? Could no one admire me? Could no one want me beside him because of who I am?"

"Do not say that, love."

"Sometimes I think you no longer want to remember who I am."

"That is not true. I only do not understand why Dargos would propose this to you."

"I do not know why you are surprised." Her voice broke. "You have blamed me no matter what I have done for this family." Nótrex went to her and held her.

"I do not want to lose you too."

"Then understand this," she said. "We do not have a choice. Not if we want to keep Gemma alive."

"You cannot seriously think of tying yourself to Dargos. I will not allow it." Krístal stepped away and looked toward the Kronko guarding the cell.

"Open the door."

The creature obeyed.

Nótrex shouted after her until his voice cracked. Long after she vanished up the stairs, he continued striking the bars. Some Kronkos rolled on the floor and covered their ears. After several nitis, one rose in anger, entered the cell, wrapped its claws around Nótrex's head, lifted him, and began to beat him.

A voice sounded from the stairs.

"Setinio karno parlete. Tute Darko tornido. (Stop hitting him. Dargos will be angry.)"

Through the pain, Nótrex saw a Ventu standing before the cell.

"Setinio karno parlete!" the Ventu repeated. The Kronko threw Nótrex to the ground. "Setinio senio soro. (Let me see her.)" Another Kronko went to fetch Krístal.

When she entered the cell and saw him, her face paled.

"Nótrex, you are badly wounded."

She knelt before him and began cleaning his wounds with the edge of her silk dress.

"These wounds are only on the body," he said, crawling toward the bars and pulling himself upright with effort. "They are nothing compared to what you are about to do."

"Do you think this is what I wanted when I agreed to hear him?"

"I know it is not. I also know none of this is your fault." His voice softened.

"Come here."

She sat beside him.

"I saw Dargos from my window," she said, tears shining in her eyes.

"What was he doing?"

"He sat in front of our garden as if it belonged to him. Then he stood and looked over the bodies of those who gave their lives for our city. There was contempt in his eyes. He walked among them like a conqueror and smiled, as if the blood on the trees pleased him." She swallowed.

"For a moment, I thought he had seen me, and I ducked. When I looked again, he was not looking at me. He was touching the mystical sphere, the same sphere my father had guarded to protect Gálax." Krístal lowered her head.

"I lay on the bed and cried for a long time. Then the door opened, and I was terrified."

"Did he hurt you?"

"No. He was the one wounded. His head was bleeding. He wiped the blood from his forehead and sat on the bed. I asked about the wound, and he said he had been hanging a foolish survivor when someone struck him with a rock."

"A rock?"

"Yes. Strange, is it not?"

She took a breath and continued.

"I asked what had happened to him. I asked how he had become so cruel. He said he had always been that way and did not know how I had failed to see it. I told him it was not true. I remembered the young man who could not kill a wounded lepedo. Something changed him, Nótrex. I saw it in his eyes. They seemed empty of soul, and I told him so."

"What did he say?"

"He became furious and told me to be silent. He said if I spoke again of his past, he would show me how much he had changed. He raised his fist near my head, then stopped himself. After that, he said he would make things clear. He is in command. The offer is generous, according to him. If I accept, he keeps us alive. If not, we die."

"What does he want from you?" Nótrex asked.

"I asked him that too. Whether he wanted to kill us or something worse. He looked at me and smiled. He said he wanted your destruction: not only your death, but the ruin of everything you had, dreamed, desired, and loved. He wants you to watch everything slip through your fingers. He wants you to feel what he believes he felt."

"And you believe he has no feeling for you? No twisted pleasure in possessing the face he once wanted?"

"It would be comforting to think it is because of who I am," Krístal said bitterly. "I thought the same and told him so. He ordered me to stop asking stupid questions and demanded to know whether we had a deal."

Her voice trembled.

"I could not answer at first. A knot rose in my throat. I turned to the window and looked at the horizon. My first thought was to throw myself from it and end everything. Do you know why? Because I wanted to keep my dignity intact. But that would have been the easiest decision." She looked at Nótrex with tearful resolve.

"I did not jump because of us. Because of our people. Because of what remains of her inside me, as though she still speaks to me from the stars. I know what you feel and do not feel for me. That has always been clear. But do not think I would betray them. I never would." She closed her eyes.

"So I told him, 'I suppose we have a deal.' Dargos smiled and left. Before he closed the door, I heard him order a Kronko to heal my wound." She looked at Nótrex.

"Do you understand now?"

Nótrex nodded without saying a word.

Rólar

Rólar walked among the dead, turning over everybody that seemed familiar. He could no longer see the grass. The fallen had covered the ground with a tapestry of bruised and reddened skin.

He was searching for his father.

"Marcus!" he shouted again and again, waiting for any sound, any movement, any sign that the man who had raised him still breathed.

He ran toward the doors of Diamondis, but only ashes remained of the entrance. The smoke of battle mingled with the ruins and darkened the air. He tried to force his way through, clawing at debris until exhaustion stopped him.

Then something strange moved through him. He remembered the swords that had cut him, the blows that had split his skin, the spear that had entered his body. Yet no pain remained.

He tore at his clothing and looked down at himself.

There were no wounds.

"Am I dead?" he whispered.

A sound answered from behind him. He turned and saw a Ventu rising from the ground, a spear still lodged in its chest.

"With that wound, you should be dead," Rólar said.

"Kirku terteluter," the Ventu rasped.

Rólar's blood chilled.

"I know you. You are the one-eyed Ventu. Why do you have both eyes now?"

"Kirku terteluter."

The Ventu lunged. Rólar swung his sword at its head, but before the blade struck, the creature vanished.

He turned in confusion—and then saw a woman's face among the bodies. "No," he breathed. "No. I thought you escaped." He ran to her.

Princess Gemma lay upon a sword. Her eyes were open, empty of life. Her dress was soaked with blood, almost indistinguishable from the bodies around her. Rólar dropped to his knees before the entrance of Diamondis and screamed until the sound echoed against the palace columns.

He lifted her into his arms and held her as if he could force her soul back into her body. Then he saw, pressed against the bloodied fabric of her dress, the golden earring he had given her on her last birthday.

A whisper moved through the wind.

Rólar, my friend. I am here. Look at me.

"Gemma!"

Rólar opened his eyes.

He was drenched in sweat. A cloak covered his body. Pain returned at once, real and terrible.

"He is awake," a voice said.

Rólar tried to rise, but his right arm could not hold him. His body was riddled with wounds. He looked around and realized he was in a cave. Footsteps approached. He used his sword like a cane, gripped a protruding stone, and tried to stand, but his legs failed him.

"Do not get up, sir," a young voice cried.

A boy—too young to look like a soldier, yet too worn to look like a child— ran into the cave and helped him. "Who are you?" Rólar asked.

"My name is Nornos, sir."

"Where are you from?"

"From the City of Light. I am a soldier like you. I proved my worth, and so did my brother, though he is no longer here." His head lowered.

"A soldier?" Rólar studied him. "I know the young men on Probation, and I do not remember you."

"I used to do lesser work, sir. But not anymore. I am brave now. Mr. Kéltrox said it with his own mouth. He called us soldiers of honor."

"Kéltrox was with you?"

"Yes, sir. With both of us. But only I remained." Rólar sat back against the stone.

"What happened to your brother?"

"He died, sir."

Nornos spoke the words with effort, tears gathering but not falling.

"We have lost many loved ones in this war," Rólar said. "I am sorry for your brother. Do you have other family?"

"Yes." Nornos hesitated. "I have another brother. But he does not even know I exist."

He cleared his throat as if hoping Rólar would ask more. Rólar did not.

"How did I get here?"

"Do you not remember? You opened your eyes several times while we carried you through the Forest of Weeping. Then you grew cold. We thought you had died because you stopped breathing. We even thought of burying you. Then, all at once, you began to cough."

"The last thing I remember," Rólar said, gripping his sword, "is a Ventu attacking me."

"The chief of the Kronkos?"

"No." Rólar's voice darkened. "Not the chief. It was the second in command, the one-eyed Ventu who repeats the same words. I had never seen any Ventu fight like him. I did not hear him coming. I felt his spear enter my shoulder from behind. When I turned, one eye was shining and the other was covered in scales. I could have sworn he was laughing at me." Nornos listened without blinking.

"He struck me again, then again. After that, I barely felt the wounds. He seized me by the neck, lowered his muzzle to the blood running from my chest, and inhaled. Then he roared, 'Kirku terteluter.'"

"Kirku," Nornos whispered. "Was that his name?"

"I think so. His claws tightened around my neck until I could no longer breathe. He threw me down. I opened my eyes and saw his shadow raising a sword toward my head. I thought I would die." Rólar looked away.

"My last thought was of her."

"Princess Gemma?" Nornos asked softly.

Rólar ignored the question.

"I closed my eyes and surrendered myself to the will of the Overlords. Then I heard a sound. I thought it was the sword. But I was still alive. When I looked again, Kirku was on his knees. An arrow had pierced his arm. After that everything went black. Someone touched my chest with something warm, and I heard words: 'Now I can do no more, but you will live, and you will find them.' Later, I heard my father cry, 'Hold on. I am going to get you out of here.' Then I knew no more."

"I brought you something to eat," another soldier said from the cave entrance.

He carried fruit in his helmet.

"That is Tartos, sir," Nornos said. "He helped rescue you."

"I remember you," Rólar said, looking at Tartos. "We must return to Diamondis."

He tried to stand again.

"Stay still, sir," Nornos said. "You are still weak."

"He has taken only liquids while he slept," Tartos added. "He had a fever."

"And he kept shouting the princess's name," Nornos said.

"Princess Gemma..." Rólar swallowed. "Is she alive?"

"The Kronkos were after her," Nornos replied. "But General Kéltrox went to help her."

"Did they catch her?"

"We do not know," Tartos said. "I pray they did not."

"How many soldiers are with us?"

"Eighteen," said Nornos.

Rólar lowered his voice. "My father. Did you see him?" Tartos looked down.

"We found Captain Marcus's body lying over you. I am sorry."

Rólar seized his sword and struck the rocks until the sound rang through the cave. Nornos stepped outside with wet eyes and said nothing.

Nornos

At dawn, Nornos awoke and realized Rólar was gone. He took his sword, gathered a few supplies, and followed the fresh footprints leading south until they climbed the side of a mountain.

Near the top, he saw a silhouette moving among the trees.

"What are you doing up here, sir?" Nornos called.

"Getting my strength back," Rólar said.

He lifted a heavy stone and threw it over the cliff.

"I am choosing the heaviest ones I can find."

"Hard work, sir," Nornos said, sitting on a rock.

"You should not say 'sir' so much."

"Yes, sir. I have been told." Rólar almost smiled.

"Take out your sword. Let us practice."

"I do not know how to use it well. I am still learning."

"I do not believe you. A boy who cannot fight does not rescue wounded men from Diamondis."

"It was luck, sir. If you are not strong with a sword and you want to live, brilliant ideas come to you."

"There is no such thing as luck on the battlefield. You kill or you are killed. How did you manage?"

"Do you truly want me to tell you?"

Rólar nodded.

Nornos picked up a stone the size of his palm.

"Do you see that tree below, the one with the highest branch?"

"What are you doing?" Rólar asked.

"I am going to hit that branch."

"No one can throw a rock that far."

Before Rólar finished, Nornos hurled the stone. It struck the branch cleanly and snapped it from the tree.

Rólar stared.

"I have never seen anything like that."

"Thank you, sir. I discovered it only a few days ago. Before that, all I had thrown were packets of fruit."

Rólar laughed despite himself.

"You are funny, Nornos. I do not know why, but I feel as if I have known you before."

"Perhaps you should have," Nornos murmured.

Then he threw another stone and struck a boulder protruding from a stream.

"What is wrong?" Rólar asked. "You fell silent."

"I had not thought of it before," Nornos said. "But sometimes skills come from disappointment."

"Did someone disappoint you?"

"Actually, sir, I disappointed him."

"What does that have to do with how you throw rocks?"

"I will tell you if you answer something first." Rólar nodded.

"Why were you calling Princess Gemma's name while you slept? Are you two a couple?"

"No, Nornos. Nothing like that. We are friends."

"You were very troubled. We thought you would not wake up. At one point, you said you loved her."

"You are more perceptive than you seem." Rólar looked toward the horizon.

"The princess's love belongs to someone else."

"Prince Altren," Nornos said.

"Yes. If I am right, he is now Prince Altren AK, heir to Ilucus. But what I want does not matter. What matters is that Princess Gemma is safe, wherever she is."

They were silent for a while.

Then Nornos spoke.

"My brother and I lived with our mother. Our father visited only a few times each teckli. Two or three at most. He came at night, as if ashamed to be seen. He did not come to know us. He came to measure us."

Rólar listened.

"He always compared us to his oldest son. His real son, he called him. We were only a disappointment. He never let us meet our brother. I think he feared we would embarrass him."

Nornos picked up another stone.

"He would make us practice with swords. It always ended the same. We could not please him. My brother would cry in bed, then spend the day drawing landscapes. I would run to the river and throw rocks at trees, at stones, at anything that did not move. I imagined every rock was my sword, and every throw carried my anger away from me. It gave me relief. I never thought it would help me in battle."

"Hardship can perfect what is hidden in a man," Rólar said. "Your father did not think you would do what you have done. Yet you saved me, Nornos. Your skill and your courage saved my life."

"Thank you, sir. That means a great deal coming from you." Nornos hesitated.

"By the way, how did we get you out of Diamondis? The Kronkos dragged bodies from the palace and left them before the front garden. Dargos would turn them over and hang anyone still alive."

"How did you see me?"

"We were hiding behind the trees by the servants' house when we saw Dargos holding you."

"Dargos was about to kill me?"

"Yes. So I took a rock, like this one, and threw it at his head. I never miss." Rólar stared, then burst into laughter.

"You hit Dargos in the head with a rock?"

"Yes, sir. He fell immediately."

"I would give anything to have seen that." Nornos smiled.

"If your father were here," Rólar said, "he would be proud of you."

"He is a soldier," Nornos answered softly.

"What is his name?"

"It is not important. I prefer not to speak of him."

Rólar did not press him. Instead, he stood and gestured with his sword.

"Get up. I will teach you a few movements."

"Do not hurt me."

They began to practice. Nornos dodged better than he struck, but Rólar saw the quickness in him.

"You evade well. As well as many soldiers I have fought. Now strike back. Keep your legs steady. There—better." Rólar paused.

"What is that hanging from your neck?"

"Tíricus slime, sir." Rólar frowned.

"Tíricus slime. I do not know why I asked. Why do you carry that in a jar?"

"To protect me. My brother taught me the trick. He called it the scarer." Nornos uncorked the bottle.

"Close it," Rólar said at once, recoiling. "Close it."

"It scares animals away from the forest. You must be careful, though. It is acidic. It burned two of my fingers once."

"It will scare people too. Put the lid back on." Nornos obeyed, smiling.

Rólar sat back on the grass.

"There is something I want to ask you."

"Anything, sir."

"Did you know my father?"

"Who did not know your father? Everyone thought Captain Marcus admirable."

For an instant, Nornos considered telling the truth. Then fear returned— the old fear that Rólar would reject him as Marcus had.

"In the cave," Rólar said, watching him, "I could swear I saw you weeping for him as one weeps for family." Nornos looked away.

"I am sorry, sir. I think you are mistaken. I should rest for a while." He returned toward the cave, leaving Rólar thoughtful.

Before dawn the next morning, Rólar came out of the cave, climbed a rock, lifted his sword, and called the soldiers together. Those who still slept woke at his voice; those gathering food hurried back. Soon all stood before him.

"They have taken us for dead," he said. "They think we are plunder, fallen men, defeated remnants. They came without provocation, using traitors and secrets to exploit our weakness. But we have not fallen. While our hearts beat, we fight for our people and our kingdom." The soldiers watched him in silence.

"Dargos is proud. He believes victory belongs to him. We will use that pride against him. We will rescue Princess Gemma and our king and queen, put them beyond his reach, and then strike with every ally we can gather. If Dargos captured them, they are in Diamondis. As long as we have life, we will not stop looking. Are you ready?" Nornos raised a rock over his head.

"We are ready!"

Some soldiers clapped. Others raised their swords and shouted with him.

Led by Rólar, they gathered fruit and moved into the Enchanted Swamp. They advanced with care, hiding among rocks and caves, keeping watch without fire, and avoiding every dry branch that might betray them.

On the second morning, near the edge of Suntras Valley and only a short distance from Diamondis, a commotion behind them froze the group.

"What is that sound?" Tartos whispered.

"Quiet," Rólar said.

"It sounds like shrieking," Nornos said. "And something else. Marching." The earth began to vibrate beneath their feet.

"Kronkos," Rólar said. "Into the trees. Now."

The soldiers hurried toward the undergrowth, but a cry came from behind them.

"Sir, help!" Rólar turned.

"Nornos, what are you doing there?"

"I am stuck."

Nornos had fallen into a sinkhole. Mud covered him to the knees and held him fast.

"Tartos, with me," Rólar ordered. Then he pointed the others toward the trees. "Hide there. If they catch us, find Princess Gemma and the king and queen. Get them to safety." The soldiers obeyed.

Rólar and Tartos ran to Nornos.

"Quiet," Rólar warned. "They can hear us from far away."

They seized Nornos by the shoulders and pulled. The mud held him like stone.

"Again," Rólar said. "One. Two. Three." Nothing.

A shadow moved across the sky. "Look," Tartos whispered. "A Bolco."

"Dargos," Rólar said.

All three lowered their heads. The Bolco flew high above and passed without turning.

"Did he see us?" Nornos asked.

"No. Again."

The sound of the Kronkos grew closer. Bushes trembled. The earth shook.

"We must go," Tartos whispered, tears in his eyes.

"You are right," Nornos said, trying to sound brave. "Leave me." Rólar looked toward the monstrous silhouettes emerging from the fog.

"No."

He grabbed Nornos again.

"With all your strength."

They pulled. Nornos pushed. The mud shuddered, released one knee, then the other. With a final wrench he flew forward over Rólar and Tartos.

"Move," Rólar whispered.

They crawled into the trees just as the Kronkos arrived.

"Lower your head, Nornos," Tartos hissed.

Nornos pressed his face into the mud.

"Lower it, not bury it," Tartos muttered.

Then the marching stopped.

A Ventu stepped away from the ranks.

Rólar's blood went cold.

"That is him," he whispered. "Kirku."

The one-eyed Ventu approached the bushes, sniffing.

"He smells blood," Tartos whispered.

Rólar looked down at the reopened wound in his shoulder.

"Nornos," he breathed. "The bottle. The slime."

"The repeller?"

"Yes. Quickly."

Nornos gave him the jar. Rólar snatched it open and poured the tíricus slime over his wound. The acid burned like fire, but he clenched his teeth and endured it.

The stench spread through the brush.

Kirku thrust his snout between the leaves, inhaled, and recoiled. He searched the ground, broke stems aside, and came so close that Rólar could feel his breath. Then the Ventu backed away, returned to the ranks, and moved on with the army.

"They are leaving," Nornos whispered.

"Toward the Nale Desert," Tartos said.

"Then there will be fewer Kronkos inside Diamondis," Rólar said. "Come." They continued toward the palace.

Diamondis had become a carcass of stone. The main entrance was heavily guarded, and the doors were clogged with rubble and bodies.

"The secret tunnel is near the pile of bodies," Rólar said.

"I do not see anything," Nornos whispered.

"It would not be secret if you could."

Four Kronkos worked nearby, dragging bodies and adding them to the pile.

"We need them away from the entrance," Rólar said. Nornos picked up a stone.

"Sir, wait. I have an idea." Rólar saw the stone and smiled.

Nornos stepped from behind the boulders and threw. The rock struck one Kronko in the head with such force that it collapsed. The others rushed toward it, shouting.

"You knocked him out," Rólar whispered, fighting the urge to laugh.

"They are carrying him inside," Tartos said. "But one stayed."

"To keep moving the bodies," Rólar said.

Nornos looked at him.

"Do it," Rólar said.

Nornos threw again, but the Kronko ducked at the wrong moment, and the stone crashed against a tree.

The creature saw him.

"Stand still," Rólar whispered, grabbing Nornos before he could run.

The Kronko charged.

When it thrust its spear between the rocks, Rólar slipped behind it, wrapped his bandaged arm around its muzzle, and drove his sword into its chest. The creature kicked, clawed, and bit into him, but Rólar held fast until its struggles weakened.

"The bastard bit me," Rólar hissed.

Dozens of Kronkos came out from the gates, searching the area.

"They heard us," Nornos whispered.

"Do not move."

Rólar shoved the dead Kronko into a lazy sprawl beside the rocks and lay facedown near it, as if he too were one of the guards shirking duty. The Ventu approached, scanned the broken branches, then looked at the bodies.

"Dircatos terc Vertanes," the Ventu muttered.

The Kronkos turned back toward Diamondis.

"It worked," Tartos whispered.

"What did he say?" one soldier asked.

Nornos swallowed.

"He said, 'Lazy. Asleep again.'" Rólar looked at him.

"You know the Ventus' language?"

"A little, sir."

"You are a genius, Nornos."

"A fearful genius, sir."

"Then keep being fearful quietly."

They reached the hidden entrance. Nornos climbed the cut log and searched for the slit, but froze at the sight of blood.

"What is wrong with you?" Rólar whispered harshly.

"The trunk... there is blood."

"Stop looking at it. Open the crack."

Tartos took his place, pulled several times, and managed to lift the trapdoor.

They descended one by one. Rólar guarded the entrance until the last man had gone below, then slipped into the passage and closed the slit above him.

The tunnel was not as he remembered it. Fallen stones narrowed the path, and the bodies of soldiers lay in the darkness where they had died trying to protect the passage.

"This smell is going to kill me," Tartos whispered.

"It is worse than tíricus slime," Nornos said.

"Look at the bodies," Rólar said. "This is where they fell. The stones that support the fountain must have collapsed." A mountain of rock blocked the way.

"Now how do we pass that?" Nornos asked.

"By moving it," Rólar answered.

For several nitis they worked in silence, shifting stones until they opened a gap narrow enough to crawl through one at a time. Beyond it, the tunnel rose toward Princess Gemma's chamber.

"We have arrived," Rólar whispered. "There may be Kronkos in the room. I go first. Tartos follows. Then Nornos. Then the rest."

He climbed, pushed the trapdoor, and entered the princess's chamber.

Empty.

"It is safe," he whispered. "Come up."

The others ascended carefully. Rólar crossed to the door and looked into the corridor. A Kronko sat near the stairs.

The creature saw him.

Rólar sprang, seized the Kronko, and dragged it into the room before it could shriek. It bit his bandaged arm, but he locked his other arm around its throat.

"Close the door," he hissed.

"The doors are smashed," Tartos said.

Nornos grabbed a cushion and held it out.

"Take this, sir."

Rólar could not let go.

"Give it to me," another soldier said.

He snatched the cushion, pressed it over the Kronko's muzzle, and slit the creature's throat. Blood soaked Rólar's body.

"Is it your blood or the Kronko's?" Nornos asked.

"It does not matter."

"The hallway is still clear," Tartos whispered from the doorway.

They descended the stairs one after another, holding the railing and trying not to slip on the rotting blood that covered the steps.

When they reached the dungeon, several Kronkos slept on the cell floor, piled over one another. Rólar signaled. In pairs, the soldiers covered their muzzles and cut their throats before any could wake.

Tartos found the keys in the claws of a wounded Kronko and tossed them to Rólar.

"Rólar?" King Nótrex asked from behind the bars. "Is that you?" Rólar opened his mouth to answer.

Before he could speak, one of the wounded Kronkos hurled a spear straight at his back.

Chapter Eleven

FALLEN FROM THE SKY

Princess Gemma regained consciousness on the sand, her head buried in her arms and grit clinging to her face. She sat up quickly and found Kéltrox beside Cortus, stroking the animal's head while Mantus hopped in short, irritated jumps, trying to shake the red dust from the wrinkled folds of his peculiar clothing.

"The princess is awake at last," Mantus said.

"What about Úniquen?" Gemma asked.

"He will be back any minute," Kéltrox replied.

"Where did he go?"

"I sent him to Trasto to buy water. The village is just beyond that mountain."

A fluttering sound cut through the dry air. They turned toward the sky and saw a dark shape approaching against the glare of the Triplets.

"Here he comes," Mantus said, shielding his eyes with both hands. "He looks half-suffocated, but at least he has the water."

Úniquen descended before Princess Gemma. The beat of his wings threw dust over their feet, and the full pitchers strapped to his back squeaked as they rubbed against one another. A few drops escaped and hissed into nothing as soon as they struck the hot sand.

"We have to hurry," he gasped. "I saw the Kronko army. They are following us and moving south."

"South?" Gemma asked. "Why south?"

"They must be going around the Endless Abyss," Kéltrox said.

"Then we have a few days," Mantus said.

Gemma looked toward the sky, where the light was beginning to dim. "It will be dark soon."

Mantus pointed toward a high wall of stone rising from the desert. "That rocky mountain should shelter us. We can find a place to camp there."

"Yes," Úniquen said, still catching his breath. "But only if we reach it before nightfall."

They crossed the remaining distance in a weary rhythm of wingbeats, jumps, and stumbling steps. At the foot of the rocky mountain, they unloaded the water from Úniquen's back, untied the blankets, stretched them over crossed poles, and fastened them into a tent. Princess Gemma kept the Book of Origins close while Kéltrox took dry sticks, a strip of cloth, and a small flask of oil from the supplies. He worked the sticks until a spark caught, fed it with the oiled cloth, and raised a torch.

"That is what those were for, smally," he said.

He set the torch at the entrance, and they went inside.

Mantus tested the crossed poles with a cautious hand. "The tent is not terrible. With some mercy from the wind, it may survive the night."

Úniquen lowered his head, more serious now. "There is something I must tell you. I heard a conversation in the village that disturbed me." The others turned toward him.

"They are speaking of a witch child in the desert," Úniquen continued. "They say she appeared in Trasto and displayed terrifying power. Afterward, the girl—Mila—and her mother vanished without a trace. Some claim Mila murdered her mother, buried her in the desert, and has been hunting travelers ever since. Others say foreign strangers kidnapped them both."

"Trasto has always been a superstitious place," Kéltrox said.

Mantus frowned.

"At least they gave me the water without charge," Úniquen added.

"Why would they do that?" Mantus asked.

"Fear," Úniquen replied. "They know Dargos has taken the City of Light. The civilian chief recognized me and knew I was Princess Gemma's companion."

"Trasto has always been loyal," Kéltrox said. "Your father should have paid more attention to them."

Gemma nodded, though her mind had already moved elsewhere.

"I am not sleepy," she said. "I will take the first watch." She moved closer to the torch and opened the Book of Origins.

Kéltrox told her to call him later. The others settled down, and soon the tent fell into a shallow, uneasy quiet. Outside, wind mixed with sand and tugged at the blankets. One loose corner swayed again and again, making the torch flame bend and tremble. Gemma read by the weak light, lifting her eyes now and then toward the darkness beyond the entrance, then returning to the ancient pages when the flame steadied.

Her eyelids began to sink. The soft slap of the loose blanket faded into the wind. Somewhere between waking and sleep, she heard a whisper. The book slipped from her fingers and fell open on the sand.

"Did you learn anything," Kéltrox asked, sitting beside her, "or were you only dreaming over the pages?"

Gemma blinked and picked up the Book of Origins. "The book speaks of someone named Muralah of Zurh, but I still do not know what he has to do with the mystical spheres."

"Tell me later."

"It also begins with a passage I do not understand."

Kéltrox frowned. "I do not remember your father mentioning an enigma."

"Listen," she said, and read aloud. "A lineage and blood chosen among the Sibling Worlds to be perpetual. Among the chosen, there will be elected ones, and although they are equal children, their destinies will be different. They all are fortunate carriers of the seed that ignites the ancient source of the mystical spheres, yet few will be able to unleash its power. It will not be the integrity of their conscience that will determine their function, nor will cleanliness of thought have the reward, but the corruption of their principles and the wickedness of their hearts will thwart its complete fulfillment." Kéltrox was silent for a moment.

"It is not an enigma, smally." She looked at him sharply.

"It means not all children of the chosen lineage can use the mystical sphere. When I was very young, your grandparents tested the sphere with your father and me. It never reacted to me because that was not my destiny. But when your father touched it—sometimes without our father's permission—it glowed."

He sighed, and the old memory seemed to weigh on him.

"Is that why they made him king, even though you were the eldest?" Gemma asked.

"Yes. Though I never wanted the crown."

"Did my father test the sphere with me?"

"Not to my knowledge. I do not think he wanted to."

"Then why can he no longer use it?"

Kéltrox looked away. "That is not mine to tell you. When we rescue your father, he will tell you himself."

Gemma's voice lowered, but her anger sharpened. "Why did none of you ever speak to me about these things?"

"Your father wanted to keep you—"

"Away from all of it," she finished. "Yes. That is what Úniquen told me as well. So he decided what I had the right to know and what I did not. That was irresponsible."

"You will wake the others."

Gemma forced her voice down. "Is there anything else they have hidden from me?"

"Smally—"

"No. Do not call me that. Not now. Please answer me."

Kéltrox's face softened. "Yes. There are other secrets."

"Then reveal them."

"Not here. Not now." He breathed out slowly. "And not because I doubt you. The Overlords know you have your mother's wisdom, and you can face more than most. But some truths are not for me to reveal, and this is neither the time nor the place to force them into the open."

Gemma closed the book.

"I am going to sleep."

She entered the tent, settled into one of the back corners, folded a blanket beneath her, and pulled the rest around her shoulders.

Kéltrox remained outside. He scanned the horizon while the stars cast their faint light over the red sand. The desert had fallen into a deep silence, broken only by the thin whistle of wind scattering sand into small, shapeless dunes.

Not much time had passed when a sob pierced the quiet.

Kéltrox turned toward the sound. In the dim starlight, he saw the figure of a woman staggering across the sand. She could barely stand, and one hand clutched her left shoulder as if she were holding herself together.

He moved toward her quickly. As he drew closer, he saw that she was young and wounded. Her clothing shimmered strangely, falling over her figure in delicate folds unlike anything he had seen in the Kingdom of Light. Gloves covered her hands, and golden bracelets circled her wrists. Something unfamiliar was fastened to her arm. Her hair was black as coal and fell beyond her waist, a striking contrast against her pale skin.

Even through the darkness and her pain, Kéltrox could not deny what he saw: the blurred shape he had first mistaken for a shadow had become the most beautiful woman he had ever beheld.

For a moment, he wondered if he was awake.

The woman stopped when she saw him. Her knees buckled, and she fell hard into the sand. With great effort, she rose again, though she swayed as if one breath could bring her down.

Kéltrox reached her.

She looked into his eyes. "Kéltrox... is that you?"

He did not know what to answer. How could she know his name? Questions rushed through him, but before he could speak, her expression changed. A faint smile touched her lips.

Kéltrox saw her blush and lower her gaze. Relief, trust, and recognition passed through her eyes, as if he were not a stranger she had met in the desert, but someone she had been hoping to find.

"Who are you?" he murmured, though the words barely left his mouth.

"They are coming for me," she whispered.

Then she collapsed at his feet. Blood spread beneath her shoulder and darkened the sand.

Kéltrox knelt and examined the wound. A sword had cut deep into her shoulder. Moving with great care so the gash would not open further, he lifted her in his arms and carried her back to the tent.

The noise woke the others.

Kéltrox saw their stunned faces when he entered and felt an unexpected relief. He had not imagined her. The woman was real. And if she was real, so was the danger: she could bleed to death before his eyes.

"Help me, smally!" he shouted.

"Put her on my blanket," Princess Gemma said. "Quickly."

"And who is that?" Mantus asked.

"I do not know. I found her walking in the dark."

"What was she doing in the desert?" Úniquen asked.

"Where did she come from?" Mantus asked at the same time.

"Silence," Gemma ordered.

She held the sphere in her right hand and pressed her left hand over the woman's shoulder. Light gathered beneath her palm. The torn flesh began to close, slowly at first, then with greater certainty, until the wound vanished beneath smooth skin.

Gemma exhaled and lowered her hand.

"I have never seen clothing like this," she said.

"She seems to come from far away," Mantus murmured.

Úniquen leaned closer. "What is tied to her arm?"

Mantus narrowed his eyes. "It looks like an electronic device." Úniquen turned to him. "A what? And how would you know that?"

"You would not believe me if I told you," Mantus replied.

Kéltrox did not look away from the woman. "She seemed to know me. She even called me by name."

"She called you Kéltrox?" Mantus asked.

"Yes. As if she was relieved to see me."

Gemma glanced at her uncle, and despite everything, a little mischief returned to her voice. "Any woman would be relieved to see you, Uncle. For an old man, you are not so wrong."

"Very funny," Kéltrox said. "Before she fainted, she said something else. She was afraid, but I could not understand it."

The sphere still rested in Gemma's hands when a roar erupted outside the tent.

The blankets tore open. Armed men burst through the entrance and the sides at once, dressed in animal skins and shouting words none of them understood. Horns and crude instruments blared in the darkness, turning the camp into confusion.

Mantus looked desperately for a gap between the blankets, as if he expected to see the sky through them. He tried to escape, but one of the attackers struck him, threw a hood over his head, and gagged him before he could speak.

At the same time, others seized Princess Gemma. In the struggle, the mystical sphere flew from her hand and landed on the sand. A woman among the attackers bent down, picked it up, and glanced at Gemma with a secretive look. Then she hid the sphere beneath her fur garment without anyone noticing—anyone except the princess.

"Where is the sphere?" demanded the man who appeared to command them.

"We searched the girl and the princess," one of his men said. "Neither has it."

The woman who had taken the sphere remained silent, watching the wounded stranger from the corner of her eye.

"Behind me," the leader ordered her.

The woman lowered her head and obeyed.

Kéltrox was trying to find Gemma through the mass of armed bodies. The attackers surrounded him. At first, they tried to take him alive, but he struck them down one after another.

No matter how many came, Kéltrox kept fighting. He cut through every man who moved close enough for his blade. Soon the attackers hesitated to approach him at all.

"Careful with that one!" one of them shouted. "He is possessed!"

The ruined tent collapsed around them. Gemma was dragged into the open. Úniquen, his wings bound, was chained to a wooden carriage. Mantus lay facedown and senseless beneath his hood. The strange woman Kéltrox had rescued had not fully regained consciousness.

Only Kéltrox remained free.

For a moment, even the attackers stopped moving.

Their leader lifted his voice. "Kéltrox. That is your name, is it not?" Kéltrox turned, breathing hard. "So you know who I am." Then he saw the others captured around him. "Of course we know," the man said. "We came for you." Kéltrox's grip tightened around his sword.

The man pressed the tip of his spear against Princess Gemma's neck. "If you do not surrender now, I will kill the princess. Then I will kill the others."

Kéltrox forced himself to speak calmly. "I am sure we can come to an agreement. If you want goldets, then you know who we are, and you know I can pay. Is that not what weed-eaters want?"

"Tempting," the man said. "But no. Drop your sword." The spear pressed harder into Gemma's skin.

Kéltrox let his sword fall.

One of the men approached from the side and struck him on the head.

Kéltrox fell to the ground like a severed branch.

When Kéltrox opened his eyes again, he was lying on wet sand.

The desert wind was gone. The suffocating heat of Nale had vanished. Beneath his hands, water lapped softly through the sand, and the tide brushed his feet like a living thing.

Where am I? What place is this?

Before him lay a small island. Waves crashed against the shore and splashed his face. He looked around, but he saw no one—only birds circling over the sea.

"Little girl!" Kéltrox shouted with all his strength. "Where are you?" No answer came.

He left the beach and entered a forest a short distance from the shore.

Gigantic trees rose around him. Strange animals watched from the undergrowth. He searched desperately, but the silence and the splendor of nature filled him with a fear he could not explain.

Waking in an unknown place was disturbing enough. Feeling watched was worse. But what truly unnerved him was the sensation that his will no longer belonged to him. His feet moved as if called forward by a force he could neither see nor resist.

Kéltrox did not fear death. He had been captured before, surrounded before, cornered before, and he had faced danger with the stubborn courage that had shaped his life. But this was different. His self-control had abandoned him.

As he moved among the trees, something shifted behind him. He turned and saw a boy walking deeper into the forest. The child wore a long white tunic and went barefoot. Now and then he looked back, silently urging Kéltrox to follow.

Kéltrox went after him, but the boy moved too quickly. He ran until his breath burned. In the distance, the child vanished into the undergrowth. Kéltrox turned back toward the beach—and collided almost face-to-face with the boy standing before him.

He leapt back.

At once, every sound disappeared. The animals, the breeze, the water, the birds—everything fell silent. Time itself seemed suspended. Nothing moved except the child.

Kéltrox's heart thundered. "How is this possible? You were—"

"Kéltrox," the boy said, "follow your instincts. Do not doubt what your heart already knows. You are asleep. Now wake up." Kéltrox opened his eyes.

His vision blurred, and pain split through his head. He lay facedown with his cheek pressed near what looked like bars. Beneath him, rocks and sand rushed past like a moving curtain.

"What a strange dream," he muttered.

Daylight burned overhead. The heat had returned, merciless and familiar.

He tried to rise, but his body resisted him.

When his sight steadied, he saw that he was inside a wooden cage. Huge iron wheels, wrapped and bound with thick chains, carried it over the desert.

A rolling prison.

They must have traveled through the night. The wagons had carried them far from the rocky mountain to an unknown place. Ahead, an oasis appeared in the middle of the Nale Desert—plants, fountains, and streams gathered impossibly around a settlement of stone.

They were entering a fortress carved into the rock, enclosed by a high wall with a single gate.

Princess Gemma was in another cage ahead of him. The wounded woman lay beside her. Úniquen was being dragged in chains, shackles fastened to every leg and his wings bound close to his body. Kéltrox could not see Mantus, but a cage covered in heavy material rolled nearby; he suspected Mantus was inside it.

"It seems we have arrived," Úniquen called to Kéltrox from several meters away.

One of the men holding Úniquen struck him with a whip.

"Silence, you stupid beast!" the man shouted, whipping him again.

"You do not have to hit him," Princess Gemma snapped. "Speak to him, and he will do what you say."

"And who asked you, insolent girl?"

The man raised the whip, this time toward Gemma.

The woman who had hidden the mystical sphere was walking behind the leader with her head lowered. When she saw the whip rise toward the princess, she lifted her eyes.

"Do not touch her!" the leader ordered. "The Grand Master wants her intact."

The words stilled the soldiers at once.

Even Kéltrox knew whom they meant, and the name filled him with dread.

Gemma saw the change in her uncle's face and understood that their situation was even worse than she had imagined.

The Grand Master, she thought. He must be their leader.

"That is right," whispered the mysterious woman beside her, pushing herself up from the floor of the cage. "He is one of the Contaminated Mages— one of the most powerful beings in the universe. That is why they fear him. He does not live among them, but he comes here often. And right now, he is inside the fortress."

Gemma stared at her. "How do you know all that?"

"Shut up!" one of the weed-eaters shrieked.

After that, the procession moved in silence until they reached the massive gate before the fortress.

"Take them to the dungeon," the leader ordered.

One of his men hesitated. “Verlou, what shall we do with the child?”

“I told you he is not a child,” Verlou snapped. “We will follow the Grand Master’s instructions. Put him in the whipping dungeon and tie him as we were ordered. And remember—take him out of the cage only after he is inside the dungeon.”

Chapter Twelve

Locked Up

Two of the shield-bearers clamped their hands around Kéltrox's chained wrists, while two others seized Princess Gemma by the waist with shameless force. The unknown woman was pushed in after them. Their captors drove them into a cave and down a narrow passage carved into the rock. They stumbled against one another, scraped their shoulders along the uneven walls, and dropped from step to step until the stairway opened into an ancient dungeon. Like the passage above, its walls had been cut directly from stone, and the floor beneath them had been worn almost smooth by time.

The chamber was large and empty. There was no bench, no proper place to sit, and no comfort of any kind. Rudimentary torches burned along the walls, offering only a weak, trembling light, while a narrow opening high above allowed a thin blade of daylight to fall into the gloom.

The Sardars untied Princess Gemma, Kéltrox, and the woman only long enough to throw them into one of the cells. They slammed the barred door shut, covered the primitive handle with a metal plate, passed a chain between two hooks fastened on either side of the lock, and fixed a square latch through the opening. Then one of them unscrewed half of the mechanism and carried it away.

Kéltrox rose at once and looked through the bars. "There are a lot of armed Weeds down here. I doubt we are the only prisoners."

"Look at that door in front of us," Princess Gemma said. "It has bars, too. They may be keeping someone dangerous inside."

"True. I saw the Sardars cross in front of it as if they were afraid."

Gemma narrowed her eyes. "I cannot see anyone inside."

"The cell has no torch."

"Our cell has no torch either," the woman interrupted from one of the corners. "But it has something better."

They both turned. She was sitting beneath the chimney-like opening, watching the sky through the thin beam of light that fell across her face.

Kéltrox glanced back toward the stairs. "I never thought the weasels would be patrolling the place where we camped. I suppose..."

"They were chasing me," the woman said.

"Then we will find a way out of here," Kéltrox replied.

She smiled faintly. "My name is Lila." Then she turned to Gemma. "You are Princess Gemma, are you not?"

"Do we know each other?" Gemma asked.

"When we were in the tent, while your uncle was fighting, I woke when I heard him call your name."

"I was not shouting," Kéltrox said.

"Then you must have thought it loudly."

Princess Gemma and Kéltrox looked at her at the same time.

"What do you mean?" Gemma asked.

"And how did you know my name in the desert?" Kéltrox added.

"I am from Green Plant."

Kéltrox's expression changed. "Ah. Now it makes sense."

Gemma frowned. "It does not make sense to me."

"The people of Green Plant possess one of the most impressive abilities I have seen in the Sibling Worlds," Kéltrox said. "They can read thoughts." Lila nodded before he had finished speaking.

"So it is true," Gemma said. "I thought it was only a myth."

"I visited your planet long ago," Kéltrox told Lila. "The First Lyson invited Nótrex and me to the Great Treehome, along with other leaders from the Sibling Worlds."

"My father always believed we should share our technological knowledge with less developed Sibling Worlds," Lila said.

Kéltrox studied her more carefully. "Then your father is the First Lyson?"

"He was. Now there is another Prime Minister. My planet was invaded."

"Let me guess," Kéltrox said. "Tolan."

Lila's eyes sharpened. "How do you know?" Then she stopped herself. "Ah... I see."

"I heard Dargos speak of conquering another Sibling World," Kéltrox said.

"Why did you come to us?" Princess Gemma asked.

"I came to ask King Nótrex for help."

Kéltrox gave a grim half-smile. "As you can see, we are in no position to help anyone. Our world has been invaded as well."

"Did you come through the Pirutus portal?" Gemma asked.

"No. The Tree of Entrances was too heavily guarded."

"The Tree of Entrances?"

"The gateway to Green Plant."

Kéltrox glanced toward the narrow shaft of light above them. "Then how did you get here? Your planet is far from ours."

"I used advanced transfer technology. Once I entered your planet's orbit, I tracked the mystical sphere with a location DRED and guided my ship toward the Nale Desert, where the energy was strongest. But the thrusters failed before I could land. I had to crash in the desert."

Princess Gemma looked at Kéltrox, confused by the unfamiliar terms.

"A ship," Kéltrox explained, "is a flying device that allows people to travel through the universe."

"You were fortunate to survive," he added, turning back to Lila. "Yours is not the first ship that has failed while entering our world."

"Failed?" Lila asked.

"As far as I know, our planet has a natural barrier that restricts advanced technology," Kéltrox said. "Few ships make it through the atmosphere, and those that do usually crash. Devices brought by allies from the Sibling Worlds often stop working once they reach the Kingdom of Light. Some scholars believe it is caused by the Triplets and the field created by their orbit around us. Whatever the cause, it interferes with the frequency on which that technology depends."

Gemma looked from Kéltrox to Lila. "I knew nothing of this."

"Your father did not like involving you in such matters," Kéltrox said.

Gemma snorted softly. "Of course he did not."

Kéltrox ignored the remark. "How did you find us in the desert?"

"I followed the last location the DRED gave me. Before my father was captured, he told me to come here. I barely escaped."

Gemma's gaze shifted suddenly toward the opposite cell. "Look. It is a girl."

The child's eyes met hers from across the dungeon.

"What is a girl doing in a place like this?" Kéltrox asked.

"She cannot be more than ten cycles old," Lila said. "Tecklis, as you call them."

Gemma lowered her voice. "Why are they guarding her so closely?"

Lila focused on the girl, then frowned. "I cannot read her mind. I do not understand why."

The girl stood, watching Lila with strange intensity. From that distance they could see thick chains hanging from her wrists.

"Quiet now!" shouted an Escardo from the rough stairway.

Kéltrox stepped closer to the bars. "Escardo, come here. This is important."

The guard approached with irritation. "What is important, prisoner?"

Kéltrox pointed toward the opposite cell. "Even you people must have some boundary. Why are you keeping a little girl chained like a criminal?"

"A little girl?" The Escardo gave a harsh laugh. "That is none of your concern. Call me again, and I will have you whipped." He returned to his post beside the girl's cell.

"Did you get anything?" Kéltrox whispered.

"Yes," Lila said. "There is something about her mother, but his mind was unclear. I could not fully understand the thought."

"The girl is not filthy," Gemma said. "That means she has not been here long."

"I told you to be quiet!" the guard snapped, returning to their cell door.

"What are you whispering about? Do not think you can escape. It could be terrible for you if you try."

"We were only talking," Lila replied.

The Escardo smiled in a way that made Gemma's skin crawl. "I would take you to my bed and let you talk all you want, but you are unlucky. Verlou does not allow me to touch you. Otherwise, we would have known each other better."

Then he saw Kéltrox's face. Their eyes locked. The guard backed away until he struck the door of the girl's cell.

"You frightened him," Lila whispered after he left.

"Why do you say that?" Kéltrox asked.

"He was thinking of all the men you killed in the desert." Silence settled over the dungeon for several minutes.

"My niece has fallen asleep," Kéltrox whispered.

Princess Gemma lay near the cold hearth, curled on her side, her head resting on one arm while the other covered her face.

"She is not the only one," Lila murmured, nodding toward the guard whose legs were crossed near the opposite wall.

"How do you know he is asleep? Did you read his mind?"

"No. He is snoring." They both smiled.

"Before he fell asleep, I scanned him," Lila added.

"What do you mean?"

"I made an incisive scrutiny of his thoughts."

"And what did you find?"

"The key to this cell is kept in a box in the room of the wizard they call the Grand Master."

Kéltrox's smile vanished. "So he truly is here. This is more serious than I thought. We need a plan."

Before — Dala from Senters (Part Two)

Pina could not ask anything else. She carried Dala up the rocks slowly, planting her feet in every crack she could find, forcing strength into her weak knees until she reached the top. Then she sat on a stone with her daughter in her arms, looked into her eyes, and began to cry.

Too many unanswered questions tormented her. Was it only her daughter's imagination? If so, how could Dala have fallen from such a height and remained unharmed? If strange beings had saved her, who were they? Why could Dala see them when Pina could not? Would it be easier to forget what had happened and continue life as if nothing had changed? Or would ignoring it place her child in greater danger?

"Come, Naughty. You are alive, and that is what matters." Pina breathed unevenly and kissed her forehead. "Tonight you will hear a story you must never forget. Treasure it, my love. Your life may depend on it." Dala kept staring toward one of the rocks below the cliff.

"What are you looking at?" Pina asked.

"Will my friends come back?" Dala whispered.

Pina could not answer. She took her daughter's hand, and together they walked away.

A few minutes later, they reached a cave whose walls were carved with animals and human faces. Forty-six people sat inside on rocks and logs, waiting in a tense silence.

An elderly man stood near the entrance. "Pina," he said, "I see you have chosen to reveal the truth to your daughter. Dala, sit with the other children. Let us begin."

Dala obeyed.

"Ten days have passed since Kata was taken from us," the old man said. "We have shared Pina's grief over the loss of her youngest daughter. Some children among us still do not know why Kata is gone forever. And she is not the only one. There have been others. Many more. Tonight we tell the story our ancestors entrusted to us, so that each generation may repeat it to the next. It is the story of those responsible for the massacres, the killers who watch our steps even now. They may be lurking in the dark as I speak."

He moved among the gathered people and lifted a wooden instrument from behind a rock. Threads stretched across its center, and on its back were drawings similar to those carved into the cave wall. He stood before the community and began to sing the Song of the Tolorons.

"I do not speak of animals, for animals possess neither evil intention nor the hunger for cruelty. Even in the vilest human, a flash of grace may still remain. But these savage creatures are architects of extreme violence. They conspire against humankind and fill the night with dread. They devise traps, stalk dreams, and appear as heralds of death. Their aspect is sinister, though they seldom reveal it. They move as swiftly as the wind. Their nails break bones as if they were shells. They delight in devouring human flesh, and the taste of it drives them mad. They have no devotion except the hunt. To flee them is useless; to stand motionless before them is death. Many have been caught in their traps, and no human has escaped them. They look almost human, for they walk as humans walk, but their wings and wild features betray them. Their cunning makes them lethal, and they are wiser than men in the art of hunting."

On the way back, Pina and Dala walked quickly through the dark.

"We are almost there," Pina said. Dala stopped. "What is that?"

"Behind me!" Pina shouted.

Before she could finish, she vanished. Dala stood alone only a few steps from the cave.

She searched frantically for her mother, but then she remembered Pina's command. She ran as fast as her legs could carry her, entered the cave, and hid beneath her blankets.

The next morning, Dala stepped outside and found the entire community gathered near the entrance.

The Lord of the Community approached her with sorrow in his face. "Your mother was taken last night. We heard her screaming in the distance."

"I will go and get her," Dala said.

"You cannot. No one can. You are only a child."

"My friends will come with me."

"What friends?"

"You cannot see them, but they are with me."

The Lord lowered his head. "Poor child. She has suffered too much." He went to his wife. "We will take her with us," he whispered.

Dala looked toward the sky and nodded, as if someone unseen had answered her. Then she turned to the Lord of the Community. "Yes. I will go with you."

Midnight came. The Lord was sleeping beside his wife when a sound woke him.

He left the cave and followed the faint noise until colored flashes shone from behind a large boulder. For a moment, he stood frozen. Then he began to back away toward the cave, but a familiar voice stopped him. "Dala?" he called, returning to the rock. "Who were you talking to?" The light had already vanished.

"My friends," Dala said. "I know where to find my mother."

"Come inside."

He took her hand and felt an unfamiliar object in her palm. "What is that?"

"My friends gave it to me so the Tolorons will not hurt me." The Lord of the Community stared at her, speechless.

The following morning, shrieks outside the cave startled him awake. He ran to the entrance and found the people gathered there, shouting so loudly that no single voice could be understood.

"Something terrible has happened!" a woman cried.

"Our children are gone!" another man shouted.

"Where did they go?" the Lord asked in horror.

"No one knows. Some say the Tolorons took them."

The Lord ran back into the cave and searched for Dala. She was gone too. Her blankets had been folded neatly before she left. Beneath them, he found a sharp dagger. He took it and returned outside.

"We must go and find our children," he said.

The men of the community armed themselves with weapons of wood and metal and set out. They had not gone far when they saw figures approaching in the distance. The children walked beside Dala. Behind her came Pina and many others who had been abducted.

The community rushed toward them. Parents embraced children. Laughter mingled with weeping. Amid the commotion, the Lord approached Dala.

"Did you rescue them?"

"My friends helped me," Dala answered.

Pina cried, though a smile trembled through her tears. "What about your sister? Did you find her?"

"They had not taken her."

"Then where is she?"

Dala sighed and looked at her mother. "Kata is somewhere else. My friends promised they would care for her, and that one day I would see her again."

Before — Kerisetale from Gálax

On the planet Gálax, there were not yet kingdoms or great cities. The First Humans lived scattered in communes they called Entities. Each Entity was made up of thirty families who enclosed portions of land, raised tents and huts, and lived together in colonies near the Golmis River, the largest river in the region.

One village climbed from the foot of a mountain to its heights. A fierce frost had struck the region, and chunks of ice fell from the sky, disturbing the river until it overflowed its banks. The waters destroyed the seedbeds, cracked the huts, floated them over the numb and trembling ground, and battered the foothills of the mountain.

The Entities fled to the top of the mountain and took shelter inside a great cavern. They waited anxiously for the storm to pass. Some sat on rocks; others leaned against boulders. In one clean corner lay a pregnant woman, her head resting on rags, her body wrapped in animal skins.

"Emma is awake!" an old man shouted, hurrying toward her.

The others gathered around. A man offered her a clay canteen, but Emma rose in panic and knocked it away.

"Where is my daughter?" she demanded. "She was ahead of me. Then I woke, and she was gone."

A man approached her carefully. "I never saw her, Emma. I searched for her among the crowd."

"A piece of ice struck your head," an old woman said, pointing to the man beside her. "Cóncor saved your life and many others."

"Emma," Cóncor said softly, "you were alone when I found you. I thought your daughter had run ahead with the others. I am sorry."

Emma stared at him in silence. Then she stood and tried to run. Pain stopped her. She placed a hand over her swollen belly and made her way toward the cavern entrance as quickly as she could.

She tried to step out, but the wind hurled her back. She would not surrender. She clung to a rock and tried again, but before she could place one foot outside, arms wrapped around her waist with tender firmness and pulled her back into the shelter. She knew whose arms they were before she turned.

She pulled away, pretending anger, though gratitude and fear warred inside her. She tried to keep her gaze hard, but one look at Cóncor's eyes and one sound of his voice softened her face.

"I will look for her," he said.

Emma closed her eyes as his warm hands cupped her frozen face. He wiped away tears chilled by the draft, then slid his fingers over her mouth as if to keep her from thanking him. Relief overcame her, but terror followed it. Her spirit companion had died half a winter earlier. If Cóncor went out, he might die as well, and she did not know whether she could survive losing him too. "I will come back," he promised.

Cóncor descended without looking back. He clung to rocks jutting from the mountain, fought the current of air, ignored the cold, and endured the cuts made by falling ice. He climbed down until he stood before the frozen water that flooded the mountain's side.

He saw only floating debris, dead animals, uprooted trees, and blocks of ice drifting in the flood.

"Kerisetale!" he shouted. "Kerisetale!"

The cold began to paralyze him. He could barely feel his hands. Shapes appeared in the ice, and his thoughts dimmed at the edge of unconsciousness.

Then he saw something among the snowflakes that disturbed him. He rose, unsure whether he was hallucinating. An ice floe had lodged itself near the shore, and on it lay a girl surrounded by what looked like a transparent bubble emitting purple light.

"Kerisetale?" he cried. "Is that you?"

The girl lifted her head. Cóncor did not recognize her face.

"Come here, child. Come."

She answered in a language he did not understand.

Cóncor climbed onto the floe and stretched out his hands. The bubble vanished. When he lifted the girl, he realized she was warm. Her warmth passed into him as he carried her up the mountain. She kept speaking, but he understood only the word she repeated again and again.

"Kata. Kata."

He reached the cavern exhausted. The crowd at the entrance began to applaud when they saw him, but Emma's hopeful smile broke when she realized he was not carrying her daughter.

Cóncor put the girl down and went to Emma. She was crying. He held her and said nothing, only listened to her grief.

The girl ran after him and stood before them.

Emma turned her tear-soaked face toward her. The girl's eyes, skin, clothing, and features were unlike anything she had seen before.

"Come here, little one," Emma whispered.

The child did not understand the words, but she understood Emma's open arms. She ran to her and embraced her.

"I think her name is Kata," Cóncor said, remembering what she had repeated.

Emma pulled back slightly. "Are you Kata?" The girl nodded.

"My daughter is dead, Kata," Emma said, weeping again. "The Overlords warned me. They also told me you would come. Do not be afraid. We will care for you. The Overlords sent you to me so I could protect you. I knew it would happen—not like this, but I always knew."

She touched the girl's hair and searched her face through tears. "From this day, I will give you my daughter's name. Kerisetale. Will you be my Kerisetale?"

The child did not understand every word, but she understood the sorrow and the love. She nodded, and Emma held her as if she had lost and received a daughter in the same breath.

Prince Altren AK from Ilucus

Tambourines shook beneath the starlight of the Purple Night. Dozens of choristers sang while fiery red lamps burned from the rooftops and washed the courtyard in the color of blood. Twelve hundred dancers leapt to the rhythm, celebrating the Man Child's grand ceremony while King Sortus AK watched from his throne beside Queen Le Clauta AK.

"Red, like this night, is the color of blood," the king said, rising. "Son of my blood, the time of childhood ends. Walk the Weeping Paths and be reborn."

He stood before Prince Altren. "Go now. Return not as a child, but as a man."

Then the king struck him on the forehead.

The blow signaled the beginning. As he had practiced in the palace, Altren turned and stepped barefoot onto the long corridor of dried branches and thorns laid out before him. Silence fell over the crowd. Each step broke it again, for thistles and splinters pierced his feet, and the bright red blood he left behind shone against the blackened leaves.

He crossed the Weeping Paths without stopping. When he reached the end, he placed his bleeding feet on the grass and turned to face the people.

"I have reached the end of this path of torment," Prince Altren said. "Neither wounds nor tragedies will change my course. May the power of the Supernals strengthen my sword, and may the guidance of the wizards bring peace to the Sibling Worlds."

He lifted his hands. The king opened his arms, and Prince Altren ran back to him. This time, soldiers removed the thorns and branches from his path.

"By the light of the Overlords, you are worthy," the king said proudly.

"From this day forward, while your path remains straight, you will no longer be known only as Prince Altren. You are Prince Altren AK, the new man."

They embraced, and the courtyard erupted in applause and cheers. Then a soldier ran out of the palace and fell before the king.

"My King Sortus AK."

"Speak."

The soldier rose, trembling. "You will not believe what has happened."

Prince Altren AK turned toward him. "What did you see?"

"There is a glow in your chamber."

The king and prince looked at one another, then ran toward the royal chambers with dozens of soldiers behind them.

At the door, prisms of different colors slipped through the tiny edges of the room.

"Cover the king," Altren AK ordered. Then he pointed to a group of soldiers.

"You, come with me."

He opened the door. Inside, they could barely make out a silhouette standing before the window.

"Identify yourself!" Prince Altren AK said, drawing his weapon. "I will not ask again."

The lights began to fade, revealing a man looking out from the window.

"Watch that animal!" a soldier shouted, pointing to a creature beside him.

Prince Altren AK moved to seize it, but the man turned.

"Prince Altren," he said. "Or rather, Prince Altren AK. It is good to meet you in person."

"Lower your sonorous," the king called from the doorway. "Is it truly you? For a moment I feared you were a tainted wizard."

At the king's command, the soldiers lowered their weapons.

"You know him, Father?" Altren asked.

"You know who he is too. I have told you stories of him since you were a child."

Altren stared at the stranger. "Are you Morico? The great warrior mage?"

He approached the wizard and knelt. The soldiers followed his example, though the king remained standing.

"Yes," the man said. "I am Morico of Ilucus. Stand. No prince should kneel before any wizard."

They rose. Morico's expression softened only slightly. "And do not believe every tale told about me. Stories are often altered." The king and wizard laughed, but the sound died quickly.

"I bring news," Morico said.

"Then I assume it is not good news," the king replied, "or you would not have come after all this time."

"The Kingdom of Light has fallen. It is under the dominion of the tainted wizards."

Altren AK looked first at his father and then at Morico. "Princess Gemma. Is she alive?"

"She is in good hands."

"By the good fortune of the Overlords," Altren whispered. "I was with her only a few days ago, closing the Treaty of Binding."

King Sortus's face hardened. "How did they conquer the Kingdom of Light without your knowing?"

"The Contaminated Wizards used a man to do it under our very eyes," Morico said. "We suspected they were preparing something through him, but we did not know he could use a mystical sphere."

"Who would lend himself to such evil?" the king asked.

Morico's eyes darkened. "You knew him in your youth. A man whose ambition and obsession have wounded many. A man who covets what is not his, corrupts others in pursuit of his desires, lies while justifying himself, and calls destiny what is only selfish hunger. Dargos did it."

"Dargos," Altren said. "The one who conquered Gálax?" Morico nodded, and the creature beside him growled.

"That he is still alive is already a marvel," King Sortus said slowly. "But that he can use the mystical sphere? Impossible."

"I do not understand," Altren said. "Dargos is not of the lineage."

"The tainted wizards have done something," Morico replied. "Perhaps they corrupted the sphere of Gálax. Perhaps they altered Dargos himself. We do not yet know. What we do know is that Dargos is using a sphere, and he must be stopped."

"What do you need from us?" Altren asked.

"For the moment, nothing. I came to warn you. Since your realm has no mystical sphere, I will create a protection that can help you resist if the Contaminated Wizards attack before I return. It will temporarily block portals in and out of your kingdom, though not aerospace access. The barrier will give you a few days to prepare your ships and armaments. Its strength will fade after about five solar days, sooner if the Contaminated Wizards unite to break it."

"Is that all?" the king asked.

"In the morning, after I cast the spell, I will leave."

Lila

The next day, a deep voice echoed through the dungeon walls. Kéltrox woke, listened to the sound, and looked around. Lila had fallen asleep against his legs, and Princess Gemma lay in a corner.

"Wake up," he said.

Lila realized where her head was and sat up, blushing.

Gemma rubbed her eyes and stood. "They are making a horrible noise."

She touched her chin and winced. Two scratches burned there, irritated by small granules of rock embedded in her skin.

"The commotion is coming from the stairs," Lila said, hurrying to the bars.

"Listen. They are arguing."

Kéltrox listened. "No. They sound excited."

"Excited about what?" Gemma asked.

"I do not know. All night I heard footsteps above us, like nórmides dragging heavy things. I heard hammering, too, and saw lights moving on the stairs."

"Here they come," Lila whispered.

The Weeds rushed down and opened the barred door. Kéltrox took a fighting stance, while Gemma and Lila moved behind him. Seven Weeds entered the cell. Five forced Kéltrox into a corner at swordpoint. Two seized Princess Gemma first, then Lila, and chained their hands and feet.

For an instant, Kéltrox considered tearing a sword from one of them and fighting his way out. But the slightest move might bring harm to Gemma or Lila, so he buried the impulse. His niece and Lila looked frightened, but their spirits were not broken. Their eyes told him plainly: do not fight them.

"What are you going to do with us?" Kéltrox asked, seeing the smiles on their captors' faces.

The guard holding Gemma pressed a dagger to her throat. Another thrust the tip of a spear against Lila's back.

"What we do with you is none of your business. Put the shackles on. I will not tell you again."

When Kéltrox hesitated, the guard holding Gemma dragged the dagger's edge lightly across her neck. She moaned.

Kéltrox's jaw tightened. "Do not hurt her. I will do it." He lowered his head and held out his hands.

"No," one of the guards snapped. "Put them on yourself."

Kéltrox obeyed. The Weeds seized him, Gemma, and Lila and dragged them up the stairs.

They emerged into a courtyard before a tall tower. A crowd of Weeds had gathered in a newly assembled stadium, its rough semicircular seats made of logs like primitive bleachers. Men, women, and children cheered and clapped as the prisoners were shoved down a short flight of stone steps onto a wooden platform in the center. Then the guards threw them into a muddy pit.

They slipped against the clay walls as they tried to brace themselves. Even untied, climbing out would have been difficult. Beside the pit stood a huge old tree whose branches stretched over the moat. Ropes hung from it, some nearly rotten, though their knots remained firm. It looked like a tree used for hanging the condemned.

The tower gates opened. The crowd fell silent for one breath, then roared even louder than before.

A gigantic Ventu emerged. His footsteps shook the platform as if an earthquake moved beneath the courtyard. He was twice Kéltrox's height, and he carried a spear larger than a man. As he stepped onto the wooden platform, the crowd began to chant with fierce rhythm.

"Terlus! Terlus! Terlus!"

Gemma tried to wipe mud from her face with equally muddy hands. "It looks as if they are going to execute us."

Lila freed one foot from the mud, reached for Gemma, and helped her stand.

"Terlus is the Ventu's name. They believe he is going to fight one of us."

The massive Ventu dragged the edge of his spear through the mud, climbed out of the pit with a few heavy steps, crossed the platform, and stopped before them. Then he pointed the spear directly at Kéltrox.

"What is he doing?" Gemma asked.

"He has chosen me," Kéltrox said.

"You can defeat him, Uncle. Please be careful."

Kéltrox did not hear the sob she tried to suppress; mud covered her face and hid the tremble of her mouth.

"No," Lila said suddenly. "He is not choosing you."

Kéltrox and Gemma watched the point of the Ventu's spear slide away from him until it stopped before Lila.

Three Weeds came to the edge of the pit, grabbed Lila, and began pulling her upward. Gemma and Kéltrox seized her feet and tried to hold her down, but the mud made their grip useless. Lila slipped free, and the Weeds dragged her onto the platform, untied her hands, and pushed her toward the titan.

With his hands still bound and mud clinging to him, Kéltrox should not have been able to escape the pit. But the thought of Lila dying under his protection drove strength through him. He leapt, caught one of the ropes hanging from the tree, swung hard, and landed outside the pit.

The guards stared at him in disbelief.

"Get him back in!" shouted the one who seemed to command them.

Before they could restrain him, Kéltrox stood and shouted with everything in him. "I will fight in her place! I will do it!"

"Shut up!" a guard roared, striking him in the stomach.

Kéltrox dropped to the ground. Several Weeds seized his legs and shoved him back into the pit.

He recovered quickly. Lila was in danger, and that thought sharpened him. He kicked at the Weeds and surged toward her again. One intercepted him, then several more. They beat him, but even with his wrists bound, Kéltrox moved with brutal agility, returning blows wherever he could. It took several soldiers to restrain him.

Then Lila ran to him and kissed him.

The Weeds did not understand what was happening until her bound arms were around Kéltrox's neck. For a heartbeat, the crowd stopped roaring, as if the act itself had become part of the spectacle. No one dared separate them.

Kéltrox stared into Lila's mud-darkened eyes. He did not know whether he was seeing tears or only damp earth clinging to her lashes. The blows had dazed him, but her kiss stole what breath he had left.

The crowd erupted again, this time chanting in the tongue of the Ventus. "Tortaris! Tortaris! Tortaris!" Fight. Fight. Fight.

The guards knocked Kéltrox down and threw him back into the pit. Then one of them thrust a sword into the platform at Lila's feet. She gripped it with both hands and looked back at Kéltrox and Gemma.

Her eyes met Kéltrox's, and he heard a voice inside him.

Please release my home.

Surprised, he studied Lila's face and understood that she had sent him the message.

"Did you hear that?" he asked.

"Hear what, Uncle?" Gemma said. Kéltrox shook his head. "The voice." Gemma had heard nothing.

"Watch out, Lila!" Kéltrox shouted.

The Ventu ran backward to gain momentum, then hurled his spear toward Lila's head, intending to end the fight with a single throw. Lila flung herself to the side. The spearhead brushed through her hair, and her sword slipped from her hands.

"The sword!" Gemma cried.

Kéltrox tried to climb out again, but a guard struck him with the handle of his sword, and he fell back into the mud.

"I will tear you apart, little bug!" the Ventu roared in his own language.

He snatched a sword from a guard and charged. The platform shook beneath his steps. Cracked wood split farther, and splinters leapt with every stride.

Lila stood unarmed before him and watched every movement. The Ventu swung at her head. She ducked. He raised the sword and brought it down as if to split her in two. She threw herself backward, rolled across the muddy wood, and sprang to her feet. Through dirt and sweat, she saw him approach more slowly now, like a warrior realizing his opponent might not be as helpless as she appeared.

For a moment, Lila ceased to hear the crowd, Gemma, Kéltrox, or the guards. The platform seemed to vanish. She saw only the Ventu. She searched his eyes, his pupils, his grief.

He struck toward her right shoulder. She dodged. He aimed between her eyes. She slid back without falling.

When the Ventu realized she was avoiding every blow, he signaled to the guards near the pit. Three ran to the tower and returned dragging a sledgehammer covered in sharp iron spikes. It was so heavy they could barely move it.

The crowd screamed with greater hunger when they saw it. Gemma and Kéltrox looked at each other.

The Ventu shoved the Weeds aside and lifted the giant mallet onto his shoulder. Its spikes hung behind him like fangs. He approached Lila and swung to crush her.

She barely escaped. The spikes buried themselves in the wood, and the courtyard shook. The stands thundered again.

"Tortaris! Tortaris! Tortaris!"

The Ventu strained to pull the mallet free. Lila moved closer, searching between the cracked boards and the buried spikes until she saw the sword's handle half-covered in mud.

"What are you doing?" Gemma shouted. "Get away from him!"

Kéltrox shouted with her, but Lila ignored them. She seized the sword with both hands and cried out in the Ventu's tongue.

"Verete dorita cotaia!"

The Ventu froze. His head lowered.

Lila rushed forward and drove the sword into his heart.

The Scardos stood motionless. The frail woman they had mocked had defeated their champion. The crowd did not shout again. They withdrew in a stunned murmur, while several in the front ranks dragged the Ventu's body away.

The Weeds pulled Gemma and Kéltrox out of the pit, seized Lila by the arms, and dragged all three back to the cell.

"What did you say to him?" Kéltrox asked once the door had shut behind them.

Lila lowered her eyes. "Verete was the name of his son. He died fighting the Kingdom of Light when Dargos attacked them. Dorita means waiting for him, and cotaia means in the afterlife. I told him his son was waiting for him in the afterlife."

"That was a good strategy," Gemma said quietly.

"I know," Lila replied. "But I feel guilty. If you had felt his pain for that son..." Her voice broke. "I used his grief to save myself. Who is the monster now—him or me?"

"You had no choice," Kéltrox said, and embraced her.

After a while, several Scardos descended the stairs carrying three rusty, filthy trays. They pushed two under the bars of Gemma's cell and slid the third with visible fear beneath the door where the chained girl was kept.

"Food," Gemma said, hurrying to uncover one of the trays. Then she wrinkled her nose. "It looks like something used for bathing." She stirred the gelatinous substance with her thumb.

"It is slimy," Lila said, "and it smells awful."

"Feed yourself, smally," Kéltrox said with a weary smile.

"No, thank you. I will pass."

Lila looked at the two trays. "Why did they bring only two for three prisoners?"

Before anyone could answer, two more Weeds came down the stairs and opened the cell. They dragged in a wooden cart carrying a silver tray larger than the others. Unlike the previous trays, this one was clean and polished.

A pair of metal tongs lay beside it.

"You are fortunate," one guard muttered. They shut the cell and went back upstairs.

"Where did this come from?" Gemma asked.

Lila uncovered the tray. "The weasels left thinking this is the first time they have given the reward of combat to a woman."

The tray held fruits, vegetables, and meat. Lila shared it gladly, and the three began to eat.

Gemma picked up a fruit and looked toward the opposite cell. The girl stood and stared back.

"Let me try," Lila said. "I have a good aim."

She threw the fruit between the bars. It landed inside the girl's cell. The child snatched it up and ate greedily.

"Poor child," Gemma murmured.

"Yes," Kéltrox said. "What is she doing here?"

"I do not know," Lila answered. "I still cannot read her mind." The girl looked at Lila again.

Lila turned to Gemma. "Princess, there is something else you should know. Before the fight, I saw a woman in the crowd trying to see you. From her thoughts, I believe she knew you."

"The woman who took the mystical sphere in the tent?" Gemma asked.

"Yes. She was thinking about how to return it to you."

"Then why did she come with the Weeds?" Kéltrox asked.

Gemma frowned. "I think I have seen her before, but I cannot remember where."

The girl in the other cell sat up suddenly and fixed her eyes on Princess Gemma.

Úniquen

"Hey, you. Tell me something," Úniquen said, pushing his snout between the bars of the cart. "Why are they screaming on the other side of the tower?"

Two Weeds sat in front of his rolling prison. Úniquen tried to shift his numb wings and only then remembered they were tied tight. His bruised skin had almost stopped feeling the sharp bite of the chains.

"You talked in your sleep all night," one of the guards said. "And even awake, you do not shut up."

The other smiled mockingly. "Terlus, a gigantic Ventu who came with Dargos's army, is fighting the prisoners who came with you."

Úniquen snorted. Then he noticed, a short distance away, a dungeon sealed with skins so no daylight could enter. Dozens of Weeds surrounded it.

"That is where Mantus was locked up, is it not?" he asked.

The guards exchanged a glance and suddenly stood.

"What is happening?" one asked.

"I do not know. They stopped shouting. The fight must be over."

"Let us see."

"And the Bolco?"

"He is not going anywhere."

They ran toward the other side of the tower.

Úniquen studied the sealed dungeon. The Scardos at the entrance were distracted; others lurked near the covered doors. He jerked hard, and the cart lurched. The chains binding the door and those wrapped around his wings held firm. He braced his hind legs against the bars and pushed. The cart rocked again, its wheels squeaking as they sank into the clay.

He struggled for a long time. At last, exhausted, he collapsed upside down, drew a deep breath, and prepared to try again. Then something made him stop.

He rose, pushed his snout through the bars, and saw a small body lying in front of the sealed dungeon. A moment later, a light began to glow.

"Who are you?" Úniquen whispered.

Then darkness swallowed him, and he fainted.

Chapter Thirteen

Germovas Peritis

The girl watched Princess Gemma through the bars when three Sardars descended the stairs, armed more heavily than usual, and stopped before the cell. Verlou, their leader, carried a long weapon shaped like a spear. Both ends were hollow, like small cannons, and three round buttons lined its center.

"What are you doing with a lightning spear?" Lila asked.

Verlou did not answer. He raised the weapon and aimed it at them. "Stand back."

"What do they want now?" Kéltrox asked.

"Back, I said. Against the wall. Heads down, or I'll kill your niece." Verlou shifted the weapon until its mouth pointed at Princess Gemma's face.

"Lightning launchers don't work on this planet," Kéltrox said.

Verlou slid his thumb over the center button. "Do you want me to test that on her face?"

Kéltrox held his stare for a moment, then stepped back. "I'll move." He went to the wall and lowered his head.

The Sardars opened the barred door. Before Kéltrox could react, they dragged Lila out and locked the cell again.

"Don't take her!" Kéltrox shouted, striking the bars with both hands.

Time passed with painful slowness. Princess Gemma watched the dim space beyond the cell while Kéltrox paced like a caged beast. At last, voices echoed from the stairs.

"I think I heard Lila," Gemma said. She hurried to the door and peered through the bars.

"Let me see."

Gemma stepped aside.

Kéltrox looked through the bars. "Yes. That's Lila. They're bringing her back with her hands tied."

"What did they do to her face?" Gemma whispered. "She's bruised." Kéltrox drew a hard breath through his teeth.

"Back!" Verlou ordered.

They obeyed. The Sardars threw the woman into the cell, slammed the door shut, and left. She landed sitting, sobbing, then crawled toward one of the corners.

"What did they do to you?" Kéltrox asked, stepping toward her.

He stopped before reaching her and punched the wall. Skin tore across his knuckles, and blood stained the stone.

"Uncle, you hurt yourself," Gemma said.

"Look what they did to her."

"I see her," Gemma replied, keeping her voice low, "but hurting yourself will not help Lila."

"I'm fine," the woman said, looking at him through her tears.

Gemma moved closer. "We were terrified, Lila. Why did they take you?"

"They wanted answers. When I refused to speak, they hurt me." She rose unsteadily and walked toward Kéltrox.

Kéltrox avoided her and sat in the corner.

A while later, the woman looked toward the cell's narrow chimney. Evening had already begun to fall.

"Kéltrox," she said, "you still have not told me what you were doing in the Nale Desert. Where were you going?"

"That is not relevant, Lila."

"Were you supposed to meet someone there? Or were you trying to reach another world for help?"

"Lila, I am trying to find a way out of here. Do you not understand that I need to think?" he said harshly.

She drew back and lowered her head between her knees.

"You did not have to be rude," Gemma whispered angrily. "Look what you did."

Kéltrox stood from the corner. "I was waiting for a moment like this."

He approached the woman as if he were about to embrace her, as if he would let her rest her head against his shoulder. Instead, he seized her by the throat and began to strangle her.

"No!" Gemma cried. "What are you doing, uncle? You're going to kill her! Let her go!"

She struck Kéltrox's back again and again, but he did not release the woman.

The woman's cheeks darkened. Her hands clawed desperately at Kéltrox's arms. Her feet beat against the floor. Kéltrox tightened his grip, feeling her resistance weaken, watching her mouth open as the gasps grew thinner and more desperate.

He did not seem to feel Gemma's blows. He did not answer her pleas. Then the woman's beauty began to collapse before their eyes. Her eyes slowly vanished. Her hair fell away. Her face turned an unnatural blue. What remained was no longer Lila, but a shapeless, amorphous creature slick with viscous liquid that spread across the floor.

"What is that?" Gemma cried.

"A chameleon," Kéltrox answered, still breathing hard. "They come from the Shared Realm of Dóriton."

He grabbed the bars of the cell as if he meant to tear them out and shouted with all his strength, "Is that the best you can do? I knew it wasn't her the moment they brought her back!"

Gemma stared at the creature, still shaken. "Why didn't you tell me?"

"Chameleons are strong, even the females."

"So you waited for a chance to surprise her."

"I waited until her guard was down enough to grab her by her only weak point."

"The neck?" Gemma asked.

Kéltrox nodded.

"Do you think I could harm Lila?" he asked. "Or any innocent person?" Gemma lowered her gaze. "I knew you would not. I thought you were under some spell."

While they were still speaking, a group of Sardars descended in formation, with Verlou at their head, and stopped before the cell.

"Get back!" Verlou ordered, pointing the lightning spear at Kéltrox.

"Verlou, put that down. You know that technology does not work on this planet."

The voice came from the stairs. A thin elderly man appeared, elegantly making his way between the guards while leaning on an old cane.

"Bravo, Kéltrox. Bravo. I did not expect that."

He stopped before the bars. "I never imagined you would discover that the battered woman was not the Lila you knew. I always thought you were brute force and little more, but I must confess I was wrong. I underestimated you. You are more cunning than I thought."

He turned his gaze to Gemma. "Princess, you must be very proud of your uncle. He is a clever man, though before long we will learn whether he is also wise."

He tapped the bars three times with the old cane, almost playfully.

"I know you have heard of me. However, to satisfy my customary formalities, I shall introduce myself. My name is Peritis of Germovas, though perishables usually call me Grand Master."

He raised his arms, spun once with theatrical grace, then lowered them again.

"You are the Grand Master?" Gemma asked.

"Does my appearance surprise you? Understandable. Wizards and humans are not so different at first glance. But do not mistake resemblance for equality. You perishables are as helpless before us as ants before a mischievous child."

His eyes narrowed with amusement. "If you had lived as long as I have, you would understand that human beings end up beneath the feet of those superior to them. You, perhaps, may be the exception. In fact, why do you not tell me about our mutual friend?"

"I do not know who you mean," Kéltrox replied.

"Do you truly not know, or is ignorance part of his plan?" Peritis asked.

"You mean Mantus?" Gemma said.

At the same time, Kéltrox asked, "Did he betray us after all?"

Peritis smiled. "For now, that matter is of little importance. Leaving your friend aside, I will tell you what you will do. You will tell me everything you know and everything you were doing in the desert. In return, I promise not to make the rest of your existence miserable."

"I am not afraid of you," Kéltrox said.

Peritis laughed. "That must be the funniest and most foolish thing I have heard in ages. Do you know why you can say such a thing, Kéltrox? Because your tiny, finite mind cannot comprehend all the evil I can do to you."

He leaned closer to the bars. "I could extract the information I need with a snap of my fingers, but I would break you. And what use are you to me broken or dead? Men like you do not appear often. Naive, yes, but brave. It would be a shame to waste your virtues. Look at Verlou, for instance." Verlou kept his gaze fixed ahead.

"Fortunately for you," Peritis continued, "I did not come here to hurt you. Not today. I only want to know whether you are working with anyone else. Have you asked anyone to help liberate the Kingdom of Light?" He paused, allowing the question to settle between them.

"I give you my word. If you accept my Seal of Allegiance, I will return the person you love so much. I will also return your brother, your family, all of them."

Gemma and Kéltrox looked at each other.

Kéltrox turned back to Peritis.

"You do not believe me?" Peritis asked. "Yes, Kéltrox. Your brother and sister-in-law are alive. They are imprisoned in a dungeon in the Kingdom of Light."

It was the most encouraging news they had received in days, and the cruelty of its source made it harder to accept.

"Working for me is a privilege and an honor not all men enjoy," Peritis said. "Now tell me. Do you have allies? Where is the mystical sphere? Did you hide it in the desert, or did you bring it with you?"

"You are wasting your time with us," Kéltrox replied.

He and Gemma exchanged another glance.

"Very well," Peritis said. "Loyalty Seals first. Questions after." He looked at Verlou.

Verlou placed a small box between the bars. Gemma opened it and saw two small square creatures, each with tiny insect-like legs, vibrating and squeaking inside.

"What is that?" she asked.

"Show them," Peritis said.

Verlou uncovered his chest. A similar creature was embedded in his skin as if it had become part of him. It glowed from time to time.

"It doesn't hurt," Verlou said.

Gemma looked from the box to Peritis. "I find it strange that you do not simply force us."

"How foolish perishables are," Peritis muttered. "You test my patience with so many stupid questions."

"You cannot force us," Gemma said. "If you could, you would have placed the creatures on us already." Peritis smiled.

Kéltrox understood. "Then we would have to put on the seals willingly for their magic to work."

In that instant, the words of the boy from his dreams took meaning inside him: Follow your instincts. Do not doubt what your heart knows.

"The free will of perishables is irritating," Peritis said with a snort. "Put them on, and you will be reunited with your family. You will leave this planet and come to me only when I call for one of you."

"We will make no deal with you," Kéltrox answered firmly.

As he spoke, he shifted his gaze just enough to meet his niece's eyes.

"Do you think so too, princess?" Peritis asked.

"Of course," Gemma said. "The Kingdom of Light is a guide for its people, a refuge and an encouragement for those who depend on it. As its rulers, we do not ally ourselves with those who disturb peace, deceive the innocent, and seek only their own benefit. We will make no bargain."

"A noble speech," Peritis mocked. "I repeat, you are fortunate. Still, I advise you not to abuse your luck."

He turned slightly toward Verlou. "I must leave. Unfinished business on another planet requires my presence. Until I return, I will give you something to think about. Bring Lila."

Then he looked back at Kéltrox. "When I return, I expect that box to be empty. If you refuse the Seal of Allegiance, I will kill Lila with my own hands. Then I will kill the Bolco you brought. Finally, I will dismember Princess Gemma before you."

His voice remained almost pleasant, which made the threat more dreadful.

"After that, you will give me the information even if you do not wish to. I will torture you in ways you have never imagined, and once you tell me what you know, and believe me, you will, I will continue until I grow bored of you." Peritis turned and walked up the stairs, followed by the Sardars.

Gemma closed the box. The creatures inside jumped, shaking it twice.

Shortly afterward, a Sardar threw Lila into the cell. Kéltrox rushed toward her. "What did they do to you?"

"They didn't hurt me," Lila answered.

"I thought I would never see you again," he said.

"I saw the chameleon they sent in my place," she said. "How did you know it wasn't me?"

"Because sometimes you walk as if you were dancing." They both smiled.

"It seems the chameleon you killed was important," Lila said. "The Weeds treated it with fear and deference, as if it had more power than they did."

"There is something I have been thinking about," Gemma said. "If the Grand Master asked about the mystical sphere, it means the woman who picked it up has not told anyone she has it."

"Then we need to find out who she is," Kéltrox said. "She may help us escape."

Lila lifted her head. "Listen. Someone is coming."

"No," Kéltrox said. "That sounds like metal."

The three stood in silence, watching the stairs.

The "Witch" Girl

Two silver trays of leftover fruit and stew landed on the top step of the stairs.

"Why did they fall there?" Gemma asked.

"Listen," Lila said. "Footsteps."

A face appeared at the entrance of the dungeon.

"Mantus?" Gemma asked. "How did you escape?"

Mantus held half of the mechanism used to fasten the cell door.

"We don't have much time," he said, fumbling with the rustic lock. Lila stared at him. "Is that boy talking like a man?"

"I am a man," Mantus replied.

"Not like that, man. You have to fit that half of the mechanism into the part inside the lock."

"I know. I'm doing it." The door opened.

"Quick," Kéltrox said.

Mantus handed him a sword. They left the cell, and Lila studied Mantus for a moment.

"There is something strange about him," she said.

"Very strange," Kéltrox agreed.

Mantus frowned. "I can't read your thoughts."

"It must be the spell," Mantus said quickly.

"Let's get the girl out," Gemma interrupted.

"Yes," Kéltrox said. "Open her cell." The girl heard them and stood at once.

They reached her cell. Mantus opened the door and looked inside. A narrow channel of liquid circled the girl like a barrier. Her eyes were swollen; the shackles had cut into her wrists, and clotted blood stained the rings of the chains near her fingers.

"Help me," she begged.

"Poor thing," Lila said. "Only one tray of food managed to fall into the channel."

"The fruit we gave her yesterday is the only thing she has eaten in days," Gemma said, tears gathering in her eyes.

"Why did they put that channel around her?" Lila asked.

"Never mind. Get her out," Mantus said.

Lila stood before the girl for a few seconds, then shouted, "Wait! She is a witch. That channel is diluted iron."

"I know," Mantus said, "but she is a child. She won't hurt us."

Kéltrox looked at him. "We do not know that she is a girl."

"Release her, Uncle Kéltrox," Gemma said. "She is a child. Besides, the Weeds have mistreated her for a long time. We cannot leave anyone at their mercy."

Kéltrox looked from Gemma to the girl. "All right. Take off her shackles." Mantus handed him the lock mechanism.

Kéltrox raised an eyebrow. "What is it? Are you afraid of the girl or the channel?"

They stepped through the diluted iron.

"The channel only affects those endowed with magic," Mantus said.

After they freed her, the five began climbing the stairs. Before they reached the final steps, they found two Weeds lying side by side, mouths open, snoring.

"That is why the trays fell," Lila said.

"Are they asleep?" Gemma asked.

"So it seems," Kéltrox said.

Gemma looked at Mantus. "What did you do to them?"

"Me? Nothing. I found them like this when I came down. There are others." They carefully passed the sleeping Weeds and reached the courtyard.

"Look," Gemma said. "More Weeds sleeping."

"This is strange," Kéltrox said. "No one is awake." The girl looked around. "It looks like magic."

"Where is Úniquen?" Gemma asked.

"Follow me," Mantus said. "I know where they have him." He ran toward the back of the tower.

Úniquen was inside the wagon.

"Gemma?" he called.

"Úniquen!" she cried.

"How do we free him?" Lila asked.

"With the latch," Mantus answered, pushing the mechanism into the lock that held the chains.

"It doesn't work," Lila said.

"Let me see," said the girl.

She stood before the wagon lock and placed both hands on it. The chains that sealed the wagon door loosened, and so did the shackles binding Úniquen.

"Thank you," Gemma said. "You are very skillful. What is your name?"

"My name is Mila, Your Highness. I need you to rescue my mother."

"Your mother?" Kéltrox asked.

"Yes. She must be in the tower. Verlou keeps her prisoner. He is terrible."

Kéltrox turned to Úniquen. "Stay here and keep watch. If the Weeds wake up, fly to the top and take Gemma away." Úniquen nodded.

They climbed the tower stairs. Artistic figures had been carved into the walls.

"Who did you say lives here?" Lila asked.

"Verlou," Mila answered. "With my mother."

"Your mother is here, and you were locked up?" Mila did not answer.

They entered what appeared to be a large room with many windows. Verlou lay on the floor beside the stairs. On the bed sat a woman, gazing out one of the windows.

"Mommy!" Mila cried.

She leaped over Verlou's motionless body and ran to the woman, who turned in surprise and embraced her daughter tightly.

"Mommy, I thought I would never get out of that cell."

"It is a miracle, Mila. It worked!" the woman said, kissing her and holding her through her sobs.

"What worked?" Kéltrox asked.

"A man, an old man, gave me a flask with a substance," the woman said. "He told me that if I wanted my daughter back, I should mix it into the stew they were preparing and not eat any of it."

She walked toward Gemma and knelt before her. "Princess Gemma, Your Highness, this belongs to you." The woman handed her the mystical sphere.

Gemma took it, stunned. "I know you. I know I do, but I cannot remember from where."

"My name is Maltra, Your Highness. You and your friend, Mr. Rólar, helped me in the City of Light long ago."

"Yes," Gemma said slowly. "That is right. I remember. I waited for you in Diamondis for several days."

"We have to go," Kéltrox interrupted.

"Take me with you," Maltra said. "The man you see over there kidnapped me."

She pointed toward Verlou, who still lay asleep.

Gemma nodded.

They descended the tower and returned to Úniquen.

"I think the nórmides are over there," he said.

They moved to the outskirts of the village, crossed through the weeds, and found the nórmides tied to buried stakes.

"Everyone take a nórmide, and let's get out of here!" Mantus shouted.

"Look, Uncle Kéltrox," Gemma said, pointing toward the enormous tree, "there is Cortus."

"How can we return to the road if we do not know where we are?" Gemma asked.

"I think I know how to get back," Mantus said.

Kéltrox looked at him. "Tell me, Mantus. How did you escape?"

"Let's say you have your skills, and I have mine." Mantus glanced at Lila.

"What is the name of the new one?"

"Her name is Lila," Kéltrox replied.

Mantus smiled at her. Lila gave him a sideways glance and snorted.

Mantus took the lead, guiding the nórmides as quickly as he could without outpacing the group. Kéltrox and Lila followed in short leaps with Cortus.

Maltra and Mila rode a little farther back, each mounted on a nórmide.

Princess Gemma flew with Úniquen a short distance above the ground.

From time to time, Gemma and Úniquen turned back, flew in the opposite direction, and watched the Sardar village in the distance to make sure no one pursued them. Then they returned to the others.

The sweltering heat had begun to beat down. The sands of the Nale Desert waited only a short distance ahead, and a stream of hot air struck them, carrying reddish dust with it.

"I need to talk to you," Lila said, her voice catching between jumps.

"I can barely hear you," Kéltrox answered. "Can it wait?"

"It has to be now."

Cortus leaped again.

"Tell me!" Kéltrox shouted while still in the air.

"What they have kept from the princess is horrible," Lila said.

Kéltrox struck Cortus's head twice. The animal dropped back into the sand and stopped. The others noticed, but Kéltrox waved them on.

He turned to Lila. "What did you say?"

Lila looked him in the eye. "It is none of my business. I know that. But Gemma deserves to know."

"Stop reading me," Kéltrox said sharply.

Then he sighed. His voice lowered. "I do not know how to tell her."

He looked toward Princess Gemma and Úniquen as they turned back in the air.

"Why are you stopping?" Gemma shouted from above, barely audible over the beating of Úniquen's wings.

"It is nothing," Kéltrox called. "Go ahead."

"Well, no one said they saw the tent ahead!" Gemma shouted back.

Úniquen turned, passed Mantus, and continued onward.

Lila leaned closer. "Look, Kéltrox. Your niece is not foolish. She already has questions, and she is going to find out anyway. It would be better if she heard it from you."

Kéltrox said nothing.

"You are the most important person in her life right now," Lila continued. "The only one she believes has not lied to her. Besides, we do not know what happened to her parents. We cannot trust the Grand Master's word."

"Do not say that. Nótrex and Krístal are alive. We will rescue them with Ilucus's help."

"Krístal?" Lila asked softly.

She sighed. "Just think about it. The princess may be stubborn, but she is a mature young woman. I believe she will forgive them."

Kéltrox sighed, set Cortus back in motion, and continued toward the Nale Desert.

Chapter Fourteen

Kidnapping

Úniquen reached the camp first and landed before the wrecked tent. Princess Gemma slipped from the Bolco's back and hurried toward the entrance. Before she could step inside, Cortus came leaping out of the air with his legs thrust forward. He landed a short distance from her, and the impact sent red sand bursting upward, striking Gemma's face and dusting Úniquen's muzzle.

"You need to calculate Cortus's jumps better," Princess Gemma said, frowning as she wiped sand from her cheek. "You almost landed on top of us."

"Forgive me, smally," Kéltrox said as he jumped down from Cortus's back and helped Lila descend. "The sand blinded me. I did not see where you had landed until we were already in the air."

Mantus arrived next and slid down the tail of his nórmide.

"We should pack the tent and find another place before nightfall," he said.

"Here come Maltra and Mila," Úniquen said.

Mila arrived first. Maltra's nórmide came behind her, slower and more exhausted, stopping every few steps to pant. When it finally reached the tent, it collapsed onto the sand.

"Maltra," Princess Gemma asked, "did you see whether the Scardos took a thick book?"

"I did not see Verlou carrying any book," Maltra replied as she climbed down from her nórmide.

Mila, worn out from the journey, let herself fall beside the animal's tail and rested her head against Maltra's waist, kicking weakly at the red dunes with her battered sandals.

"Here it is!" Princess Gemma said. She lifted one of the blankets and pulled the book from beneath it.

They searched for another place to shelter, raised the tent again, and spread the blankets over the sand. One by one, they entered and lay down, their bodies heavy from exhaustion.

"We must thank Maltra for guarding the mystical sphere," Princess Gemma said. "If not for you, the Grandmaster would have taken it."

"If not for you," Maltra replied, "my daughter and I would still be locked away."

Princess Gemma studied her for a moment, and a softer memory crossed her face.

"Rólar and I waited for you in Diamondis," she said. "I always had a feeling we would meet again."

Maltra smiled faintly.

"So this is the daughter you told me about?" Gemma asked, looking at Mila.

"Yes," Maltra said, drawing the girl close. "My little Mila."

"Was she not ill?" Princess Gemma asked.

"I thought she was," Maltra said. "Mila spent much of her time speaking to herself, so I believed something was wrong with her mind. But she was not speaking to herself. She seemed to be communicating with people on other planets, or seeing things none of us could see. Later, I understood that she had been born with a magic far stronger than visions."

"Is that why you left the City of Light?" Kéltrox asked from the entrance of the tent.

"When Mr. Rólar gave me the goldet, I left the City of Light and bought a property in Trasto," Maltra said. "We lived quietly on the outskirts, right at the edge of the desert. For a long time, I searched for answers about what was happening to my daughter."

Mantus narrowed his eyes at Mila.

"Witches are not born witches," he said. "They become witches by practicing magic for many years." Mila looked back at him without fear.

"You are strange," she said.

"And you are not?" Mantus replied.

"People have told you that more than once," Úniquen muttered.

"Please," Princess Gemma said. "Do not argue. Continue, Maltra."

Maltra breathed in slowly. "I found no answer. I searched for books, consulted wise men, and asked anyone who might understand what was happening to Mila. No one could tell us anything. After a while, we ran out of money, so we began earning a living by lodging travelers and performing small exhibitions of magic."

"And how did you fall into the hands of those vermin?" Kéltrox asked.

"One night," Maltra said, "Verlou, chief of the Scardos, stayed at my house with his men. They had come from an expedition along the edge of the desert. The people in Trasto whispered that they were looking for someone." Mantus stared at the sand.

"My ship crashed near that town," he said. "I wandered alone for several days. Perhaps they had come for me."

"That is what I heard," Maltra replied. Princess Gemma leaned forward.

"What happened with Verlou?"

"The next morning, before he left, he stopped by the tent Mila and I raised in front of the house each sunrise for our magic show. When the performance ended, he approached us."

Maltra's expression hardened, and her voice changed as she recalled his words.

"How does your daughter move those objects?" he asked me. "And the knives—who throws them? It is an impressive trick."

"Part of the trick," I told him, "is not revealing it."

"My name is Verlou," he said, "and these men are with me."

"Well," I answered, hoping he would leave, "if you require nothing else, I must continue gathering our things." Maltra looked away for a moment.

"He smiled at me with lust and violence, as if the thought of frightening me amused him."

"I hope your bound one does not mind my saying this," Verlou said, "but you are very beautiful."

"My... my bound one?" I answered.

"Are you and your daughter alone," he asked, "or does someone else live with you?"

"Some relatives live with us," I said. I thought the lie might drive him away.

"You are lying," Verlou said. "Do you think I mean to hurt you?" Maltra swallowed.

"Then he smiled as if he enjoyed knowing that I did."

"It is a pity," he said, "for a woman like you to be alone with a child in a town like this. I could take good care of you. Come with me. Stay in my house. I will place everything you need at your disposal."

"His men smiled behind him," Maltra said, "and I understood exactly what kind of protection he was offering."

"No, thank you," I answered. "My house is here."

"They laughed. But when they finally left, I thought the danger had passed."

Maltra tightened her arm around Mila.

"It had not. Two days later, Verlou returned to the tent with his men."

"I hope you have considered my proposal," he said, without even greeting me.

"Would you stop harassing me?" I told him. "You make me uncomfortable."

Verlou's face changed.

"What is this?" he said. "The truth is, I am never as kind as I have been with you. I do not usually ask. I take what I want. I tried to behave differently, but you have left me no choice." Then he turned to his men.

"Grab her. We are leaving."

"What about the child?" one of them asked.

"Bring her too," Verlou said. "It will be useful to have them both." Maltra's voice trembled.

"They tried to seize us. Mila and I ran out of the tent and around the house. They followed, shouting insults behind us. Then we collided with one of them, who had circled from the opposite side."

"We were trapped."

Mila looked down at her hands.

"Then Mila screamed," Maltra said. "The sound was so powerful that every man froze. None of them believed a child could make such a cry."

"Unfortunately, it did not stop them for long. They recovered and closed in on us. Mila looked at the sky. The trees began to shake, a black cloud covered the glow of the Triplets, and a violent whirlwind formed above us. It struck the men and threw them several meters across the ground."

"It is a witch!" Verlou shouted. I saw terror in his eyes and in the eyes of his men.

"Careful—it is coming again!" one of them cried.

"Where did that whirlwind come from?" another asked.

"From the girl," Verlou answered. "Run."

Princess Gemma turned to Mila with awe. "That is extraordinary, Mila. How did you do it?"

Mila only smiled.

"That kind of power does not appear at random," Mantus said.

"Now you are an expert in magical powers too?" Úniquen asked.

"Mantus is right," Lila said. "Someone must have granted such power for a purpose. It is one thing to know magic or cast spells. It is another to bend the weather itself."

Princess Gemma looked back at Maltra.

"What happened next?"

"Two days later, the same men entered our tent in silence while Mila and I slept. They took her first, then me. They bathed Mila in water diluted with iron. I learned later that they use it to weaken powers."

"Even wizards have that weakness," Lila said quietly.

"Why did they lock your daughter in the dungeon?" Úniquen asked.

"Because Verlou told me he would kill her if I did not stay with him," Maltra replied. "He kept her imprisoned to keep me in his house. They neutralized her powers because they were terrified she might escape."

"No wonder," Lila said. "Your daughter's magic is powerful. I tried to read her mind and could not. It takes great force to resist me like that." Lila turned toward Mantus.

"I still wonder why I cannot read yours either." Mantus said nothing.

The next morning, Princess Gemma opened her eyes and saw neither Kéltrox nor Úniquen inside the tent.

"They left after midnight to make sure the weasels were not following us," Lila said from the entrance.

"Listen," Maltra said. "They are coming."

A moment later, Kéltrox and Úniquen entered the tent.

"No sign of the weasels," Kéltrox said. "We will try to reach the Pirutus in two dawns."

Maltra took Mila by the hand.

"Then our paths part here."

"Where will you go?" Princess Gemma asked.

"Back to town," Maltra said. "We will gather our belongings and look for a place outside the City of Light."

"I hope to see you both again," Princess Gemma said.

"Thank you, Your Highness," Maltra replied, and bowed.

Unexpectedly, Mila hugged Úniquen. The Bolco looked startled, then lowered his head with unusual tenderness.

Then Maltra and Mila left.

Kéltrox and Mantus began dismantling the blankets that formed the tent. Princess Gemma and Lila were folding the rest and arranging them on Cortus's back when Mila came running back across the sand.

"Mila is returning," Úniquen said.

"And Maltra is right behind her," Lila added.

Mila reached them breathless.

"I know I must go with you," she said, stammering.

She moved toward Princess Gemma and began to kneel, but before her knees touched the sand, Gemma took her hands. Inside the princess's dress, the mystical sphere glowed. Mila's eyes shone for an instant. Then both girls released each other.

"What was that?" Kéltrox asked.

"The mystical sphere reacted to Mila," Mantus said.

"Without her touching it?" Kéltrox asked.

Lila stared at Mila.

"Does she belong to the lineage?"

"It seems so," Úniquen said.

"I felt her calling me," Mila whispered.

Maltra arrived and stopped before Princess Gemma.

"My daughter insists that we must go with you," she said. "May we?"

"We are in great danger," Gemma replied. "I cannot promise I can protect you."

"I had a vision," Mila said. "I know I have to go." For a moment, no one spoke.

Then Princess Gemma nodded.

"So be it."

They traveled at great speed throughout the day. Princess Gemma flew with Úniquen. Kéltrox and Lila leapt across the dunes on Cortus. Maltra, Mila, and Mantus followed on nórmides, pushing the animals as far as they dared. Before nightfall, they found a place to camp, unpacked the blankets, and raised the tent again.

"Maltra."

A voice whispered beside her right ear.

Maltra knew at once where she was. Though a fierce beam of light pressed against her eyelids, she remembered not to open them.

"You left me alone," she said, and her breath trembled. "They kidnapped me. They locked me away. They imprisoned my daughter and almost killed us both. Where were you?"

"Remember," the voice said, "do not open your eyes, or you will wake."

"Do you think I have forgotten? Perhaps I should open them every time I hear you. Then maybe you will try to return, or disappear forever."

"Are you truly that angry?"

"Why do you keep appearing if you cannot come back?" she said. "I want you to stop."

Her eyes remained shut, but tears escaped from beneath her lashes. She wiped them away with trembling fingers, pressing her eyelids tighter as if holding them closed could hold him near.

"Listen to me, love," the voice whispered. "I have not left you alone. I have always protected you."

"If you protected me, how was I kidnapped?"

"Could Verlou touch you while you were with him?" Maltra went still.

"He tried," she whispered. "So many times. But... wait. Was that you? He never could. Every time he wanted to force himself on me, he fell asleep. The next day, he believed we had..." She heard a low laugh.

"Do not laugh," she said. "Are you mocking me?"

"You amuse me," the voice said gently, "but I am not mocking you. You are so special, and I miss you." Maltra's tears deepened.

"I promise I will always watch over you," he said. "And one day, we will finally be together again."

She felt warm fingers brush across her closed eyelids.

"Will you leave so soon?" she asked.

"I must. Pay attention to what he tells them. But as I warned you, do not speak of me to anyone."

Maltra opened her eyes.

It was still dark. Beneath the faint rays of the Triplets beginning to rise along the horizon, she saw Mila sleeping beside her, Kéltrox nodding near the entrance, and the others still wrapped in their blankets. She was about to lie down again when Mantus cried out.

"Help... help!"

Maltra sat up and ran to him. The others woke at once.

"What is it?" Kéltrox asked.

"It is Mantus," Maltra said. "He seems to be sleeping."

Mantus was pale, flailing his hands as if trying to defend himself from something none of them could see. They shook him until his eyes opened.

"What happened?" Mantus stammered.

"You were asleep and screaming nonstop," Princess Gemma said.

"I had a bizarre dream," he replied.

"You mean a nightmare?" Úniquen asked.

"Not exactly," Mantus said. "I think it was real."

"Good," Kéltrox said. "Gather your things. We leave now."

"Wait." Mantus grabbed Kéltrox by the arm. "I have a feeling we are going to be attacked. In my dream, I saw Dargos launching his army against us."

"Are you a seer now too?" Úniquen asked sharply.

"Believe me," Mantus said, still breathing hard. "I know I am right, even if I cannot explain it."

"We must go anyway," Kéltrox said. "Hurry. We continue."

"No," Mantus interrupted. "You do not understand. We cannot continue this way. If we do, they will catch us."

"What do you suggest?" Princess Gemma asked.

"We turn back, cross the Endless Abyss again, and take the southern road." Úniquen wrinkled his snout.

"So we cross back over the Endless Abyss, then go around it?"

"Exactly," Mantus said. "We will move behind Dargos's army instead of ahead of it. By the time they realize we are not where they expect us to be, we will have reached the Pirutus."

"That road is long," Princess Gemma said, "not to mention the time we would lose by returning."

"I think we should listen to the strange boy," Mila said.

Maltra looked at her daughter, then at Mantus.

"And how will we enter the portal if Dargos's army is ahead of us?" Lila asked.

"We will find a way to slip through," Mantus said. "It is still better than being caught in the open."

"I think Mantus is telling the truth," Maltra said.

Lila's gaze sharpened.

"How are you doing that, Maltra?"

"Doing what?"

"I cannot see what you are thinking right now. It is as if you are hiding something."

"You should not do that," Maltra replied. "It is disgusting."

"Quiet, please," Mantus said. "We must focus on the problem."

"There is no problem," Kéltrox said. "We follow the same path. We are not going back several days because you had a bad dream."

Without another word, they dismantled the tent and set out again.

They had gone only a short distance when Cortus stopped. Kéltrox and Lila jumped down from the séritroc, while Princess Gemma and Úniquen turned in the air and landed in front of him. The others arrived behind them on their nórmides.

"Why did you stop?" Princess Gemma asked.

"Cortus," Kéltrox said. "He refuses to jump."

"Then leave him," Mantus said. "We have no time to lose." Cortus rolled onto his back and lifted all five paws into the air.

Kéltrox crouched, examined the animal's eyes, and placed his ear near Cortus's snout.

"He is panting," Kéltrox said. "He seems exhausted."

"But he is a séritroc," Mantus said. "These animals are strong. Look at the nórmides. They are breathing harder than he is."

"He has been running long distances with little rest since the attack on the Kingdom of Light," Kéltrox said.

Lila knelt beside Cortus and stroked his head.

"He looks sick to me."

"Sick or tired?" Mantus demanded. "Is sleeping at night not enough? Lazy animal. We must leave at once. We are in grave danger."

"Help me lift him," Kéltrox said.

When everyone pulled, Cortus sat up with a tired groan.

"We walk for a while until he recovers," Kéltrox said.

"We are all going to be captured," Mantus said.

Kéltrox turned on him.

"Listen, smarty-pants. According to my calculations, Dargos's army should still be two days behind us, and we are two days from the Pirutus. By the time the Kronkos reach this place, we will already be at the portal and on our way to Ilucus."

"Do you think Dargos is going to rest?" Mantus asked. "He will not stop, not even at night."

"Even if we leave Cortus and continue on the nórmides," Lila said, "we would have to place two people on one animal."

"Exactly," Kéltrox said. "Which means we would not make much progress anyway."

Princess Gemma looked from Cortus to the horizon. "We will rest for a while," she said, "and then continue." Mantus's face went pale. He pointed behind them.

"Oh no," he whispered. "I told you."

Chapter Fifteen

Secret Legacy

Before — Krístal

"I know what I saw, Nótrex," Krístal whispered. "I am not losing my mind."

"No one said you were," Nótrex replied, keeping his voice low.

"Then why do you look at me like that?" she asked. "Why do you listen to me as if I were already broken?"

"Krístal—"

"With pity," she interrupted, her voice rising. "That is how you are looking at me."

"Lower your voice," he said, glancing toward the bed. "Look. You woke her."

Princess Gemma lifted her head from the pillow and rubbed her eyes. "What is wrong, Mommy?"

Krístal's face softened at once. "Nothing, my doll. You fell asleep on Úniquen on the way back from the Weeping Forest."

"Your mother and I brought you to bed," Nótrex added. "Now rest."

Gemma smiled sleepily and sank back into her pillow. "Dad, Mom... it was my best teckli celebration ever."

Nótrex waited until her eyes closed again, then eased the door shut.

"Listen to me, Krístal," he said. "For the sake of our family, stop. Do not continue with this. I saw nothing in the Weeping Forest. Kéltrox saw nothing. None of the guests saw anything."

Her eyes filled with tears. "Do you think I am lying?"

"Of course not. I know you believe what you saw. But you must trust me. We will seek help. We will find a way to quiet the nightmares and the visions. But you cannot let this frighten our daughter."

"And what if you are right?" she whispered. "What if I am unwell? What is happening to me?"

She folded into his arms. Nótrex held her tightly, and for a moment neither of them spoke. They only clung to each other, shaken by a fear neither could name. Then hurried footsteps sounded in the corridor.

"You will not believe whom the Pirutus Watchers have brought," Kéltrox announced from the doorway.

Krístal wiped her face. "Whom?"

"Come and see for yourselves."

They descended the stairs and found a young man seated at the Fountain Table with a child beside him. Both were filthy, trembling, and stained with blood.

"Sortus!" Nótrex embraced him, then stepped aside so Krístal could do the same.

Krístal's gaze moved to the boy. "And little Altren... You missed Gemma's fifth teckli celebration."

The boy did not answer. He only trembled and watched Sortus without blinking.

"Nótrex, Krístal," Sortus said, running a hand over the child's grimy hair, "I am in trouble. I have been telling Kéltrox that we were stripped of our kingdom. We barely escaped Ilucus. We reached the Pirutus at least seven days ago, and the Watchers brought us here."

Servants hurried to him, cleaning the blood from his face and hands with aromatic cloths.

Krístal turned to one of them. "Take the boy to the blue room. Give him everything he needs."

As the child climbed the stairs, Krístal watched him closely. His eyes met hers for an instant, then flicked away.

"How did it happen?" Nótrex asked.

"Le Clauta AK," Sortus answered. "She set a trap for me."

"Your wife?" Nótrex asked, stunned.

"She tried to kill me. A counselor helped me escape." Krístal kept staring at him.

Sortus frowned. "Krístal, why are you looking at me that way?" She did not answer.

"Krístal is exhausted," Nótrex said quickly. "She has been working all day on the celebration."

"I understand," Sortus said, breathing heavily. "So am I."

"I will take you to a room so you can rest," Kéltrox said.

"Yes," Nótrex added. "We will speak calmly tomorrow."

They all went upstairs and withdrew to their rooms. Krístal walked to the balcony, sat on the floor, and lifted her eyes to the stars.

Nótrex joined her. "Are you not tired?"

"It is not that."

"Tell me."

"No, thank you." She lay on her back, folded her hands beneath her head, and watched a comet flicker across the heavens.

Nótrex leaned closer, playful for a moment, brushing his nose into her hair the way he used to. "Tell me."

"That was not Sortus AK downstairs," she said. "And the boy with him is not Altren."

Nótrex rose at once. Krístal stood with him.

"Krístal..." He exhaled slowly.

"If they are not Sortus and Altren," she asked, "then who are they?"

He stared at her. "So now you want me to believe you?"

"I want you to see what is in front of you."

Nótrex looked toward the door, then back at her. "By the grace of the Overlords... you may be right. The more I think about it, the less I believe they are who they claim to be."

"Did you see their eyes?"

"Yes. There was something wrong in them. And the boy..." He shook his head. "I cannot explain it. I will speak with Kéltrox and investigate. Stay here. Do not open the door until I return."

He took his sword, fastened it to his side, and left.

Krístal sat again on the balcony floor and began counting stars, trying to steady her heart.

Nótrex knocked on Kéltrox's door. Half asleep, Kéltrox opened it and stepped into the corridor, pulling the door almost shut behind him. Nótrex glimpsed a woman lying in the bed beyond.

"Is something wrong?" Kéltrox asked.

"I believe the visitors are not Sortus AK and his son."

Kéltrox stared at him. "Brother, let us discuss this in the morning. And whatever you have been drinking, stop before you start looking for lepedos in the Nale Desert."

He tried to close the door, but Nótrex wedged his foot between the frame and the edge.

"I am serious."

Kéltrox sighed. "What do you want to do?"

"We go to the room of the man pretending to be Sortus and ask him a few questions."

"You are going to embarrass us all," Kéltrox muttered. "But that is what kings are for, is it not?"

He girded his loincloth, took up his sword without waking the woman, and followed him.

They moved quickly through the corridors with several guards. At the door of the guest room, Kéltrox knocked.

"He seems to be asleep," Kéltrox said. "Let us go." Nótrex knocked again, harder. No one answered.

"Break it down," he ordered.

Kéltrox looked at him. "Are you sure?"

"Break it down."

Kéltrox kicked the door open. The bed was unmade. The window stood wide to the night.

"Where did he go?" Kéltrox asked.

"The boy's room."

They ran to it and forced that door open as well.

"He is not here either," Nótrex said.

Together they raced to Princess Gemma's room. The door was open. Heart pounding, Nótrex entered with his sword drawn.

Gemma sat on the floor with the boy, both of them playing with her wooden toys. In the corner behind them lay a knife.

"Take the boy and stay with the princess," Kéltrox ordered.

The soldiers seized the child.

Gemma looked up, confused. "Why is Altren's daddy in jail?"

Nótrex did not answer. "Where did the other one go?"

The question answered itself before anyone could speak. He turned and ran back to his chamber.

The bed was empty. He rushed to the balcony and saw Krístal on the floor, covered in blood, a dagger buried in her chest.

Nótrex screamed, but he could not hear his own voice. He could not hear the soldiers behind him. He fell beside her and gathered her into his arms.

Her blood soaked through his clothes.

Krístal's eyes were half open, yet for a fleeting instant they found him.

"She looked like you," she gasped. "But I knew she was not you. There was no kindness in her eyes."

"Do not close your eyes," he said, drawing out the mystical sphere with a trembling hand. "Stay with me, love. Hold on."

He squeezed the sphere in his right hand and pressed his left over the wound. Tears mixed with her blood and ran down his face.

Krístal's mouth curved into a faint smile, as if relief had come to her before death did.

"Do not be sad," she whispered. "Take care of her." Then she breathed out.

Before — Nótrex

Night came without Nótrex noticing. He remained beside Krístal's body, clinging to her as if grief alone could keep her from leaving him. When he heard someone enter, he lifted his eyes toward the door.

"We caught up with him," Kéltrox said, coming onto the balcony. "He had your form when we found him. The soldiers hesitated, thinking for a moment that he was you, so I had to bind him myself." Nótrex said nothing.

"I asked around," Kéltrox continued. "No one knows what kind of creatures they are or where they come from. But they can take our form, and we do not know whether there are more."

Nótrex only stared at him, then lowered his gaze again.

"I brought him to Diamondis," Kéltrox said. "After the interrogation, I killed him."

"So he is dead?" Nótrex asked, as though the words had not reached him the first time.

"Yes."

"Good."

"His appearance changed again as soon as he died. A rare creature." Kéltrox paused. "But we have a grave problem. He confessed that Dargos sent him, and that Gálax is under attack even now. We must help Queen Katty and Nilda."

Nótrex did not respond.

"Listen, brother. You have been in this room since last night, and the morning is almost gone. Decisions must be made. Do you want me to take charge of everything?"

Nótrex finally looked up. "Where is the little creature?"

"The boy? In the dungeon."

"It is not a child," Nótrex shouted, rising. "It is a monster. Kill him. We go to Gálax in the morning."

"I will not kill him."

"Kill him!"

Nótrex struck Kéltrox again and again. Kéltrox did not defend himself. He only embraced his brother until the blows weakened, and Nótrex collapsed against him, weeping. Together they stood there, holding each other in the ruin of the morning.

A knock came at the door. Kéltrox released him and opened it halfway. A soldier waited outside.

"What is it?" Kéltrox asked.

"Princess Gemma has been asking for the king and queen."

"I will come out in a moment."

Kéltrox closed the door and turned back to Nótrex. "Did you hear him?"

"Who else knows Krístal is dead?" Nótrex asked.

"Only the soldiers who have been with me since last night, and those guarding the entrance." Kéltrox's voice softened. "You know you must speak with Gemma."

"Not yet. Kill the beast's spawn and prepare your men. We leave for Gálax tomorrow morning."

Kéltrox left the room and returned after some time. Nótrex stood at the balcony, staring into the distance. Krístal lay on the bed behind him, washed clean, dressed anew. There was no longer blood on her or around her, and yet the room still seemed made of it.

"Half the army is ready," Kéltrox said. "I will leave the other half here to guard the city. Your weapons will be secured on Úniquen at first light, and we have provisions for twenty-five dawns. But we must remember that the Germovenese army has armaments far superior to ours, besides King Teritinio Deluken's sphere."

"What did you learn from the creature?" Nótrex asked.

"They come from the Shared Kingdom of Doriton."

"So it is a chameleon?"

"So it seems. He said his father was a Destroyer of Men."

"Like the stories Mother used to tell us." Nótrex was silent for a moment. "Did you ever hear our parents speak of any diplomatic approach to that planet?"

"Not to my knowledge."

Kéltrox noticed that his brother's gaze had returned to Krístal's pale face. "What else did he say?" Nótrex asked quietly.

"That a group of Destroyers of Men tried to conquer Green Plant and failed. He knows nothing more."

"And did you kill him?"

"No."

Nótrex turned. "Must I repeat myself, or send someone capable of obeying?"

"Nótrex, you are not acting like yourself." He snorted.

"I know you are wounded. We all are. But look at what the creature did. He was ordered to kill Gemma. Instead, he entered her room, dropped the knife, and played with her. He is not human, but he is still a child."

"Fine," Nótrex said. "I will do it myself."

"Do not do this, brother."

"Move."

Kéltrox followed him to the dungeon. The little chameleon lay curled on the floor of the cell. Nótrex ordered the door opened, seized the creature by the neck, and drove his blade into its chest.

The child did not die. A viscous liquid spilled across the floor. Nótrex stabbed again and again, his grief turning each thrust into rage, until at last he cut the creature's throat. Only then did the chameleon boy fall still.

Night returned. Two of Nótrex's servants placed Krístal's body in a box of acacia wood. Inside it were drawings Princess Gemma had made, and around Krístal they laid selected diamonds. In darkness, with only a few trusted soldiers nearby, Nótrex and Kéltrox carried her to the Weeping Forest and buried her beneath the starlight.

"Mark the place," Nótrex said. "No one will speak of her death until I bring her back."

Kéltrox looked at him. "What do you mean, bring her back?"

"I will find a magician who can resurrect her."

The soldiers and servants lowered their eyes. Kéltrox opened his mouth, but no words came.

The following day, King Nótrex left Diamondis mounted on Úniquen. Kéltrox and half the army followed overland. On the fourth day, they reached the Pirutus.

The Watchers received the king, fed him and his army, and allowed them a brief rest. Then they led them below until they reached a vast chamber.

On a silver-covered plateau stood thirteen diamond rocks, their points embedded in thirteen holes. Light of different colors streamed from the holes, staining the diamonds with radiance.

"To Gálax, my king?" asked the oldest Watcher, a woman with a shaven head.

The king nodded.

She pressed down a diamond lit with turquoise and pronounced the words, "Erudinit regolertus teracus."

The turquoise glow filled the chamber and grew brighter with every breath.

Nótrex turned to his army. "As you all know, we are going to fight the army of Germovas and take back Gálax. The Iceberg Portal may be guarded by invaders."

"Raise your swords!" Kéltrox shouted.

Nótrex mounted Úniquen and rode into the light. Kéltrox followed, and behind him the army advanced in ranks of twenty.

Before — Dargos

Germovas' army celebrated in the corridors of the Acropolis. It seized the possessions of the igloos while the terrified inhabitants of Concor City watched the invaders march through the streets in purple uniforms, their ranks moving like rivers of blood.

Dargos walked briskly beside King Teritinio Deluken through the Pillars of Ice when an A-t commander hurried toward them.

"We killed Queen Katty," the commander said.

"Good," King Teritinio Deluken answered. "Did you capture Nilda?"

"The princess is nowhere to be found. We have searched everywhere."

"Then keep searching," Dargos snapped. "She cannot simply disappear." King Teritinio Deluken studied him. "Why do you want her alive?" Dargos said nothing.

The king smiled with dark amusement. "Do not tell me. I understand. At least everything happened as Peritis predicted."

Before — Nilda

In a dim room, a soldier stood before two black curtains with a boy of about nine beside him. The soldier wore a purple uniform. Two naked men lay dead on the floor in front of the curtains. Behind the opaque fabric, the outline of a woman could barely be seen.

"Are you ready, princess?" the soldier asked.

"It will not work, Marcus," Nilda said from behind the curtain.

"The other option is surrender. And believe me, princess, I want to see my son grow up."

"Then I suppose there is no choice."

Marcus looked at the boy. "Are you ready, Rólar? Remember, do not move and do not make a sound."

"Yes, Daddy."

Rólar climbed into a sack that contained a wide tube and several metal objects.

Nilda pulled back the curtain. "I have the soldier's uniform."

Marcus looked her over. "It is too large for you, but it will do."

"Will it not seem strange that you are carrying Germovenese armament?" she asked.

"I took it from these soldiers when I killed them." He pointed to the bodies. "From what I have seen, the Germovenese carry these devices wherever they go."

"They did not even need them to defeat us," she said, and fresh tears filled her eyes.

"I am sorry about your mother," Marcus said gently. "She was a good queen."

"Yes." Nilda wiped her face. "Dargos knows this hideout. We must hurry."

"Gather your hair and put on the helmet." She obeyed.

"Now comes the most important part."

Marcus drove his sword into one of the dead men, soaked the face and uniform Nilda wore with blood, then splashed some over himself. He lifted Nilda onto his shoulders and dragged the sack containing the armament and Rólar.

Dressed as a Germovenese soldier, Marcus dragged the sack through the enemy ranks. Now and then he gave little jumps, as if the weight of the body over his shoulders burdened him, hiding the tremors running through Nilda.

Her small hands barely reached through the uniform's wide sleeves.

They crossed the main corridor of the Acropolis with little difficulty, passed within sight of the Pillars of Ice, and reached the gate. In the distance, Marcus spotted Dargos and King Teritinio Deluken entering the Acropolis.

He continued through the streets of Concor City, moving among soldiers and senior officers, until a voice called from behind him.

"Enlisted Z! Where are you taking that wounded man?"

Marcus stopped and turned. An A-t commander approached. Instead of walking steadily, Marcus began to stagger, as though the body he carried weighed him down. Nilda trembled against his shoulders.

"He is not wounded, sir," Marcus said. "He is dead. Seneschal Dargos ordered me to remove him from Concor."

"Why would the Seneschal ask that of you?" the commander demanded.

"He said Enlisted Z touched something contagious and died instantly."

The commander recoiled. "Get him away from me." Marcus began to turn, but the commander stopped him.

"Wait. Why do you speak with that accent?"

Marcus lowered his head. "I was one of Seneschal Dargos's spies on this planet. I was born here, in the City of Concor, like him."

The commander eyed the armament. "And why do you carry your ejector?"

"I never part from my weaponry, sir."

"Good. You are an exemplary Z enlistee. Go."

Marcus walked away without looking back. He did not stop until they reached the statue of Kerisetale in Gálax.

"I think it is safe," he said, after making sure no one watched them. He lowered Nilda to the ground and released the sack. Rólar crawled out.

"How did you think of all that?" Princess Nilda asked.

"Before I attacked the soldiers, I heard them speaking," Marcus replied. "One told the other that an A-t commander had disciplined him for walking without his weaponry."

"And how do you know their language so well?"

Marcus's voice cracked. "Rólar's mother was Germese."

"Did she die?" He nodded.

"I am sorry."

"It was a long time ago. Come, princess. We have a long road to the Iceberg Portal."

The three crossed the borders of Concor City on foot. They entered the inhospitable lands beyond, endured snowstorms for the rest of the day, and spent the night inside a cavern.

The next morning, seeing no sign that they were being followed, they cut logs, built a crude boat, and followed the Iceberg River through two days of violent current.

When Glacier Falls appeared in the distance, they paddled to shore. Soaked and shivering, they climbed to higher ground and lit a fire.

"The Iceberg Portal is crawling with Germovenese soldiers," Nilda said.

"Where is the portal, Daddy?" Rólar asked.

Marcus lifted him onto his shoulders. "Do you see the waterfall?"

Rólar held on to his father's head and stretched his neck. "Yes."

"The curtain of water and ice hides the entrance." Marcus pointed through the spray. "The main path runs along the edge of the mountain."

"You cannot see the stone road from here," Nilda said, climbing onto a rock and patting Rólar's bristly hair.

"Look," Marcus said. "The entrance lit up."

"Someone must be coming out of the portal," Nilda whispered.

"Help me assemble the armament."

Marcus poured out the sack. Metal pieces clanked against the rock. He picked up a cylindrical tube and began joining the parts.

"Do you know how to assemble it?" Nilda asked.

"No idea. But we will try."

"Look, Daddy," Rólar said, handing him a tiny magnetized piece shaped like a screw. "Here is another one."

Nilda looked at the wet pieces. "Do you think it will work?"

"I do not know," Marcus said.

Before — Nótrex

King Nótrex, able to see only the restless beat of Úniquen's wings and the silhouettes of his army moving like shadows through the blinding turquoise glare, held the mystical sphere in his right hand and fixed his eyes on the end of the luminous tunnel.

Kéltrox rode a séritroc behind him, keeping enough distance from the Bolco's tail for the army to follow.

On the other side, on Gálax, dozens of Germovenese soldiers guarded the Iceberg Portal. Through the opening, framed like a vast painting bordered in marble, they watched the enemy army racing toward them. In combat formation, they raised their loaded ejectors.

"What does the analog transmitter tell you?" asked an A-t commander.

"The enemy possesses rudimentary weaponry," an Enlisted Z replied.

"What planet are they from?"

"The Kingdom of Light, Commander A-t."

The commander frowned. "How could King Nótrex dare come without an ally, knowing we possess superior armament?"

He looked more closely at the analog transmitter. "What is that?"

"The analog emitter is detecting a powerful energy source."

"Of course," the commander said. "A mystical sphere."

"That is right, A-t. The king and Dargos are far from here. Without a mystical sphere, we are no match."

"Silence, cowards. Prepare to attack!"

The soldiers, arranged in staggered lines several meters from the portal, watched the enemy emerge without blinking.

Nótrex pressed the mystical sphere to his chest while Úniquen flew forward, but nothing happened. At the same instant, the Germovenese army opened fire on the soldiers of the Kingdom of Light as they poured from the portal. Though smaller in number, the defenders wounded them severely.

Kéltrox saw that Nótrex had not used the sphere. Leaping between séritrocs, he shouted, "Why do you not use it?"

He landed on one of the ejectors and crushed the soldier carrying it.

"It is not working!" Nótrex shouted.

"How?"

"Hand-to-hand combat!" Kéltrox roared.

He charged into the enemy ranks on his séritroc. The beast crushed several ejectors, and the larger army of the Kingdom of Light forced its way through.

Then a sharp blast erupted near the waterfall's entrance.

Nótrex saw an ejector shot strike the mouth of the cavern. Ice, stone, and dirt collapsed onto the Germovenese guarding the entrance. Those who staggered back to their feet watched their ranks breaking and fled toward Concor City.

"Find out who fired that shot!" Nótrex shouted.

Úniquen swept out of the cave toward the rocks beyond the falls.

Before — Nilda

"It worked!" Nilda cried. "You hit the soldiers."

She looked toward the sky and saw Nótrex flying on Úniquen. "There he is. It is Nótrex."

"He saw us," Marcus said. "He is coming this way."

Úniquen landed on the rock beside the canyon. Nótrex climbed down, and Nilda threw herself into his arms.

"I lost my mother, Nótrex," she said, tears breaking through her voice.

"Queen Katty is dead?" he asked, stammering.

"If not for Marcus, I would be dead too."

Nótrex turned to Marcus. "We owe you much."

His gaze fell on the boy. "Is that your son?"

"Yes, King Nótrex."

"Look," Nilda said. "The Germovenese are leaving."

"For so few soldiers," Nótrex said, "they killed many of my men."

Úniquen lowered himself. "Come up, Nilda. Marcus, we will wait for you at the portal."

He flew with Nótrex and Nilda across the waterfall and into the cave. Kéltrox saw Nilda arrive and leaped down from his séritroc.

"You managed to escape dressed as one of them," Kéltrox said. "Ingenious."

Then his expression changed. "And the queen?" Nótrex shook his head.

Kéltrox bowed his head. "I am sorry, Nilda."

"They attacked us with two mystical spheres," she said. "They did not even need their armaments."

"Two mystical spheres?" Nótrex asked.

"Dargos used the one he stole from us," Nilda said, "and King Teritinio Deluken used the sphere of Germovas."

"Dargos?" Kéltrox said. "He is not even of the lineage."

"I do not know how he did it, but I saw it."

"We cannot recover Gálax now," Nótrex said.

"No," Kéltrox agreed. "It would be two mystical spheres against one, and they have superior armament."

"Not one," Nótrex said. "For some reason, the mystical sphere of the Kingdom of Light is not functioning. It would be two spheres against none."

"How is that possible?" Nilda asked.

"I have never heard of such a thing," Kéltrox said.

"Perhaps if we find a copy of the Book of Origins," Nótrex said, "we will discover the reason."

A soldier approached. "Sir, at the entrance, we captured a Germovenese soldier and his son. He claims he works for you."

"He is dressed as one of them," Nilda said, "but he is ours. That is Marcus, and the boy is Rólar."

"Release them and bring them here," Nótrex ordered.

Kéltrox looked toward the portal. "Let us go home, brother."

Nilda lowered her eyes. "I do not know how I will tell Krístal what happened to our mother."

Nótrex and Kéltrox looked at each other.

Nótrex rubbed his eyes. "Come, Nilda. There is something we must tell you about Krístal."

Chapter Sixteen

The Oracle

Nótrex — Continued

On the highest level of the Pirutus, seven Watchers studied the lights that shimmered from the diamonds set into the silver plateau. Sometimes the dust, the wind, and the glass of the great window twisted those lights into strange figures, as if the portal itself were dreaming.

A few nitis before the Triplets hid, one of the Watchers saw movement on the horizon. Through the stirred dust came King Nótrex, mounted on Úniquen and flying with desperate speed. Behind him, Kéltrox and Marcus rode séritrocs, each beast leaping over the earth as if chased by ruin itself.

The Watchers descended at once, opened the hatches, and stood ready to receive the king.

The youngest among them, barely nineteen tecklis old, stepped ahead of the other six. Unlike the older Watchers, whose heads were shaved and whose bodies were broad from years of service, she had a slender frame and a thick fall of hair that reached past her waist.

Úniquen landed first. A breath later, Kéltrox and Marcus arrived behind him.

"Your Majesty," the young Watcher said, bowing, "we did not know you were coming without your escort."

"I see I have taken you by surprise, Larnesa," Nótrex said as he slid from Úniquen's back.

"We have nothing prepared, but I will give the order at once." She pushed back a lock of hair that had fallen over her nose and eyes.

"Hurry, Larnesa," Kéltrox said. "We travel before the Triplets hide."

"Where will you travel, Your Highness?"

"To Germovas," Nótrex answered.

The other Watchers exchanged uneasy looks.

"My king," Larnesa said carefully, "since the recent attack on Gálax, the three main portals of Germovas have doubled their security."

"Then we will not use the main portals," Nótrex said. "Come inside, and I will explain. Give water to the séritrocs and tell the others to prepare."

Larnesa turned to the other six Watchers, issued her orders, and entered the pyramid gates with Nótrex, Kéltrox, Marcus, and Úniquen.

When they reached the front hall, the king stopped.

"It is incredible," he said.

"What is it, Your Majesty?" Larnesa asked.

Nótrex, Kéltrox, Marcus, and Úniquen were all looking around. The statues had been repositioned, the paintings straightened, the ornaments arranged with a symmetry the room had never possessed before. "You put everything back in order," Kéltrox said.

"Yes, Your Highness. I hope it is to your liking."

"I never thought the Pirutus could look this immaculate," Nótrex said.

"The statues, the paintings, the ornaments... everything has its place."

Larnesa blushed. "Thank you, Your Majesty."

"I see why Dirtera recommended you as her replacement," Kéltrox said, patting her shoulder twice. "Even if you are very young and have broken a few rules of the Pirutus."

"It is true," Marcus said thoughtfully. "When I came from Gálax only a few days ago, Dirtera was still in charge."

"She was my mentor," Larnesa said, and her eyes reddened. "Without her, I would have learned nothing. I owe her everything." Another Watcher approached and bowed.

"They are preparing food and aligning the diamonds. You can travel in half an hour."

"Good," Larnesa said. "Bring the records on Germovas to my study." Then she turned back to the king.

"I know it is not my place, Your Majesty, but this unexpected trip to a world outside the Alliance troubles me. Bypassing Germovas's security will be almost impossible."

"I know," Nótrex said. "That is why I need every record you have on the rugged portals."

"Your Majesty, those portals are nearly inaccessible. The risk of death is—"

"Make a list," Kéltrox interrupted, "and bring it to us." Larnesa bowed and left.

Inside one of the smaller halls, Nótrex turned to Marcus. "Are you certain he can do this?"

"That is what I heard since I was a boy," Marcus replied.

"And the rumors about his death?"

"Vólartor assured me the Oracle spread them himself."

"Then we shall see for ourselves."

A short time later, Larnesa returned with a wooden record tablet.

"These are the rugged portals of Germovas," she said. "The Aralin Volcano, one hundred and fifty nitis from Deluken City."

"No," Marcus said at once. "Too far, and we would roast before reaching the city."

Úniquen snorted with laughter.

"Go on," Nótrex said.

"The Big Rock, a few nitis from Deluken City."

"I have been there," Marcus said. "There is no way to climb in those winds."

"Selva Bardos. Seven nitis away."

"Too many dangerous animals," Marcus said. "Not to mention the herd of brown kirkis the Delukens brought from Green Plant a hundred tecklis ago."

Larnesa glanced at him with surprise. "You know a great deal about Germovas."

"Enough."

"Some Sibling Worlds call it the Planet of Islands," she added.

Marcus nodded, and for a brief moment they smiled at each other. "Go on, Larnesa," Kéltrox said.

"Vertigo Leap. Four nitis away."

"That one," Marcus said. "Give me the details. I have been there."

"The portal opens at the center of the falls. The drop is immense."

"With Úniquen and the séritrocs..." Kéltrox began. "Wait," Larnesa said. "That portal has surveillance."

"Even though it is rugged?" Marcus asked.

She nodded.

"How much?" Nótrex asked.

"According to our records, it remains classified as rugged because no army could pass through it, but soldiers were placed there to prevent spies."

"We will use it," Nótrex said.

"Prepare supplies," Kéltrox ordered. "Then leave us." Larnesa bowed and went out.

Kéltrox looked at his brother. "Once we go, there is no turning back."

"I know."

"You should have told Gemma what happened to Krístal before leaving. If something happens to us..."

"Nilda will tell her if necessary," Nótrex said. "And if we succeed, Gemma will never have to know her mother was dead."

"If I may, my king," Úniquen said.

"Speak," Nótrex replied, more sharply than he intended.

"The truth revealed is always less bitter than the lie discovered. And the lie is always discovered."

Nótrex lowered his gaze. "You are right, Bolco. If we fail, I will tell her when I return."

Larnesa entered again. "Majesty, everything is ready."

"Do the records include the territorial distribution near Vertigo Leap?" Nótrex asked.

"Of course, Your Majesty." She handed him a small wooden tablet marked with careful inscriptions. "The surrounding villages are listed in the third line and fourth column. The portal map is marked in the lower corner. If you leave now, daylight will be on that hemisphere of Germovas when you arrive."

Kéltrox leaned over the tablet. "Then let us determine where we should jump with the séritrocs."

"And where the soldiers may be positioned," Úniquen added.

Marcus pointed to a marking on the map. "There is a causeway on the left side of the falls. If they are guarding the portal, they will be there."

On Germovas, five Z Enlisted stood watch over the rugged portal of Vertigo Leap. The night guard had just withdrawn, and the day relays had begun their rounds along the wet stone causeway near the falls.

The God of Day, as the people of Germovas called their main star, threw fierce light against the falling water. The roar of the river was almost deafening, yet the soldiers still tried to speak as they walked, their boots splashing through the puddles. From time to time, one leaned against the metal railing that separated the causeway from the cliff.

Then the center of the waterfall blazed.

Three silhouettes burst from the torrent, interrupting its fall for an instant.

At first the guards saw only water and motion. Then they recognized a Bolco, a king mounted upon him, and two séritrocs flinging their legs toward the causeway.

The soldiers raised their cannons.

They were too slow.

Úniquen seized two of them with his claws and hurled them over the cliff.

Marcus's séritroc crushed another against the stones.

But Kéltrox's séritroc landed badly. Its front legs struck the causeway and shattered part of the railing, but the hind legs and center leg found no solid ground. The beast slipped. Kéltrox leapt away, reaching for the broken railing, missed, and plunged into the abyss.

At the last instant, he caught one of the vines hanging from the stony wall.

Gunfire cracked through the spray. One soldier fired at Nótrex while another turned on Marcus.

"Úniquen!" Nótrex shouted. "He is falling!"

"I am slipping!" Kéltrox called from below.

"Take my claw!" Úniquen cried.

"I am tangled!"

"Get him!" Nótrex ordered.

"I cannot reach him without tearing away the foliage!"

"Do it!"

Úniquen drove his claws toward Kéltrox's shoulders and ripped through the vines. Several stems snapped.

Kéltrox fell.

"No!" Nótrex and Úniquen shouted together.

"Help!" Kéltrox's voice faded as he plunged into the mist.

A cannon blast struck Nótrex's right arm. He collapsed against Úniquen's back. Úniquen wrapped his tail around the king, hooked him with his paws, and swooped downward after Kéltrox.

On the causeway, Marcus saw the soldier who had shot the king. The last remaining guard fired at Marcus's séritroc, striking the animal in the head. The beast kicked wildly, and Marcus fell hard onto the stones. He drew his sword, but a second cannon blast struck his side. His weapon dropped from his hand.

"If you move, I will kill you," one of the soldiers said.

Marcus looked toward the falls, then at the cannon pointed at his chest. He did not move.

King Teritinio Deluken

King Teritinio Deluken stood at the library window of the King's Tower, watching mechanical quadrupeds gallop through the avenues of Deluken City. In one hand he held a leather-bound book titled The Memoirs of Dóriton of Norko, a thin tablet marking a page near the end.

The chief councilman entered behind him.

"We have a situation you will want to attend to, my king."

"Silence," the king said. "Let me finish."

Berjo Kolari stopped. After a moment, he stepped closer and followed the king's gaze to the avenue below.

"Look carefully," Teritinio said. "Tell me what you see."

"Quadrupeds on the avenue. People returning from their duties."

"Oh, Berjo Kolari. Has anyone ever told you that you have too little imagination to be Councilman A-t?"

"Yes, Your Majesty. You tell me every time you ask the same question." The king burst out laughing.

"At least you answered differently this time. Are you losing patience with this old man?" His eyes sharpened.

"No, Your Majesty. Never."

"Do not look so grave. I will not kill you as I killed the other Councilman A-t, not for something so insignificant. Now, what happened?"

"Three men, riding two séritrocs and a Bolco, entered through the rugged portal at Vertigo Leap."

"From where?"

"Scarlet Science's preliminary data indicates the Realm of Light."

"Ah." The king turned slightly. "Did you kill them?"

"Two fell from the cliff. I sent three search teams. We captured the third."

"Interrogate him as necessary, then kill him," Teritinio said. "Capture the Bolco unharmed if you can. I have always wanted one's loyalty."

"So we will, Your Majesty." Berjo began to leave.

"Berjo."

"My king?"

"I changed my mind. Since you interrupted me, bring the prisoner to the Throne Habitat. I will speak to him myself."

"Should I notify the other Councilors?"

"Yes. And contact the Islander Hierarchs who are in the city. Let us see what they have to say."

Nótrex

Nótrex woke to the clatter of water against stone. Droplets fell over him like drizzle. Úniquen was drinking from one of the channels nearby, and Kéltrox knelt beside him.

"You bled a great deal and fainted," Kéltrox said.

Nótrex looked at his shoulder. It had been bandaged.

"Where did you get these?" he shouted over the roar of the falls.

"Larnesa packed them. Bandages, wound bottles, clothes, and enough food to shame an army."

"What happened to Marcus?"

"We do not know," Úniquen said.

"He was likely captured alive for questioning," Kéltrox added.

"They will be hunting us," Úniquen said.

"Then we hide first," Nótrex replied. "After that, we go for him."

"According to Larnesa's map, there is a village to the east," Kéltrox said.

"We cannot go there. We would never pass unnoticed with Úniquen."

"Then where?"

Nótrex unfolded the map. "Downstream. There is a forest. We hide there until we decide how to reach Marcus."

Marcus

King Teritinio Deluken sat on his throne, surrounded by the Scarlet A-t, Councilors, and Islander Hierarchs. Berjo entered with three A-t Commanders and two Z Enlisted, dragging Marcus in chains.

"My king," Berjo said from the doorway, "as ordered, I bring you one of the intruders."

"Come closer."

Marcus entered bound at the hands and feet. The soldiers held him by both arms.

Teritinio rose from the throne and walked toward him as quickly as his age allowed. His eyes met Marcus's. Neither man looked away.

"You have always been daring," the king said.

Marcus twisted his mouth.

"Do you know the intruder, my lord?" Berjo asked.

"If you look beyond the dirt on his face," the king said, "you should recognize him too."

Silence spread through the hall.

Teritinio took Marcus's shackles and placed his fingers on the small plate at their center. "What is the combination?"

"Evedele thirty-four," one of the enlisted men answered.

The king pressed several buttons with trembling fingers. The shackles opened and fell from Marcus's hands and feet.

"I have something important to tell you," Marcus said.

"Tell me."

"You are too fat."

The Councilors and Islander Hierarchs stared as if the prisoner had struck the king. Teritinio's face remained severe, but his gaze did not leave Marcus.

"Who shot you?" the king asked calmly.

Marcus did not answer.

"Was it you?" Teritinio asked one of the soldiers.

"No, Your Majesty."

"It was me, my king," said the other enlisted man.

Teritinio looked him in the eyes, drew a silver dagger, and cut off his head with three brutal blows. Blood splattered Marcus, the king, and the soldiers nearby. The head rolled into the middle of a spreading pool.

"That," Teritinio said, pointing the dagger at everyone present, "is so you remember that ignorance does not justify transgression. The blood of a Deluken is shed only by a Deluken." No one moved.

"Prepare his tower," he ordered Berjo.

The dagger slipped from his hand and fell into the blood, splashing the Islander Hierarchs before him. Slowly, almost irritably, the king picked it up and wiped it against the uniform of the soldier beside Marcus.

"For some reason, I cannot let go of this dagger," he murmured. Then he looked at Marcus again. "Now, nephew, why did you enter my kingdom like a common spy?"

"I did not know whether you would welcome me or kill me."

"Because you are heir to the throne?" Teritinio asked cynically.

Marcus said nothing.

"You committed the most unforgivable transgression a Deluken can commit. That is why you have not dared face me all this time. That, nephew, is the truth. Come. Walk with me."

They left the hall and took the main corridor.

"You know I do not regret what I did," Marcus said.

"For your sake, do not say that too freely."

They reached the library. Teritinio stood before the window.

"Look and tell me what you see."

Marcus stood silent for a moment. Then he drew a deep breath.

"I have always wondered why mechanical quadrupeds."

"What do you mean?"

"Many Sibling Worlds preserve the culture of riding animals. Others travel in carts or ships along their avenues. But we prefer to combine machinery with tradition."

"An interesting point," the king said. "It is the same with the mechanical kirkis. We could have made cargo machines that resembled nothing living, as other worlds do. Instead, there they are. Do you know why, nephew?"

"No, uncle."

"Because Germovenese culture has been shaped by our blood since the Age of the First Kings. We Deluken do not abandon one thing to possess another. We want all things at once. The mechanical quadruped is both animal and machine."

"No doubt," Marcus said, and for the first time his voice softened. He looked toward the sky. "I did not realize how much I missed the sunsets of the God of Day. Do you remember how I used to sit by this window?"

"I remember." Their eyes met again.

Marcus noticed the book near the window. "The Memoirs of Dóriton of Norko? How many times have you read it?"

"I have lost count." Teritinio drew the dagger again and pressed the blade against his right palm until blood appeared. "Now tell me why you are here. And by the blood of the Deluken ancestors, speak no deceitful words."

Marcus looked at the dagger. Then he took it and pressed its edge against his own palm. Their blood mixed and dripped to the wooden floor.

"By the blood of the Deluken ancestors," Marcus said, "if I cannot speak truth, I would rather die silent than lie."

"What are you doing here?"

"I came to see the Oracle."

"The Oracle is dead."

"No. He lives, and I know where he is hiding."

"Scarlet Science says you came with others from the Realm of Light."

"Yes."

"Who are they?"

"Friends."

"You will not tell me?"

"I would rather die silent than lie."

"Marcus Deluken, if not for my brother, I would have cut you in two long ago."

"I know."

Marcus lifted his hand toward the king's face. Teritinio leaned back, gripping the dagger, but Marcus only brushed his thumb between the king's eyebrows.

"You have blood there," Marcus said.

Teritinio stared at him.

"Were you in the Kingdom of Light all this time?"

"No."

"Where, then?"

"On my home planet."

Teritinio's expression hardened. "If you say that again in my presence, I will kill you, brother's son or not."

"Very well."

"Where were you, nephew?" the king asked again, his voice softer now.

"In Gálax."

"How curious. You appear here shortly after I conquer Gálax."

"Coincidence."

"Does your reason for being here threaten my kingdom?"

"By the ancestors of the Deluken, no. My business here has nothing to do with your kingdom. I seek the Oracle because a desperate soul longs for the life companion he lost."

Teritinio held his gaze for a long moment. Then he sighed.

"Good. You do not know how glad I am to hear that." Marcus saw the king's hand tighten around the dagger.

"In that case," Teritinio continued, "take two A-t Commanders and whatever enlisted men you need. Find the Oracle and go."

"Thank you, uncle."

"Do not thank me. Thank your father."

The king looked toward the sky and raised his hand. Marcus did the same.

Together they said, "May your energy, directed by the Supernals, expand through the universe like the light of the stars. We remember you, Nornos Deluken."

Their hands were still lifted when Berjo burst into the library.

"My king, I must interrupt you again."

"What is it now?" Berjo glanced at Marcus.

"Speak," Teritinio said. "Is it about Peritis?"

"Yes."

"Then say it in front of Marcus. He was in Gálax, so he knows who our allies are. Is that not right, nephew?"

"Yes, uncle."

"The Grandmaster sent word through one of his servants," Berjo said.

"King Nótrex of the Realm of Light entered Germovas through the Vertigo Leap rugged portal."

Teritinio's gaze returned to Marcus. "So that is why you did not wish to name your friends."

Marcus said nothing.

"Berjo," the king said, "take my nephew to two of the most prestigious A-t Commanders. Order them to accompany him wherever he needs to go. Their orders will be mine. Afterward, escort him to the Scarlet Portal."

"But, sir," Berjo protested, "King Nótrex is an enemy."

"Not today."

"I do not understand, Your Majesty. The Kingdom of Light belongs to the Five Kingdoms Alliance. They attacked the Gate of Gálax. King Nótrex killed many of our people."

"Do you know the value of a Deluken's word, Berjo Kolari?"

"I beg your pardon, Your Majesty."

"Do you know it?"

"Of course."

"Then there is your answer." Teritinio turned to Marcus. "And you, nephew. Finish your business and leave. Unless you change your allegiance, I do not wish to see you again. By the same Deluken blood that binds me to my word, I swear on this dagger: if we meet again and you remain allied with my enemies, my blood will spill yours. Word Deluken."

"Word Deluken," Marcus whispered.

His eyes filled. He lifted his head for a moment, kissed the king's furrowed brow, and left with Berjo.

Berjo Kolari

Marcus and Berjo walked in silence through the main corridor of the King's Tower. A-t Commanders and enlisted officers passed through the intersecting halls. Then a Z Enlisted hurried toward them.

"Councilman A-t, I have news. The teams are catching the fugitives. They are heading downriver, as you predicted."

"The ones who came with me?" Marcus asked.

"Yes, sir."

"Contact one of the commanders," Berjo ordered. "Inform him the intruders have received the king's consent and that Marcus Deluken awaits them."

"Wait," Marcus said.

The soldier stopped.

"Make sure they understand: they are not to harm them. Bring them as guests."

The enlisted man bowed and left.

"Where are you taking me?" Marcus asked.

"To the Nornos Deluken Tower, Your Highness. It has been uninhabited since your father's death, but the king ordered it kept spotless. Between us, I believe he always wanted you to return."

"It appears so."

"Before I became Councilman A-t, I served your father," Berjo said. "I have held this office longer than you have been alive. May I give you counsel?"

"Speak."

"Take advantage of open doors, Your Highness. Sometimes, once they close, there is no way to open them again. You are heir to the throne, and your uncle still regards you with affection."

"What are you truly saying?"

"That your uncle is old. Four auroras ago, he reached his glorious ninety-seventh."

Marcus stopped. "Where are you going with this?"

"King Teritinio Deluken has no children. If he respects you, then when the time comes..."

"No, Berjo."

"If his actions today do not show a willingness to overlook what happened, nothing will."

"He will never forgive me."

"Perhaps his clemency is not only about you."

"What do you mean?"

"If you do not inherit, your cousin Biserlo Deluken will. And he is a fierce man."

Marcus looked away.

"It is yours to consider," Berjo said. "For now, you may rest in the Nornos Deluken Tower and wait for the first light of the God of Day."

Nótrex

King Nótrex, Kéltrox, and Úniquen traveled downstream for a long while before stopping to rest.

"It will be dark any moment," Kéltrox said, watching the last rays of the God of Day break through the clouds.

"The map says the forest is close," Nótrex replied, lifting the bandage on his wound and lowering it again.

Úniquen's ears rose.

"Did you hear something?" Kéltrox asked.

Before the Bolco could answer, three A-t Commanders and thirty Z Enlisted surrounded them on mechanical quadrupeds, cannons in hand.

Kéltrox drew his sword.

"Put it down," Nótrex whispered.

"Which of you is King Nótrex?" one commander asked.

"I am."

"Marcus Deluken is waiting for you in Deluken City." Nótrex, Kéltrox, and Úniquen exchanged looks.

"Did you say Marcus Deluken?" Nótrex asked.

"As you heard. Mount up. The first Twilight Goddess has risen."

Nótrex looked to the sky and saw the reddish silhouette of the moon pushing through the clouds.

"We will reach the city by nightfall," another commander said. Then he ordered two enlisted men to surrender their quadrupeds to the guests.

"I will ride with Úniquen," Nótrex said.

"His Majesty will excuse us," the commander replied, "but you are under our care until we deliver you to Marcus Deluken. The Bolco may follow from the air."

They rode up the slope, through a small suburb, then onto a forked road that soon became stone. The mechanical quadrupeds galloped faster toward the city while Úniquen flew overhead.

They entered Deluken City after midnight through a massive iron gate that divided the city from the borders of Vertigo Leap. Around the barrier stood dozens of enlisted soldiers, their red uniforms glowing beneath the lights of the Three Goddesses of Twilight. The soldiers made way for the A-t Commanders and their company. They watched Úniquen circling above, but because the commanders had brought him, no one challenged him.

The group rode down a broad avenue. The deeper they entered the city, the more mechanical quadrupeds surrounded them, their metal legs striking the stone in clattering, uneven rhythms. Sometimes Úniquen's shadow passed over the multicolored light of the three moons. Countless electric torches burned along the streets, and the eyes of the quadrupeds shone like small lamps.

Buildings rose on every side, elongated and cylindrical, built of colored stone bound with clay. At last they reached a luxurious district and stopped before a white tower. Úniquen landed near the hatch.

An A-t Commander stepped out. "Marcus Deluken is waiting for the guests. You may leave. We will take it from here." The other commanders and enlisted men withdrew.

Nótrex, Kéltrox, and Úniquen entered the tower and climbed to the highest floor.

Marcus stood before a balcony, looking down at the avenue. When he turned, he seemed both familiar and entirely changed.

"So," Nótrex said, "Marcus Deluken."

"Yes, Your Majesty." Marcus turned to the commander who had escorted them. "Leave us."

When they were alone, Kéltrox crossed his arms. "Why did you not tell us?"

"Because I did not want to speak of it. I was banished by my father long ago. Let us do what we came to do and leave."

Nótrex studied him for a moment, then nodded. "What is the plan?"

"At the first light of the God of Day, we find Vólartor. He will guide us to the Oracle."

They agreed in silence.

"The rooms are this way," Marcus said.

Vólartor

The following day, King Nótrex, Kéltrox, Úniquen, two A-t Commanders, and twenty Z Enlisted left Deluken City with Marcus at the head of the company. They rode north through suburbs and avenues, some paved in stone, others cut from dirt.

After a while, the tall towers thinned. Barren land stretched around them, broken only by dwarf towers and scattered people on foot.

Marcus stopped at a three-branched junction.

"What is it?" Nótrex asked.

"I barely recognize the road. So much has changed." Marcus looked from one path to another. "This way."

One of the A-t Commanders glanced at the other. "I know that road, Your Highness. It leads to only one place."

"That is right," Marcus said.

"The City of the Banished," the other commander said.

Marcus nodded.

"The king will not be pleased with that visit."

He drew his quadruped back two steps. Nótrex and Kéltrox discreetly touched the hilts of their swords. The enlisted men shifted their cannons.

Úniquen circled above the king.

"My uncle gave me authority to do what I needed," Marcus said. "Are you rebelling?"

The commander stiffened. He looked at the other commander, who shook his head slightly.

"No, Your Highness. I am not rebelling." He turned to the enlisted men.

"What are you staring at? Move."

They entered the village. Its borders were marked by an iron fence, and beyond it stood dwarf towers that seemed clean from a distance but, up close, were cracked and poor. They stopped before a metal arch that served as the entrance.

Úniquen descended.

"The Pact of the Banished forbids us from entering with quadrupeds or weapons," Marcus said.

Nótrex and Kéltrox dismounted and laid down their swords.

"Wait here," Marcus ordered the company.

"Your Highness," one commander said, "it is dangerous for you to enter alone with two foreign men."

"Stay here."

Nótrex leaned close to Úniquen. "Stay near them. If anything turns strange, warn us. And be careful." Úniquen nodded.

Nótrex, Kéltrox, and Marcus entered the city. Around them, men, women, and children in ragged clothes worked the earth, mended cracks in dwarf towers, or carried tools through the dust.

"Why do the men have that mark on their cheek?" Kéltrox asked.

"It is part of the Pact," Marcus said. "Before adulthood, every male Cerparos must receive the tattoo of a broken sword on his right cheek."

"That is humiliation," Nótrex said.

"Yes, Your Majesty. It is."

Some children ran past them. Many adults who recognized Marcus bowed with quiet reverence.

"I see they know you," Nótrex said.

"I was once one of them."

Nótrex looked at him. "Are these people Deluken?"

"No. Quite the opposite."

"What does that mean?" Kéltrox asked.

"Marcus!" called a hoarse voice from the largest tower.

A tall, thin man emerged. He had a long beard beneath his chin, shaved cheeks, and patched purple clothing. Though poor, he carried himself with stubborn dignity.

"Vólartor," Marcus said.

They embraced.

"King Nótrex, Kéltrox," Marcus said, "this is Vólartor, the man I told you about."

"So you are Marcus's friend who will take us to the Oracle?" Kéltrox asked.

"I do not know what Marcus told you," Vólartor said, "but he is more than my friend. He is my brother."

"You are Deluken too?"

"No," Vólartor said sharply. "Never say that, sir. It could cost me my life." Nótrex frowned. "I do not understand."

"Vólartor was the brother of the woman who was the light of my life," Marcus said, his voice thickening.

"My name is Vólartor Cerparos. My sister, Rólaris Cerparos, was Marcus's life partner."

"Life partner?" Kéltrox asked.

"Linked," Nótrex explained softly.

"Yes," Marcus said, and for a moment he could say no more.

Kéltrox's expression changed. "Then you are Rólar's uncle."

"The last time I saw my nephew," Vólartor said, "was on the day he was born."

His voice cracked.

Marcus cleared his throat. "We must not speak of this in front of the commanders or enlisted men. I do not know how far my uncle's patience will stretch."

"The king knows?" Kéltrox asked.

"Of course he knows. That is the problem." Nótrex stepped in. "How far is the Oracle?"

"Far. He is on Cerparos Island," Vólartor said. "The distance does not trouble me. Breaking the Pact of the Outcasts does."

"I have considered a way around that," Marcus said. "Your Majesty, will Úniquen carry him?"

"I have no objection," Nótrex said. "But the Bolco chooses whom he carries."

They returned to the entrance. The commanders and enlisted men had formed a crescent of cannons around the gate.

"Your Highness," one A-t Commander said, "accompanying you here is one thing. Allowing one of those rats out of hiding is another. The king will not forgive that, not even from you."

"Correct your language," Marcus said, his voice cold. "If you call these people that again in my presence, I will take your head. Now, recite the part of the Pact concerning their departure from the city."

The commander hesitated. "If any Cerparos dares to leave the City of the Banished, he will die, and if a group imitates his daring, they will all die. Word Deluken."

"Wrong," Marcus said. "The Pact says: If any Cerparos sets foot in Deluken City or rides into it, he will die, and if a group mimics the boldness, they will all die. Word Deluken."

The second commander lowered his eyes. "That is the wording."

"Úniquen," Nótrex called.

The Bolco approached.

"Dear Bolco," Marcus said, "we are in a delicate position. Will you carry Vólartor? If he does not set foot in Deluken City, and does not ride into it, the law remains unbroken."

Úniquen's ears twitched. "I like how you think, Marcus. I accept." Vólartor climbed onto his back.

"I still disagree," one commander muttered.

"Then go tell my uncle that you opposed a Deluken's interpretation of Deluken law," Marcus said. "I swear by Deluken blood, when he hears my argument, even if he is displeased, he will know I did not break our law. You will be the one who dies for leaving your post."

The commander bowed his head. "Very well, Your Highness."

"We go to Villa Costera," Vólartor said, "then from the Coloro Sea to the Silver Ocean."

"And to Cerparos Island," the commander said under his breath.

"If we move quickly," Vólartor continued, "we can reach Villa Costera by dawn."

Blarco

They passed through Deluken City by day, traveled through the night, rested only when necessary, and reached Villa Costera the following day.

The city was vast, home to millions, and the closest coastal city to Deluken City. On both sides of the stone avenues stood suburbs with towers as tall as those in the capital. People walked in crowds or rode mechanical quadrupeds that clattered over the roads.

In the distance, hundreds of metal-decked ships moved through the ports. Some glided across the waters of the Coloro Sea; others rose from beneath the surface or plunged into it.

"That vessel just came out from under the water," Nótrex said.

"Submersibles can move above and below the sea," Marcus replied.

The sound of mechanical kirkis reached them from the shore. With rubber claws, the machines dragged packages from the boats while workers operated controls from wide corridors lined with booths.

Marcus stopped his quadruped in the middle of the avenue. The others stopped behind him. Úniquen descended.

"It looks like bad weather is coming," the Bolco said, pointing to the sky.

One A-t Commander pulled a triangular device from a pouch on his quadruped and studied it.

"It is more than bad weather, Your Highness. A colossus is coming from the Silver Ocean."

Marcus twisted his mouth.

"What is a colossus?" Nótrex asked.

"The best answer," Marcus said, "is a hundred storms from the Realm of Light."

"Then we use Port Deluken, not one of the traditional ports," Vólartor said from Úniquen's back.

Marcus nodded.

They arrived shortly after. Port Deluken was heavily guarded. Four rows of seven Z Enlisted stood before a wooden gate.

A short, solidly built man emerged from behind them, marching with his hands clasped behind his back. His bulging eyes examined each quadruped with quick intensity, but they lingered on Vólartor seated upon Úniquen.

"I am the A-t Commander custodian of Port Deluken."

"Marcus Deluken, with the king's authorization, requires one of the vessels," said one of the commanders.

The man's eyes widened. "Marcus Deluken? Son of Nornos Deluken?"

"That is right," Marcus said, dismounting.

"Your father..." The man looked to the sky. "May his energy, directed by the Supernals, spread through the universe like the light of the stars. He did much good for my family."

"My father was a good man," Marcus said. "I remember you, Nornos Deluken." He lifted his eyes, then looked back at the commander. "What is your name?"

"Blarco Kolari."

"Berjo's family?"

"Yes, Your Highness. Berjo is my cousin."

"Then give me your best submersible. I need expert men who know the seas."

"Sir, it is not advisable to sail. A colossus approaches."

"We travel with or without it."

Blarco glanced at Vólartor again. "Your Highness, I could not help noticing that the man on the Bolco has a tattoo resembling the mark of the Banished. If he is with you, I assume it must be a strange coincidence."

"It is no coincidence. Do as I ordered."

"Yes, Your Highness." Blarco turned. "Deploy the portico."

An enlisted man on the watchtower pushed a lever, and the gate rose. They entered a boulevard facing the Coloro Sea. On the shore stood the cabins they had seen from afar, and mechanical kirkis carried packages back and forth.

Kéltrox pointed to four narrow holes beside one cabin. "What are those?"

"For this," an A-t Commander said, guiding his quadruped forward and placing its paws over the holes.

"Chargers," Marcus said. "For quadrupeds and kirkis."

"Will we use quadrupeds on the island?" Nótrex asked.

"We may have to," Vólartor said.

"Shall we charge them, Your Highness?" asked an enlisted man.

"Load them onto the vessel," Marcus said.

Blarco returned with two dozen enlisted navigators.

"These are my best men," he said. "And your ship is on its way. The king ordered your father's vessel kept in perfect condition. You may use it if you wish."

A submersible rose from beneath the sea.

Marcus went still.

It resembled the other vessels, but when he saw the front of it, his breath stopped and his heart faltered.

"Your Highness?" Blarco asked. "Are you well?"

"How did you recover this submersible?" Marcus asked, his voice breaking.

"What is it?"

"My father's boat. How did you recover it?"

"I did not know it had been lost." Nótrex and Kéltrox exchanged a look.

"Not lost," Marcus said. "Destroyed."

"The king has sailed many times and never wished to use this vessel, though it is the best in the port. Being the only son of Nornos Deluken, perhaps your uncle expected your return."

"Berjo said the same about my father's tower." Marcus examined the vessel. "Why did they not restore the front?"

"The experts restored it, Your Highness."

"No. Not that part."

"Well..." Blarco hesitated. "The only place the king explicitly ordered them not to touch was the upper left front."

"I see."

"Will you go with us?" Marcus asked.

"I am the best driver," Blarco said.

"Very well. Cerparos Island is about eight divines away?"

"Yes, eight divines, Your Highness."

"Divines?" Nótrex asked.

"Nitis," Marcus translated.

"Can we reach Cerparos Island before meeting the colossus?" Vólartor asked from Úniquen's back.

Blarco looked up at him and did not answer.

"Answer," Marcus said.

Blarco studied his triangular device. "We could arrive in six or seven divines in this submersible, but I cannot promise we will avoid the colossus. Projections are uncertain. It would be wiser to wait four celestials."

"We leave now," Marcus said.

Nótrex nodded.

"Your Highness, I have the operators I need, but there are more people here than the submersible can quarter."

Marcus turned to the two A-t Commanders. "Wait here. I will need you to escort us to the portal when we return."

They sailed from Port Deluken. The submersible glided across the water, then accelerated toward open sea. Some crew members worked the controls, others watched the waters, and a few, including Nótrex and Kéltrox, watched Villa Costera fade behind them.

"Can the vessel not submerge with this load?" Marcus asked.

"It can," Blarco said. "But I thought the guests might want to admire the view for a while."

Úniquen raised his ears. "To tell the truth, I am disappointed. I heard the Coloro Sea had several colors, but I see only one."

"I can explain," Blarco began. "The water is dark green, like some seas on other Sibling Worlds, but when the Goddesses of Twilight rise—"

"Do not damage with words what they can experience with their own eyes," Marcus said.

Blarco nodded.

They watched the God of Day begin to sink. Under its last rays, the first Goddess of Twilight rose and spilled scarlet light over the restless waters of the Coloro Sea.

"Look," Úniquen said. "Now I see what he meant."

"Red, yellow, green," Nótrex murmured.

"That is only the first Goddess," Marcus said. "Soon the second will rise."

"And the third?" Úniquen asked.

"The third rises sometimes," Marcus said. "Today, like yesterday, we will certainly see her."

"Then at least we will have a beautiful view," Kéltrox said.

"Yes," Blarco muttered, "but at what cost?"

"What do you mean?" Nótrex asked.

"The third Goddess will rise because a colossus is forming," Marcus said.

Blarco continued, "The Twilight Goddesses influence our seas by gravity. Most of the time two appear, sometimes the third. But every so often, the third Goddess moves closer to Germovas's gravitational field. We call it the Serial Goddesses. The swelling becomes violent, waves rise as high as towers, and if that meets a storm formation, the result is catastrophic: a colossus."

Úniquen lifted his head. "Did you hear that?"

"No," Nótrex said. "What?"

"Something is happening there."

Blarco pointed east. "The waves from that direction are growing violent."

"It is more than waves," Úniquen said.

He flew over the submersible, passed the obelisk, and looked eastward.

"What do you see?" Nótrex called.

"I see nothing, but I hear something loud approaching."

"Driver A-t!" cried a Z Enlisted from the stairs.

Blarco turned toward him. The soldier was pale and breathless.

"What is it?"

"The instruments located the colossus formation."

"So soon?"

"Yes, sir."

"Direction?"

"Northeast of Cerparos Island, in the Silver Ocean."

"How close?"

"Four divines."

"Order submersion. Full speed."

"Submersion!" the enlisted man shouted.

The submersible lurched. Metal bars lined with rubber unfolded from the edges and snapped together over the vessel like a giant tent. Nótrex and Kéltrox gripped the railing. Úniquen braced all four legs and lashed his tail for balance.

The turbines spun faster, and the vessel sank.

"We avoid the colossus at all costs," Blarco said, descending the stairs.

The others followed.

"How soon can we reach the island?" Vólartor asked.

Blarco did not answer.

"Answer him," Marcus said.

"Four divines, if there are no setbacks," Blarco replied without looking at Vólartor.

Below, they entered a large control room. Two dozen Z Enlisted sat before a wide screen that lined the wall. Beneath it stretched a glass plateau filled with groups of seven buttons. A silver lever projected from the center, and below it lay another cluster of larger buttons. Before the lever stood a wide scarlet chair marked with the initials A-t.

Above the screen, a glass ledge revealed creatures moving through the waters of the Coloro Sea.

The submersible shook violently.

Kéltrox fell sideways. Nótrex and Marcus grabbed Úniquen. Several drivers tumbled from their seats and scrambled back up.

"What was that?" Nótrex asked.

"A droporter," Blarco said, eyes on the controls.

"A what?" Kéltrox said.

"Giant animals. Clumsy. They swim erratically and fast."

"Submersibles collide with them sometimes," Marcus added.

"Do they damage the vessel?" Kéltrox asked.

"Not much," Blarco said. "These vessels are built for such impacts."

Nótrex pointed toward one window. "What is that?"

A creature clung to the glass. It was slightly larger than Úniquen and had seven arms. At the end of each arm were three eyes and a flattened snout lined with sharp teeth.

"A serpentine," Vólartor said.

Blarco turned sharply. "How do you know that?" Vólartor looked at him, then at Marcus.

"Answer me," Blarco demanded. "How do you know sea creatures when you and your ancestors have never left the City of the Banished?"

Before Vólartor could respond, a navigator shouted, "Sir! An arm of the colossus is heading toward us!"

"Turn toward—" Blarco began.

The submersible spun.

Everyone inside rolled across the ceiling, then the floor, then the ceiling again as the vessel twisted through the water. The ship stopped suddenly.

Dazed bodies tried to rise.

Blarco leapt to the controls, pressed two buttons, and shoved the lever aside. The submersible righted itself. He pressed two more buttons.

"Here it comes again!" someone shouted.

The ship spun a second time.

Blarco clung to the lever with arms and legs. "Someone hit the escape button!"

They all rolled away. Úniquen flapped desperately, struck the floor, then the ceiling, then the floor again.

"Which button?" he shouted. "Which button?"

"The green one!" Blarco and Marcus yelled together.

Úniquen bit the edge of the table to anchor himself and whipped his tail toward the green button.

The turbines roared. Blarco, wrapped around the lever, pulled the submersible one way, then the other. At last they broke free of the spiral, and the vessel steadied.

Everyone crashed back to the floor.

"We are not safe yet," Blarco gasped. "The colossus can still pull us back."

Kéltrox staggered up and searched for Nótrex. He found him pinned beneath Vólartor. Before Kéltrox reached him, Nótrex sat up.

"I am fine," the king said.

Marcus crawled out from beneath two drivers and hurried to the screen. "We are moving away," he said.

"Yes," Blarco replied, pointing. "For now."

They continued through the turbulent waters, crossed into the Silver Sea, and after three divines, Blarco said, "We cannot remain below. We are already near the north beach of the island."

"Surface, then," Marcus said.

"You heard him!" Blarco ordered.

The submersible rose. They climbed to the upper deck. Wind struck them hard. Though the Twilight Goddesses lit the early morning, the island itself remained hidden in darkness and rain.

"We wait for the God of Day," Marcus said, "and then we search for the Oracle."

At dawn, they reached the beach.

"Do you think anyone lives here, Your Highness?" Blarco asked.

Marcus and Vólartor looked at each other.

"Yes, Blarco," Marcus said. "I think someone does. You will come with us. Bring five of your best men." Blarco nodded.

"Check the quadrupeds," he ordered.

"I already did," an enlisted man replied. "They were damaged in the turbulence."

They walked over golden sand so bright that they often had to cover their eyes. The God of Day reflected off it like a mirror.

"Cerparos Island is beautiful," Kéltrox said.

"Look," Úniquen said. "Those little animals are coming out of the sand."

"They look like fish with three legs," Nótrex said.

"Little trikes," Marcus said. "They spook easily."

"They are tasty," Blarco added. "Especially the paws with viands." Úniquen stuck out his tongue.

"All this vegetation, the birds, the sand... it reminds me of Artistic Island,"

Nótrex said. "I do not understand why it is forbidden to visit."

"Cerparos Island is victory to some," Marcus said, "and misfortune to others."

"This island is a reminder of Deluken greatness," Blarco said, lifting his chest. Then he glanced at Vólartor. "Would you not agree?"

Vólartor's face tightened, but Marcus cut in. "Let us change the subject, Blarco. Vólartor, where do you think the Oracle is?"

"We must go to Concentric."

"The city?" Marcus asked.

Vólartor nodded.

They traveled south for two divines, cutting a path through dense vegetation. At last they reached ruins: piles of stone swallowed by grass, towers broken and scattered across the land.

"What happened here?" Nótrex asked.

Marcus and Vólartor exchanged a look. Blarco watched them closely.

"After the Era of the First Kings," Marcus said, "Germovas came under the dominion of three families. One hemisphere belonged to the Deluken. The other was ruled by the Cerparos and the Vocartos. The Cerparos and Vocartos were peaceful families and aided one another."

"Which family possessed the mystical sphere?" Nótrex asked.

"The Deluken," Blarco answered.

"The Cerparos!" Vólartor snapped, stepping toward him.

Blarco's men raised their cannons.

"Lower your weapons," Marcus ordered.

They obeyed.

"I will tell the story to my guests," Marcus said, looking at Blarco and the five enlisted men. "There will be no discord while a Deluken speaks." Blarco nodded.

"Our writings say the Deluken received the mystical sphere from Surmar of Morsul."

"Muralah's messenger from Zurh," Nótrex said.

"Yes, Your Majesty. But the Cerparos writings say the sphere was given to them and that the Deluken stole it. Both accounts agree on one thing: the Deluken possessed the sphere when they declared war on the Cerparos and the Vocartos. That is where Vólartor's name comes from." Vólartor lowered his eyes.

"The Deluken won," Marcus continued. "They destroyed the Cerparos and the Vocartos. Only the Cerparos royal family survived. King Yolicon Deluken died shortly after the war, and his son Mayon, later called the Wise King, ruled in his place. He refused to erase the Cerparos from history, so he gave them this island to inhabit and govern." He paused before the ruined city.

"About three thousand tecklis ago, King Formin Deluken saw that the Cerparos had grown strong here. They had built a prosperous city and appointed a governor, for the Deluken would not allow them to call themselves kings. Formin intervened. The Cerparos drove his soldiers from the island, and he returned with force. He did not need much. The Deluken ruled the planet, their weapons were superior, and they did not even use the mystical sphere. The slaughter was atrocious." Vólartor's jaw tightened.

"Formin emptied the island and took the few survivors to Deluken City. Some advisors urged him to kill them. One opposed them."

"Cerlo Kolari," Blarco said.

"Yes," Marcus replied. "Your ancestor. Cerlo reminded the king that if the Wise King had not destroyed the Cerparos, Formin should not do so. The king followed his advice and gave the survivors a city he named the City of the Outcasts. Then he created the Pact of the Outcasts, forbidding them from leaving and marking their males with the broken sword." Silence settled over the ruins.

"Your Highness," Blarco said, "may I ask a personal question?"

"I know what you will ask."

"Then it is true. You committed the unforgivable transgression."

"Yes, Blarco. The woman who was, and always will be, the love of my life was Rólaris Cerparos."

"How did the king forgive—"

"Forgive me?" Marcus asked. "Perhaps because the time has come for this planet to understand that there is no transgression in loving someone from another family. Do you understand?" Blarco said nothing.

No one spoke for a long while.

They followed Vólartor through Concentric's ruins, climbing broken causeways and skirting piles of stone. After three divines, Vólartor stopped.

"Are we there?" Úniquen asked.

"I think so."

"So you do not know?" Blarco said.

"There is the tower broken in half," Vólartor answered. "Follow me."

He ran toward it. The others followed. The two halves of the tower leaned together like a broken triangle, and they entered through the crack. "Help me look," Vólartor said. "The Oracle must be nearby." They searched for two divines, calling through the ruins.

"Oracle! Oracle!" No answer came.

"How do you know he is here?" Blarco asked.

Vólartor ignored him and continued searching.

"Vólartor," Marcus said at last, "are you certain?"

"Yes."

Blarco approached Marcus. "Your Highness, may I have a moment?"

Nótrex and Kéltrox joined them while Vólartor, Úniquen, and the others continued examining every opening in the tower.

"Speak, Blarco," Marcus said.

"I do not wish to offend your friend, the banished—"

"His name is Vólartor."

"Yes, Your Highness. Vólartor. But how can a man who has been locked away all his life know where the Oracle is hiding?"

"Because he told me," Vólartor said from behind them. "I heard his voice."

Blarco turned. "So we are all here—with the royal submersible, His Highness Marcus Deluken, a king from another Sibling World, and a Bolco— after nearly dying in a colossus, because you hear voices?" A thin musical note answered him.

It sounded like a flute.

"What is that?" Nótrex asked.

Úniquen lifted his head from one of the holes and followed the sound.

They climbed out of the ruined passage. At the top, where the two broken halves of the tower met, an old man sat with a wooden box pierced by several holes and fitted with a knob.

"Vólartor, my friend," the old man said. "Jely," Vólartor breathed. "You never change."

"I will travel at once," the old man said.

"Where did he go?" Kéltrox asked.

"He disappeared," Úniquen said.

"Here I am," the old man said behind them.

Some turned in astonishment. Others jumped back.

"What did you expect?" the old man asked, laughing. "People call me Oracle for a reason."

Vólartor ran to him and embraced him.

"How do you know the Outcast?" Blarco asked.

"I know him as well as I know you, Blarco Kolari."

Blarco's expression tightened. "You heard us speaking. That is how you know my name."

"A clever assumption," Jely said. "You expect me to prove otherwise. I will not. Your disbelief will serve you better if it remains unanswered."

"Everyone said you were dead," Marcus said.

"Highness Deluken," Jely replied, "you are one of the true Deluken, the kind who helped build this planet, not the kind who destroyed families and called it glory. You, more than anyone, should know that sometimes the difference between the living and the dead is merely the power to make one's presence known." He smiled.

"But let us not drown in philosophy. Vólartor, noble friend, why have you called for this meeting?"

"You do not know?"

"No one knows everything."

"See?" Blarco muttered.

Jely turned to Nótrex. "I know King Nótrex of the Kingdom of Light wishes to revive his wife, Krístal."

"Did you tell him?" Marcus asked Vólartor.

"No."

"Then I will be brief," Jely said. "If your wife is dead, leave her dead."

Nótrex's face hardened. "Mr. Jely, we came because we understand a wizard may help us. Faltron of the Kingdom of Light refuses to meet with me."

"I know, dear king. You have already paid the price for your bitterness. Your need to control what cannot be controlled has caused the problem you have with the mystical sphere, the one few know about."

Nótrex looked at Marcus. "Tell them to leave us." Marcus turned to Blarco. "You heard." Blarco and his men withdrew.

Only Nótrex, Kéltrox, Marcus, Úniquen, Vólartor, and the Oracle remained.

"Why can I no longer use the mystical sphere?" Nótrex asked.

"You know why. But when a heart hardens itself against obvious truth, it sometimes needs a stranger's voice to say what it already knows."

"Then say it."

"Why not you, Kéltrox?" Jely asked.

Kéltrox shook his head. "I do not know."

"Of course you know. So does your brother."

Jely's voice changed, solemn now, almost like one reading from a sacred record.

"The Book of Origins says: A lineage and blood chosen among the Sibling Worlds to be perpetual. There will be chosen ones among the selected, and although they are equal children, their destinies will differ. They all are fortunate carriers of the seed that ignites the ancient energy of the mystical spheres, yet few will be able to unleash its power. It will not be the integrity of their conscience that will determine their function, nor will the cleanliness of thought have the reward, but the corruption of their principles and the wickedness of their hearts will thwart its complete fulfillment." Jely looked at Nótrex.

"You are a just man who committed a great injustice. You knew. Your heart cried out against you. Your brother begged you not to kill the chameleon child. Yet you did it. And since that day, you have dreamed of the little boy who chose to play with your daughter instead of killing her." Nótrex lowered his head.

"But we move on," Jely said. "What you want is dangerous. No wizard with scruples would help you."

"You think no wizard will help me?"

"I did not say that. I said none with scruples. The Tainted Wizards seek allies. They would give almost anything to gain one. The question is whether you are willing to ally yourself with them."

"No," Kéltrox said.

"If I get my wife back, yes," Nótrex answered.

"Dear king," Jely said, "listen to your brother."

"My brother is not the one who lost the love of his life."

"Is His Majesty unaware of his brother's feelings for the one who now pretends to be his wife?"

Kéltrox looked away. Nótrex lowered his eyes.

"My king," Úniquen said, "I have lived longer than any man here. Perhaps a Bolco's wisdom should not be overlooked."

"Oh, Bolco of Bolcos," Jely said, stroking Úniquen's muzzle. "At last you speak. Your destiny awaits you, and she needs you."

"Who needs me?" Úniquen asked.

Jely did not answer.

Instead, he turned back to Nótrex. "Have our words persuaded you?"

"I cannot lose her," Nótrex said.

Jely's face saddened. "I am sorry for your answer. It is your decision, and you will regret it. Mostly because you will not reap the fruit you expect. You will be left with the disappointment of refusing the right path, and with the punishment already born from the innocent blood you shed."

"Are you saying a Tainted Wizard cannot resurrect her?"

"I am saying what I say. What you want to hear no longer matters. You have chosen, and you will see for yourself."

"Are you a friend of the Tainted Wizards?"

"That question would offend me if it did not come from a man determined to seek them. I am a friend of justice. The Tainted Wizards pursue injustice. Therefore I ask again, just king walking the path of injustice for the second time: do you still want to speak with one?"

"If that is what it takes to bring Krístal back, yes."

"Then return to your planet. Five days after arriving in Diamondis, go to the place where you buried her. A Tainted Wizard will meet you in the Weeping Forest."

"Are you certain he will come?" Jely only whistled.

A flute-like sound rose behind them, thin at first, then louder. Kéltrox turned. The others followed the sound, but no one was there.

When they looked back, Jely had vanished.

"Where did the Oracle go?" Nótrex asked.

"Your Highness!" Blarco shouted, running toward Marcus. "We must leave the island now. Look."

He pointed northeast. Black clouds and lightning swallowed the horizon.

"The colossus will hit the island for several celestials," Marcus said.

"We are done here," Nótrex replied. "Let us go."

"What about the Oracle?" Úniquen asked. "The island could flood."

"He will be fine," Vólartor said.

They ran back toward the submersible. Rain caught them halfway. The wind pushed against their bodies, but they forced themselves onward. Úniquen stopped trying to fly and moved with them on the ground, digging his claws into the earth and shoving the others forward when the wind threatened to throw them back.

They reached the submersible exhausted. The rain and wind grew fiercer with every breath. They set sail, fighting the turbulence they could avoid and enduring what they could not. After several divines, they returned to Port Deluken.

When they emerged, they found the two A-t Commanders Marcus had left behind, along with other commanders and nearly fifty men, all aiming long hand cannons at the submersible.

Marcus motioned for Nótrex and the others to remain behind him.

"What is this?" Marcus asked.

No one answered.

"Why do you not speak? The king gave me his word that I would be safe and escorted to the portal."

The cannons lifted toward Marcus's head as he stepped forward.

"They have orders not to speak," a man's voice said.

The ranks parted, and a medium-height man in red robes stepped through.

He had blond hair, a shaped beard, and a mocking smile.

Marcus studied him. "I almost did not recognize you. You were small when I left."

"I did not recognize you at all," the man said. "I only knew because they told me who you were."

"So this is you now, boy? The mighty Biserlo Deluken. Is this how you welcome me?"

"You are not welcome. Traitors are never welcome in Germovas."

"The king did not send you. He gave me his word."

"He gave it. He gave it," Biserlo said with contempt. "You seek the Oracle with the king of the Kingdom of Light, our enemy. I do not understand my uncle sometimes. He is harsh on so many things, yet he lets you make a mockery of the Deluken legacy. He almost made me believe he might forgive you. I dislike that."

"You are not interested in the Deluken legacy," Marcus said. "If you act against me, it will stain your reign before it begins."

Biserlo's eyes narrowed. "So you confess it is my turn, not yours?"

"I am leaving. You are staying. I am not interested. You are. What more do you want?"

Biserlo smiled. "Then let us forget this little altercation, dear cousin. There is no need to bother our uncle with such trifles. I will escort you to the gate immediately. If you leave this instant."

"Then let us go, cousin."

The caravan rode on fourthlegs toward the Scarlet Portal, Biserlo leading the armed ranks. Nótrex followed on Úniquen with Kéltrox and the others behind. Several divines later, they reached the main portal, which, unlike Vertigo Leap, was packed with soldiers.

They arrived in the Kingdom of Light at dawn, rested two nitis in the Pirutus, and then departed for the City of Light. On the fourth day, as they entered the central garden of Diamondis and before Úniquen landed, Princess Gemma ran out to meet her father.

"Land before her," Nótrex whispered.

Úniquen obeyed.

Gemma rushed into Nótrex's arms the moment he dismounted.

"Where were you? You took too long."

"I am here," he said, kissing her forehead. "Why are you crying?"

"Nothing. I just missed you so much."

"Gemma, tell me."

She wiped her eyes and tried to hold back the tears. "Mommy does not love me anymore."

Nótrex's heart tightened. "What do you mean?" Úniquen lowered his head.

"She is strange," Gemma said. "She did not play with me, not even once. And she looks at me... weird."

Nótrex's eyes reddened more than his daughter's. Kéltrox and Marcus descended from their séritrocs behind him.

The king kissed Gemma's forehead again and held her tight, turning his face away so she would not see him cry.

Five days later, as the Oracle had instructed, Nótrex set out for the Weeping Forest, this time with half his army.

At dusk, Kéltrox ordered the soldiers to remain alert. If they heard anything, they were to come to the king's aid. Then he left the ranks with Nótrex, Marcus, and Úniquen.

They reached the place where Krístal had been buried.

A garden of red and white roses had grown around the grave.

"Where did this come from?" Úniquen asked.

"It does not seem natural," Marcus said. "Someone must have planted it."

"Do you think he will come?" Nótrex asked.

"The magician?" Kéltrox said. "To be honest, I hope not."

He had barely finished speaking when a ball of light the size of a fist appeared before them.

The four stepped back.

The light grew, first shaping itself into a head, then lengthening into limbs. A humanoid figure formed, changed color, and became a young man with bulging eyes and a piercing stare.

"Nitato, King Nótrex. Nitato, Kéltrox. Nitato, Marcus. Nitato, Úniquen." He paused long between each name, watching them as he spoke. His lips did not smile, but his eyes did. "I am Fondirus of Kekarta."

"I understand the Oracle explained the details of our proposal," Nótrex said.

"The Oracle," Fondirus said, looking toward the forest. "The Perishers invent memorable names."

A rustle sounded among the trees. Something large leapt from branch to branch and landed nearby. It was as big as a bear, with long claws, small piercing eyes, and a prominent snout.

Kéltrox stepped before his brother, hand on his sword.

"He comes with me," Fondirus said.

The creature watched them, shaking its head from side to side. Its black, hairy skin began to change. The hair fell away. The body lightened. It straightened, and the face reshaped into that of a sullen man with broad cheeks and thick eyebrows. His claws slowly became hands and feet.

"Nitato to the four of you," he said, "whatever your names are."

"Mansate," Fondirus said, "be more polite. Even if they are Perishers, they may become allies."

"Fine. I am Mansate of Salfinio, and we will see whether we can agree."

Fondirus continued, "So you will not doubt the seriousness with which we consider a possible agreement with the Kingdom of Light, I speak on behalf of my companions, especially Senior Wizard Permones. We came together in case the daring Faltron dares appear."

"Then you can resurrect her?" Nótrex asked.

"Yes," Fondirus said. "For that, the power of four wizards must be united."

"We need the body," Mansate said. "We will return in seven sunrises."

"Where will you take her?" Nótrex asked.

"To Salfinio, my planet," Mansate answered gruffly. "The other wizards will meet us there."

"I must warn you," Fondirus said. "We have never wished to do anything like this before. Whatever happens to her afterward will be your responsibility, not ours."

"I understand."

"What kind of things?" Kéltrox asked.

"I do not know," Fondirus said. "If she dies again soon, or if her mind breaks, or if something worse occurs."

"I will take the risk," Nótrex said. "Tell me your terms."

"First," Mansate said, staring at the grave, "where has the body been moved?"

Nótrex's eyes sharpened. "What do you mean? We did not move it. She is here."

"She is not," Fondirus said.

He stretched his hands toward the grave. His eyes lit. The earth trembled and rose, scattering the roses. The coffin lifted from the ground and opened.

Krístal's body was gone.

Only the jewels remained.

"Who took her?" Nótrex asked, his voice low and dangerous.

Kéltrox turned on the wizards. "Do you know?"

"You are mad," Mansate snapped. "You are wasting our time."

"Of course we do not know," Fondirus said. "Find the body. Or, if you still wish to make an agreement with us, know this: we are willing to guarantee you peace amid the coming war."

"I will find her," Nótrex said, staring into the empty coffin. "And whoever did this will pay in spades."

Chapter Seventeen

THE GREAT RACE

Germovas Peritis

A diurnal blizzard swept through the village of the Weeds, flinging dust over the bodies scattered across the clay. The Triplets burned high above them, bright and merciless. Every so often, one of the savages rolled over without opening his eyes, groaned, and sank again into the same enchanted sleep.

Nitis passed. Then the sky darkened, and a dense cloud descended over the courtyard before Verlou's tower. Through the vapor, the glowing face of an old man appeared.

Peritis de Germovas stepped out of the mist, escorted by three creatures of medium height who held the edges of his cloak. They had no feet. They floated. Their bodies were round and transparent, like wraiths made of glass, and their broad arms ended not in hands but in hooks that opened and closed with delicate menace.

Once Peritis crossed into the courtyard, the creatures withdrew into the cloud. The cloud folded in on itself and vanished.

Peritis looked around. Sleeping weasels covered the courtyard. Weapons lay abandoned in the dust. Fresh tracks from nórmides cut through the sand.

He snapped his fingers.

The savages began to wake.

Verlou, who had been standing by the tower window with his eyes half closed, saw Peritis and hurried down. He dropped to his knees before him.

"Why are they all on the ground?" Peritis asked.

Verlou swallowed.

"You incompetent fool," Peritis said. "You let the prisoners escape."

"Escaped? Maltra too?"

"Did you expect him to wait for you? If I had not returned earlier than planned, we would have lost our chance to catch them again."

"I do not understand how this happened," Verlou said. He noticed a tray lying on the floor, picked it up, and stared at it. "That is why Maltra refused to eat. She must have put something in the food."

"Do not flatter yourself. They did not need cleverness to defeat you. They used magic." Peritis lifted his gaze to the sky. "Faltron's magic." Then, under his breath, he whispered, "Vegala serticated." His grip tightened around his staff.

"I cannot feel your Moltred. I cannot sense it anywhere. Where are you? Why did they take the girl? Do they know what she is?"

"Do you want me to gather the men and go after them?" Verlou asked.

"That will not be necessary." Peritis stared into the head of his staff. A faint light stirred inside it. "There they are. Dargos and the Kronkos are catching up with them. You will come with me, and we will meet them in the desert. And if Faltron dares to interfere, he will find that I have not come unprepared."

Rólar

"Watch out, Rólar!" Tartos shouted.

Rólar saw the spear only when it was almost upon him. Before he could move, Nornos threw himself against him, and they both hit the floor in front of the cell. The spear shot between the bars and scraped King Nótrex.

"Kill the Kronko!" Nornos cried.

Tartos cut the creature's throat.

Rólar pushed himself up. "My king, are you hurt?"

"Only a scratch." Nótrex's eyes searched beyond him. "Where is my daughter, Rólar?"

Rólar opened the cell door and could not answer at once.

"I hoped she was with you," he said.

Nótrex fell to his knees and wept.

"She may still be alive," Rólar said quickly. "In the tunnel, I saw Kronkos slain by Kéltrox's sword. He may have reached her. And if there is anything worth trusting in this world, it is that Gemma is too stubborn to surrender." Nótrex looked up through his tears.

"We must not give up hope, must we?"

"If anyone can escape," Rólar said, helping him to his feet, "it is her."

"Someone is coming," Nornos whispered.

A Kronko appeared at the foot of the stairs and shrieked.

"They found us!" Rólar shouted.

He seized Nótrex by the right arm. Nornos took the king's other side, and they started up the stairs while the remaining soldiers fought ahead of them, cutting a path through the enemy.

The Kronkos pressed hard. The soldiers were dwindling.

"There are too many!" Tartos shouted.

"We are being slaughtered," Nótrex said. He tore himself free from Rólar and Nornos, grabbed a sword from a wounded soldier, and charged.

They fought their way to the room where the queen had been held. She stepped into the hallway when she heard the uproar.

"We have to go!" Nótrex said.

"Rólar! Is Gemma with you?" the queen asked.

"No," Rólar answered. "She must have escaped."

"Hurry!" the king shouted.

"This is a mistake," the queen said. "We will be captured."

She had not finished speaking when a roar shook the columns of Diamondis.

A mass of Kronkos surged through the doorway.

"There is no time to argue," Nótrex said, taking the queen by the hands.

They ran toward Princess Gemma's chamber and pushed the broken doors together. The Kronkos hurled themselves against them. Nornos, Tartos, Rólar, and the few soldiers still alive braced the doors with their bodies, but the Kronkos tore cracks through the wood with their claws. Splinters flew at every blow.

The queen rushed toward the tunnel. A stone broke loose from the wall, struck her head, and knocked her unconscious.

"Krístal!" Nótrex cried, dropping beside her. "No. Wake up, love. Nilda... forgive me, Nilda."

Rólar turned at the name, startled, but kept his shoulder against the door. "Wake up!" Nótrex pleaded. "Please, wake up!"

"My king!" Rólar shouted. "The Kronkos are about to break through. Run!"

The soldiers held the door. Nornos suddenly disappeared into the tunnel.

"What are you doing?" Rólar shouted after him. "Come back! Do not run now!"

Nornos did not answer.

For one terrible second, Rólar believed he had fled. Then Nornos reappeared from the room's bath chamber carrying a bucket full of water.

"Take this, sir!"

Nótrex seized it and poured the water over the queen's head. She gasped and opened her eyes.

"I do not know if I was dreaming," she whispered, "but I heard you call my name after so long."

"Let us go," Nótrex said, avoiding the question.

They descended into the tunnel.

"Sir, move!" Nornos shouted.

Rólar, Tartos, and the soldiers let go of the door. Nornos jumped into the passage, and the others followed.

"Run!" Rólar shouted. "They are catching up!"

The Kronkos poured into the tunnel behind them, closing the distance with terrifying speed. Nilda could hardly walk. Rólar and the soldiers turned again and again to slow the creatures, then broke away and ran. After several nitis of frantic movement, they reached a pile of rocks blocking part of the passage.

Nótrex stopped.

"To the right!" Rólar shouted.

Nótrex pushed the queen through a narrow cleft in the stones and crawled after her. Rólar tried to push Nornos next, but the young man resisted. "You first, sir."

"Rólar, come through now!" the king shouted from the other side.

Rólar slid his sword into the scabbard and forced himself into the cleft. As he crawled, the hilt caught on the rocks, and the belt holding the scabbard snapped.

"Here they come!" Tartos shouted.

"Get in, Tartos!" Nornos cried.

"You first. We will cover you. What are you waiting for? Move!"

Nornos began to crawl through the opening, but before he could pass, the Kronkos reached them.

On the other side of the rocks, Nótrex, Nilda, and Rólar heard the screams of Tartos and the soldiers left behind. Nornos wriggled through the cleft. A Kronko caught his leg.

Rólar seized Nornos by the arms and pulled, but the creature would not let go. Nótrex and Nilda grabbed him too.

A shriek ripped through the tunnel. Nornos cried out and lost his grip on Rólar's hand.

"My leg! He bit my leg!"

"I am not leaving you!" Rólar said.

"Leave me here, sir. Go!" Nornos shouted. "Hail to our king!"

"We will not leave you," Nótrex said. "I owe it to your father."

The king grabbed one of the bloody spears and thrust it through the cleft until it struck flesh. The Kronko shrieked.

"He let go!" Nornos cried.

"Then move!" Rólar shouted, dragging him through the opening.

"I cannot walk, sir."

Rólar took him under the left shoulder and pulled him forward.

Behind them, a Kronko forced its head through the cleft. Though the gap was narrow, its strength dislodged the rocks that blocked it. The creature dragged itself through. Only its legs remained trapped.

Nótrex, Nilda, Rólar, and Nornos could hardly move fast enough. The Kronko was almost free, and more creatures shrieked behind it, desperate to pass.

"Sir, rocks," Nornos shouted. "Many rocks!"

The first Kronko tore itself loose and charged. Another shoved its head through the cleft behind it.

"Rocks!" Nornos pointed to a small pile near Nilda.

Nilda and Nótrex exchanged a quick glance. Then they looked at Rólar.

"Give them to him!" Rólar shouted. "Now!"

Nilda let go of Nótrex, tore a strip from her clothing, and gathered stones into it.

"Hurry," Nótrex said, helping her. "It is coming!"

"Smaller, ma'am," Nornos said.

The Kronko leapt toward them. Nilda lifted the bundle. Nornos grabbed a stone and hurled it with astonishing force. It struck the Kronko's skull and dropped the creature at once.

Nótrex and Nilda ran. Rólar lifted Nornos onto his shoulders, the young man's head hanging down his back, and ran after them.

Nornos held the cloth of stones in one hand and, with the other, kept hurling them at the Kronkos trying to cross the cleft. Unable to understand what was happening, the Kronkos on the far side pulled the unconscious bodies away, not realizing they were blocking their own path.

Nilda reached the tunnel exit first. Nótrex followed. A few moments later, Rólar emerged with Nornos on his back.

"Follow me!" King Nótrex shouted.

They fled toward the Suntras Valley, north of the Enchanted Swamp.

They had barely advanced when more than twenty Kronkos appeared in front of them. Rólar took Nótrex's sword and stepped before the king and queen.

"Everything will be fine," Nótrex began, looking at Nilda.

A Kronko thrust a spear through Rólar's body.

Rólar fell on his back. Nornos tumbled beside him and began to weep.

Nótrex knelt to help, but another Kronko struck him in the back with a spear and seized Nilda's hair.

Nornos grabbed one of the stones still in his hand and hurled it at the Kronko holding the queen. The creature fell backward. Another Kronko rushed at him, and Nornos struck it down as well. The rest approached. Before he could lift another stone, one of them slammed a spear shaft into his head, and the world went black.

"Nornos," Rólar whispered, barely breathing. "Nornos, listen to me. Do not give up."

Those were the last words he heard before darkness swallowed him.

When Nornos opened his eyes, he was lying on a thin mat inside a square tent whose fabric had been woven from strips of palm leaves. At first, he saw only a blur. Then faces took shape: several men, women, and children staring at him as though waiting for a verdict.

Beside him, Rólar was also lying on a mat, his chest bandaged. He breathed weakly.

Nornos tried to sit up and moaned.

"Easy," a familiar voice said.

"My king?" Nornos whispered.

Nótrex knelt at his side. "How do you feel?"

"As if I were bitten, struck, carried, and then used as a bag of stones, Your Majesty."

Nótrex smiled faintly despite the sorrow in his face.

Nilda stood behind him, pale and bruised but alive.

"What happened?" Nornos asked.

"A hooded woman saved us," Nótrex said. "She appeared while the Kronkos were taking us away. I do not know who she is, but she fought as though the Overlords had placed a storm in her bones." Rólar opened his eyes.

"Gemma?" he asked.

Nilda came closer. "The hooded woman told us Gemma and Kéltrox are alive."

Rólar closed his eyes again, and his throat tightened.

"By the fortune of the Overlords," he whispered. "She is alive."

"She is not on this planet," Nótrex said. "For now, that may be the only mercy we have."

Nótrex rose with difficulty.

"The woman also said that a group of people, led by a brave and brilliant woman Nornos knows well, escaped Artistic Island and is sailing here. They should arrive in less than a niti. We will wait for them at the port."

The survivors made their way toward the harbor. Along the road, they passed dozens of dead Venturians. Some had been cut by daggers. Others looked as though fire had burned through them from within.

"Did the hooded woman do all this?" Rólar asked.

"Yes," Nótrex said. "Last night, after leaving us in the tent, we heard Kronkos scream for nearly two nitis. Then she returned drenched in blood and told us we would be safe for a short while. She told us to travel with the people coming from the island to the Pirutus, and from there to an allied world."

"And she said Gemma and Kéltrox were safe," Nilda added.

Rólar stopped. He rubbed his eyes several times, but the tears came anyway.

"She is safe," he said, voice breaking.

"Yes," Nótrex answered. "Though from what the woman told us, she is no longer on the planet."

"Good," Rólar said. "Anywhere is safer than here."

They reached the port. In the distance, a ship cut through the restless Shining Sea.

On deck, the passengers had seen the figures waiting on the beach.

"Larnesa!" someone called. "Look! There are people in the port!"

"By the fortune of the Overlords," Larnesa said, stepping back as if the sight had struck her. "The king and queen escaped. I cannot believe it. And look who is there..."

"Who?" asked an old man, squinting toward the shore.

"Give me something," Larnesa said. "Quickly."

"What?"

"Anything. One of those beam shims."

A man pulled a rectangular piece of metal from a beam and handed it to her.

"You want to throw that to the beach?" a woman asked. "You cannot possibly reach it."

Larnesa threw the metal fragment.

It flew almost straight, cutting the wind with hardly a tremor, then descended and landed at Nornos's feet.

"It is my mother," Nornos cried. "My mother!"

The restless waves struck the reefs of the Shining Sea. The ship from Artistic Island reached the harbor. Larnesa climbed over the bow before the moorings were cast. A gust of wind tossed her luxuriant hair; she twisted it into a near-perfect cylindrical bun, leapt from the ship, and landed on the pier in front of Nornos.

They embraced.

Then she pulled away and inspected him from head to foot.

"Stand straight," she said.

She noticed his nightgown, folded and stained with blood, straightened it, and removed a piece of lint from the lapel.

"And that hole in your shirt? No. Do not answer that." She sighed when she realized the blood was not all his.

"Mother, stop," Nornos murmured, glancing at the others.

"Where is Mayon? Ah. You did not want to wake him, did you?" she asked, pointing toward the tent with a faint smile.

Nornos could not speak.

Before he could answer, Nótrex stepped in.

"They tell me you led a tremendous revolt," the king said.

Larnesa bowed. "Yes, Your Majesty. But the Kronkos killed many of our people, including the ruler of the region."

"Did you learn anything of the other regions?" Nótrex asked.

"Yes. We captured a Ventu while sailing here and extracted what we could from him."

"And what did he say?" Rólar asked.

"There were revolts in other regions as well. The Venturians crushed them."

"What did you do with him?"

"We threw him into the sea after the interrogation."

"Extraordinary work, Larnesa," Nótrex said. "I did not know you carried such fire."

"We owe much to Nornos too," Nilda said. "He helped Rólar free us from the Venturians. Now I understand where he gets the strength in his arm."

"My children have always carried more potential than they know," Larnesa said. "They are different, each in his way. Nornos finds peace alone in nature. His brother prefers home, sleep, and a late morning." Nilda's eyes softened.

"Larnesa," she said gently, "you must speak with your son." Larnesa looked at Nornos. "Why are you so serious?" Nornos lowered his head.

"Mayon is not sleeping, Mother."

Larnesa stared at him. Then her knees gave way. She fell to the wooden floor and struck it with both hands. Nilda dropped beside her and held her as she wept.

Nornos stood before them, tears streaming down his face.

"Mother," he said, "my brother died a brave man. He saved Mr. Kéltrox. Now it is our turn to be brave like him."

"Saved Mr. Kéltrox?" Larnesa cried. "They did not hide? Their father taught them to hide. He warned them they were not ready for war."

"It is true," Nornos said. "He told us hiding was the only thing we could do. But I am tired of being a coward. Even if I tremble at the sight of a sword when I die, I will die like my brother—with honor."

"By the good fortune of the Overlords," Larnesa whispered through her tears. "You are unrecognizable, my son."

"What do you mean?"

"You have your father's eyes."

She looked at Rólar for the second time, then cupped Nornos's face.

"Before, you could barely stand when fear came. Now you are comforting me."

She wiped her cheeks and forced herself to stand.

"What happened to your father?"

Nornos's voice broke. "He died too."

"The last time I saw him," Nótrex said, "he was gravely wounded."

Larnesa breathed out slowly. Again her gaze crossed Rólar's, and again neither spoke.

The survivors finished descending from the ship.

"There are at least one hundred and twenty of us," Nilda said.

"One hundred and thirty-seven," Larnesa corrected, wiping her eyes.

"Forty-four women, sixty-eight children, and twenty-five men."

"Your Majesty," a woman called, "another ship is approaching."

"More survivors?" Nótrex asked.

"I doubt it," Larnesa said.

Rólar climbed the ship's ladder and ran to the stern. One look was enough.

"Venturians!" he shouted as he came back down. "Your Majesty, the ship is full."

"What is our plan?" Larnesa asked.

"We travel to Ilucus through the Pirutus," Nótrex said.

Rólar let out a grim breath.

The crowd crossed the pier and hurried across the beach, stepping around the bodies of Venturians. They climbed the hill that divided the harbor from the edge of the Nale Desert. With the Triplets blazing before them, they advanced toward the Pirutus as fast as exhausted bodies could move. Some parents blew air over their children's flushed faces. Others fanned garments to stir any wind they could. From time to time, someone glanced back and saw the Venturian ship cutting into the harbor through the restless waves.

"The ship will arrive soon," Nótrex shouted from the center of the crowd. "Hurry!"

"Venturians are fast," Larnesa said. "If we do nothing, they will catch us."

"Then we need a way to delay them," Rólar said.

"How far are we from the Pirutus, sir? I mean—Your Majesty?" Nornos asked from behind them.

"About two days," Nótrex said. "Is that right, Larnesa?"

"To be precise, Your Majesty, if we maintain this pace and camp approximately six nitis each night, I estimate we will arrive in fifty-seven nitis."

Rólar glanced at her. "Greater accuracy would be desirable."

"Two days and seven nitis," Larnesa said, ignoring the sarcasm.

"Sir," Nornos interrupted, "the ship stopped."

"It did," Rólar said. "But why?"

"They seem to be fighting among themselves," Larnesa said.

"They threw several into the sea," Nornos added.

Rólar turned to him. "Can you see that from here?"

"Yes, sir. Clearly. The ones falling into the sea look human."

"Does anyone have a visor?" the king called.

Several people searched their packs. Others shook their heads.

"I have one, Your Majesty," Larnesa said, pulling a square blue metal device with a transparent strip from her bag.

"That is not like our scopes," Nilda said.

Rólar's face tightened. "It looks like one my father owned."

"Marcus gave it to me long ago," Larnesa said. "He liked it very much. He told me it was given to him in Germovas." Rólar said nothing.

Larnesa raised the visor to her eye.

"The Venturians are cutting down humans and throwing them overboard."

"Let me see," Nótrex said.

Larnesa gave him the visor.

"It is true," the king said. "They just threw the last two."

"I know who they were," Larnesa said. "A group that did not escape with us. It looks as though they tortured them."

"For what purpose?" Nótrex asked.

"I think they wanted to know how to activate the portal on Artistic Island."

"Artistic Island has no working portal," Nótrex said. "The one in the Lake of the Chroniclers, Your Majesty." The king stopped walking.

"No one has activated that portal since the era of the First Kings."

"That was true," Larnesa said. "Until last night. I saw a hooded woman come through it with my own eyes."

"You saw her?" the king asked.

"She was there?" Nilda asked at the same time.

Rólar and Nornos exchanged a look.

As they kept moving, Larnesa began to tell them what had happened.

Before — Larnesa

More than a legion of island soldiers stood watch at the harbor of Artifice under the light of the Matron. Warriors seasoned by service and novices who had never faced war stood side by side under Ruler Laryon's command, torches in hand, staring across the Shining Sea.

One of the ships emerged from the mist.

Then another.

Then dozens.

Vessels filled with Venturians rushed toward Artistic Island like ghostly hosts, their silhouettes fading in the fog and reappearing closer with every surge of the waves. From the distance came a sound unlike the wind or the sea. Several Ventus were singing, and a chorus of Kronkos answered with shrieks. It was as though their war song pulled the boats forward. The creatures rowed in unison, their claws striking rhythm from bow to stern though the height of the vessels kept them from touching the water.

"Here come the Venturians," said one soldier.

"What are they singing?" asked another.

"The Horror Song to the God of Embers," a feminine voice whispered.

No one noticed her.

"Look," a soldier said. "They are changing course. They are heading east, sir."

"They want the beach of Artifice," Laryon said.

"They will never bring those great ships to shore," another soldier said.

"The Venturians are half amphibian," the same hidden voice said. "They are known for unusual methods in war."

This time Laryon turned. He searched the battalion but saw only male soldiers.

The battalion marched after him and stationed itself along the breadth of the beach, trampling the fresh footprints of visitors who had been evacuated the previous morning.

Just before the Triplets illuminated the silver sand, the ships stopped in the distance.

"They anchored," said a soldier.

"They have some kind of sword," said another.

"Trocoras," the voice said again. "Ancient weapons." This time the tone was rougher, deliberately forced.

Laryon ignored it.

"What are they doing?" a soldier asked.

"Throwing themselves into the sea," the hidden voice answered. "I told you. Half amphibian." Laryon stiffened.

"I know that voice. I should have known it was you."

At the same moment, a soldier said, "Sir, we recognized your daughter among the battalion."

"Where are you?" Laryon shouted. "Do not hide, Larnesa."

The ranks stirred. Soldiers broke formation and looked from one face to another.

"I am here," Larnesa said.

She stepped out wearing the uniform of a Kingdom of Light soldier. The clothing was too large for her; she could barely walk without dragging it. She stood before her father, removed the helmet, and unwrapped the red scarf that had compressed her luxuriant hair.

"I suppose there is no point hiding now," she said. "This informer ruined the experiment."

"What are you doing here?" Laryon demanded. "My islander duty. I came to fight." She smiled.

"No. Return to your mother."

"I hid so we would not have this argument, Father. I am an adult, and I can decide what I do."

"You are an adult woman who has not bonded. Therefore, you remain under your father's protection."

"I do not need protection."

"Sir," another soldier interrupted, "the Venturians went underwater and have not surfaced. We do not know where they went."

"They are using the same strategy that gave them victory on several Germovas islands," Larnesa said.

Laryon frowned. "I have never heard that Venturians fought in Germovas."

"That is because many historians have ignored the event," Larnesa replied, already gathering speed. "An ancient book of the Espénicos describes in careful detail how the Venturians nearly outwitted the Deluken after singing the Horror Song to the God of Embers. Their maneuver was as unexpected as it was accurate, and it continues to surprise military scholars who mistakenly believe Venturians lack advanced strategic intelligence. But if we examine two philosophical observations by the wizard Moric, who tacitly expressed that—"

"Enough, Larnesa!" Laryon shouted. "Tell me the strategy. Quickly."

"Well, if we analyze the military pattern used in Cerparos Island, it is practically identical to what they are doing here. In Cerparos, they left their submersibles at dawn, at the first light of the God of the Day, which would correspond to our first nitis. Here, they also abandoned the ships before the Triplets rose."

As she spoke, the soldiers stared at the precise geometric motions of her hands. Every few gestures, she had to roll back the oversized sleeves of her uniform; every time, they fell again.

"Meaning?" Laryon asked.

"Meaning they will wait until nightfall. When the second Goddess of Twilight appears, they will attack the city. The Deluken knew about the attack in Cerparos, but they did not intervene because, as you know, the Deluken and the Cerparos—"

"Larnesa, focus!"

"They will surround Artistic Island and search for an undefended point. The most appropriate place is the Lake of the Chroniclers."

"Of course," Laryon said. "It connects to the Shining Sea. Move!"

Artifice looked like a tomb. No musical duets echoed through the streets. No crowds gathered before the theaters. The people barricaded themselves inside their homes. Some peered through windows. Others refused to look upon the signs of their extinction.

Larnesa and her father stood with the island army on the shore of the Lake of the Chroniclers. All day they stared into the still water with a calm so strained it felt unreal, as though they wished their gazes could plunge beneath the surface.

Night came almost without their noticing.

Shortly after the Triplets hid, the Matron's reflection warped at the center of the lake. A sudden movement stirred the water. The gentle ripples became violent currents. The lake overflowed and covered the ankles of Larnesa, Laryon, and the soldiers in the front lines. The rocks trembled. Some wooden benches around the lake groaned as if ready to crack.

"Here come the Venturians," Laryon shouted. "Ready the arrow throwers!"

"They stopped," said a soldier. "They know we are waiting."

"Of course," Larnesa said. "Venturians see better in our nights. Their own planet has a thick atmosphere, so darkness is—"

"Now, Larnesa," Laryon snapped. "Take her away." Two burly soldiers seized her arms.

"What are you doing?" she cried. "Let me go! Let me die beside you, Father. They will kill us all anyway."

"Wait," Laryon said.

The soldiers stopped.

He embraced her and kissed her forehead.

"I love you, daughter. Always. And I have always held my head high because of you."

Then he looked at the soldiers.

"Protect her with your lives."

Larnesa pleaded, resisted, and hurled insults sharp enough to make one soldier blush. Still, they dragged her away. As they retreated, she saw the Venturians burst from the lake like projectiles. "Put me down," Larnesa said. "I am not lame." The soldiers obeyed.

She straightened her oversized uniform.

"Let us do something useful for the love of Artistic Island."

"Your father ordered us to hide you," one soldier said.

"No. We will gather every helpless person we can find."

"To fight with civilians?"

"To save them from a massacre." Her voice cracked as she looked back toward the lake. "Our army will not last long."

"And if by a miracle of the Overlords we reach the port with civilians," the other soldier said, "there are Venturian ships in the Shining Sea."

"One thing at a time," Larnesa said.

The soldier nodded. "Then we start with our families."

Both battalions fought fiercely through the night. By morning, the Venturians had seized the city. They took no soldiers hostage. Bodies covered the shore of the lake, and the dead of Artistic Island far outnumbered the enemy.

By Larnesa's call, one hundred and thirty-six civilians had gathered during the night. With the two soldiers' help, they crawled through courtyards, slipped between houses, and avoided Venturian patrols. By morning they were passing the Lake of the Chroniclers on their way to the port.

Then the Ventu chief discovered them.

He and his battalion trapped the civilians between the street to the port and the lake.

"They caught us," a boy whispered through clenched teeth, clutching Larnesa's hand.

The crowd stopped crawling and rose together. Some of the elderly groaned from pain. All around them, claws and trocoras pointed inward.

"Kill them all for trying to escape!" the Ventu chief ordered.

The two human soldiers charged with their weapons raised. They fell almost at once.

Larnesa stepped forward.

"Kill me. I am the daughter of Ruler Laryon. Let the others go. They are no threat to you."

"You are not the ruler's daughter," the Ventu said. "You were. Your father is among the bodies. I killed him myself with my trocora." Larnesa held back her tears.

"I guessed as much. You did not have to confirm it."

"Seize that one," the Ventu chief said. "Kill the rest. Dargos may enjoy having a noble slave."

The Venturians advanced.

Then an orange beam burst from the center of the lake.

"What is happening there?" the Ventu chief demanded.

"The portal," Larnesa whispered. "It opened."

An oval capsule, gold-colored and sealed with a transparent crystal cover, shot out of the lake. It passed over the humans, fell into the Venturian battalion, and smashed a wooden bench.

"Who is that?" asked a Ventu.

The chief approached. Inside the capsule lay a slender, fair-skinned woman in a tight velvet suit. Black gloves covered her hands. Red hair fell across part of her mouth. A staff rested in her grip.

"That looks like a wizard's staff," a Ventu said.

"By the God of Embers, do not say that," another muttered.

"It is not a wizard," the chief said. "I have seen all of them. That is neither Dala nor Amber."

"What do we do?"

"Get her out and interrogate her."

The Venturians struck the crystal with trocoras, claws, and fists, but the capsule did not break. The humans watched in tense silence. Some thought of running to the lake, but Larnesa shook her head. She was waiting for something.

"Move aside, useless ones," the Ventu chief growled.

He touched a button on the lower corner.

Nothing happened.

"It does not work," another Ventu said.

"Nothing technological works on this wretched planet," the chief snarled. "Kill the humans and take the capsule to the port. We will deliver it to Dargos, and the Grand Master will know what to do with it."

"Sir," a Ventu whispered. "Open your eyes."

The chief looked back through the crystal—and met the woman's gaze.

She sighed, closed her eyes, opened them again, and drove her fist through the glass.

The crystal shattered. Shards tore into the faces and eyes of nearby Venturians. The woman sprang out of the capsule.

The Venturians raised their weapons, stunned by what she had done. She ran through them with terrifying speed and precision, knocking down every creature that blocked her path. When she reached the humans, they opened a way for her. Behind her, the Venturians helped their leader to his feet, his face glittering with glass and blood. The woman faced Larnesa.

"Am I on Artistic Island?"

"What?" Larnesa asked, eyes wide.

The Venturians looked at one another.

"Yes," another woman in the crowd said. "This is Artistic Island."

"Where is the ruler?"

Larnesa's eyes filled. "Dead."

"Are you his kin?"

"His daughter."

"Then take these people to the Region of Light, to the port of Brilliant Sea."

"How?" Larnesa asked, pointing at the Venturians. "We are trapped."

"Like this."

The woman pulled a hood from her garments and drew it over her face. Then she struck the Venturians with swift audacity, using fists and staff with equal force. The crowd moved behind her, passing through the broken line of enemies while she cleared the way.

Larnesa

"After that," Larnesa said, finishing the account as they crossed the desert, "we reached the port without further loss. Three Venturians were asleep in the stern of the ship we boarded. We killed them together, set sail, and came here."

"By the good fortune of the Overlords," Nilda said, "you did not meet the enemy at Brilliant Sea."

Then she noticed Nótrex's expression.

"What is wrong?"

"She entered through the portal of the Lake of the Chroniclers," Nótrex whispered.

"How could she open a portal that has been useless for thousands of years?" Nilda asked.

"That is the question," Nótrex said. "Planets far more advanced than ours have tried and failed."

"Whoever she is," Rólar said, "she helped us. Could she be human?"

"Look," Nornos interrupted from farther back. "They have arrived." The Venturians leapt from their ship and charged toward them.

The crowd ran in terror, but it did not take long for the Venturians to close the distance. King Nótrex, Rólar, Nornos, the elders, and the young men moved to the rear and formed a ragged line between the civilians and the enemy.

Princess Gemma

An innumerable horde of Kronkos was racing across the desert, growing larger on the horizon with every breath. Sand rose in a vast cloud around them. Dargos flew above them on Bartigo, his Bolco, shouting orders to the Ventu leading the pursuit. At his feet, the Kronko troops shrieked for the fugitives. Their heavy steps shook the earth, and the points of their spears carved long furrows into the sand.

"Get on, Gemma!" Úniquen shouted.

The princess leapt onto her friend's back, and they took flight.

Kéltrox and Lila bounded away on the séritroc. The others climbed onto the nórmides and fled.

"Now you jump," Mantus shouted from a distance at the séritroc.

"Fly faster!" Gemma cried.

"I am trying," Úniquen said.

"They are too fast," Mantus shouted. "They will catch us!" Gemma looked back. The nórmides were falling behind.

"Úniquen, turn back! They will catch the others."

"No," Úniquen said. "I have to get you out of here."

Then Gemma screamed. "Look! No—what is she doing?"

Úniquen turned his head.

Mila had stopped. She threw herself from the nórmide and stood alone in the sand, waiting for the troops to reach her. Before the Kronkos could strike, she lifted her face to the sky, raised both hands, and called a furious wind. Sand twisted into a wall and slammed into the troops, shoving even Dargos back.

"Mila, get on!" Maltra shouted.

"Go!" Mila answered, climbing onto the nórmide again. "The whirlwind will not hold them for long." They fled.

But Dargos's army drew closer again.

"They broke through the whirlwind!" Lila shouted.

"Mila, do not fall behind!" Maltra cried.

"I am dizzy," Mila said, clinging to the nórmide as her body swayed.

Kéltrox reined in the séritroc. One glance was enough. The Kronkos had surrounded them.

Three Kronkos threw a net into the air. It spread wide, fell over Úniquen and Gemma, and dragged them down.

Dargos was only a few meters away when he saw the princess clearly.

For a moment, he forgot the desert.

Her face struck him like a memory he had tried to murder.

She looked like Krístal.

"If you could see what you have caused, Krístal," Dargos whispered.

Bartigo heard him.

"She looks very much like her," the Bolco said, wings beating heavily.

Krístal—the woman who had wounded him more deeply than any battlefield ever could—had borne a daughter with the same face. The sight tore open the oldest chambers of his memory, the ones he had sworn to bury in the darkest place of yesterday. Her rejection had left a wound only hatred could seal. It had destroyed what little tenderness his nature had once allowed him to feel.

After Krístal, he had loved no one. Or perhaps he had become unable to love. Once freed from the fragile affection that had made him vulnerable, he gave himself to a hunger for greatness that never slept. Ambition became his companion, his breath, his beginning.

And now the daughter of Krístal lay trapped at his feet.

"At last," Dargos said into Bartigo's ear, "I will complete my revenge. To capture the daughter of my worst enemy is more satisfying than any victory I have won—even Gálax. The sphere of the Kingdom of Light will be mine. My power will rise beyond that of any perishable being, and no one will stand against me."

He pressed his mystical sphere against his chest.

Gemma fell into the sand beside Úniquen. Still tangled in the net, she reached for her own sphere and tried to bring it to her chest.

A hand seized her from behind.

"Mantus," she shouted. "Let go of me!"

Úniquen kicked and clawed, trying to tear the net apart.

"Traitor!" Kéltrox roared from the séritroc, drawing his sword.

Maltra looked at the Kronkos closing in. "Mila, can you do something?"

Mila did not answer at once. She looked at Mantus. Mantus looked back at her.

Understanding passed between them.

"Now I understand, Mother," Mila said softly. "It is not necessary." Dargos levitated closer.

Mantus released Gemma's hand, raised both arms, lifted his gaze to the sky, and bellowed: "Supinor derno portenus sirlus trulinsbar!"

A light as bright as a star surrounded him. His body transfigured into that of an old man. A silver staff appeared in his hands.

"Faltron?" Kéltrox and Lila shouted at the same time.

The wizard struck the ground with his staff.

A beam of light exploded outward, blinding everyone.

Gemma, Kéltrox, Úniquen, Lila, Maltra, and Mila fell as if fainting. A heartbeat later, one by one, they began to vanish before the astonished eyes of their enemies.

When Princess Gemma opened her eyes, she found herself once more in the Convergent Spectrum.

Made in the USA
Monee, IL
18 October 2026

66036545R00142